THE ARTARIANS II

Edna W. Christenson

authorHOUSE®

AuthorHouse™
1663 Liberty Drive
Bloomington, IN 47403
www.authorhouse.com
Phone: 1-800-839-8640

Published by AuthorHouse   12/22/2014

ISBN: 978-1-4969-5869-3 (sc)
ISBN: 978-1-4969-5868-6 (e)

PREFACE

My name is Mike Packard. About three years ago I was abducted along with four other Humans by the Artarians. It was an experiment to see if Humans and Artarians could co-exist.

Artarians are telepathic and had to live by certain laws around Humans. One was not to read a Human without permission. The second was not to use telepathy to control Humans without first asking.

The experiment proved successful. I enjoyed their world so much I joined them and became a Spaceship Captain. I also became telepathic, although not as strong as most Artarians. This is my first experience to an alien world as Captain Mike Packard.

CHAPTER 1

Caltomacoe, my Second-in-Command, and I met with Dalcamy and his Second-in-Command, Mocki, at Main at eight in the morning. I am the only Human Captain on Artara. I had met Captain Dalcamy several months before. He is quite tall for an Artarian and has strong mental powers. However, he shares the same warm friendliness as all Artarians I've met. We went in together and Commodore Mackalie greeted us.

Gentlemen, he transmitted through mental telepathy, *we have decided on a world in Sector 4 System 92 Orbit R301. It's closer than any of the others that Captain Dalcamy has found. It will take you six months to get there.*

He loaded in a map of Sector 4 on the computer screen and pointed to a small planet fourth from the sun in System 92.

The atmosphere has the normal gases, hydrogen and carbon dioxide, but has no oxygen, so you will have to carry your own. Captain Dalcamy took samples on the night side so we have no idea what the inhabitants look like. There are groups of huts that are surrounded by large walls.

The screen changed and showed the round huts. They looked like the mud huts of Africa that I've seen pictures of on Earth.

Only one ship is to land, continued the Commodore, *the other one will stay in orbit and monitor everything that happens. You can decide between you which is to land. Send 'greetings' in all frequencies while you're orbiting. Also, you should leave your Second-in-Command on ship when you make contact in case there is trouble. That's all we know gentlemen.*

When will your ship be ready Captain Packard?

My ship is ready now Sir, except for the extra oxygen, I answered.

Captain Dalcamy?

They are still making the improvements on the engines, one week.

Then you will plan to leave a week from tomorrow, and be very careful. We don't know what kind of reception you're going to get from these people, they could be very primitive.

Have a good journey gentlemen, I'll be waiting to hear from you.

Thank you, Sir.

We went to maintenance to see about having the oxygen loaded on our ships.

"We can install a catalyst that will produce all the oxygen you want," stated Naygee, the chief engineer.

"How long would that take?" I asked.

"A day at most."

"All right then, go ahead," Dalcamy and I agreed.

We worked with Naygee on designing the tanks and breathing apparatus.

We should carry two tanks, that would give us four hours of oxygen, I explained. Make them work independently from each other. I can use tubes like these, I drew the standard oxygen tubes used on Earth. We can breathe the air there, we just have to add oxygen so we don't need to wear masks.

We can use something similar, said Caltomacoe, *only they will attach to our necks*. Artarians don't have noses, they have gill slits on the sides of their necks. They are very small and could be easily over looked.

We should have twenty-eight tanks, I continued. *That would give everyone a second set of tanks to change to if needed. Twelve Artarian breathing sets and two breathing sets for me. Captain Dalcamy should have fourteen, also. How long will it take to have this ready?*

Four days.

Fine, I turned to Dalcamy and transmitted, *anything else?*

No, that should be all. Let's go to the Buch Restaurant and have lunch.

The Buch Restaurant is Dalcamy's favorite. We went over the menu and the waiter served asil and appetizers.

This is your first planet isn't it, Mike? Mocki said after we ordered.

Yes.

You take this one, said Dalcamy. *I'll take the next one.*

You sure? You discovered it you should have the pleasure of exploring it first, I answered.

You go ahead, Weather Man, I've already explored a few, you'll enjoy it.

I started to laugh with my mouth full when he called me 'Weather Man' and had to wash the food down. "I don't think I'm going to live that down," I said laughing.

"I'm not going to let you," he answered with a sparkle in his eyes.

Dalcamy is the only Artarian that calls me Weather Man. I got that name when Borkalami was showing a group of Military Generals and some Scientists from Earth what powers telepaths have over Humans. The day had been overcast with clouds all morning and one of the Generals angered Borkalami.

Borkalami asked me if I trusted him with my life. I said yes. The next thing I knew I was flying up into the sky beyond the cloud covering. It was beautiful above the clouds with bright sun and warm air. I transmitted to Borkalami that the weather was much better and the atmosphere warm. The story went around the entire planet and I became known as the Weather Man.

Did you leave your ship at all when you got the air samples? I asked.

No, we just hovered close to the ground. I didn't see any movement at all, it could be a dead planet. We didn't register any life forms in the city. Picked up animals outside the city though, but we didn't see them either.

I wonder why such a huge wall, I said. *China built a wall like that on Earth to keep other people out.*

Or it could be to keep something in, Mocki said.

What about the other side of the planet?

We stayed on the night side, we didn't want to show ourselves. I was only to find the possible planets, not make contact. Dalcamy told us about some of the other planets he found as we finished our meal. We left the restaurant and split up planning to meet again in a week. I went home to Tomiya.

That means you'll be gone for over a year, she said. *I knew this could happen, but it doesn't make it any easier to live with.*

I know, I transmitted as I held her, *I'm going to miss you, too. We have a week, let's make the best of it now,* I said as I took her to the bedroom, *maybe someday they'll let me take you with me. But right now I would feel better knowing you're safe at home.*

Our week together was almost a second honeymoon and Tomiya was smiling when I kissed her goodbye.

Keep that smile, I said. *I'm going to remember it for the next year, love ya honey.*

Dalcamy and I lifted at ten in the morning and headed to the fourth planet of System 92. Six months in space is a long time. We had routine details to take care of but otherwise, there wasn't much to do. I kept going through the library and picking different topics to study to help pass the time. Finally we could see the planet on screen.

It was red and had a ring. We followed Dalcamy down to orbiting level and started to scan the surface. We could see the areas where the cities were located, but we were still too high to see any detail. There were bodies of water, but not as high a percentage as Artara. Dalcamy started transmitting our greeting message and I monitored all the frequencies for any response from the planet. Twenty-four hours elapsed and Dalcamy came on screen.

"Doesn't look like we're going to get any response from them. You ready to go down, Weather Man?"

"Yes," I smiled, "I'm all set."

"I'll be listening, be careful."

I nodded, signed off and gave Caltomacoe the order to descend.

We descended slowly and hovered over a city. Creatures looked up at us, gawking. We magnified them on our screen. They had tentacles for arms, four of them, one on each side as our arms are and one on the front of each shoulder. Their heads were on short necks and the body was round and straight down from the shoulders to the ground. I couldn't see how they propelled themselves they didn't seem to have legs. They didn't appear to be afraid of us, at least no one started running away. We lifted slowly and moved to the outskirts of the city were we saw a barren area much like a desert and landed. Then we just waited to see if they would come. An hour later we could see ten approaching us from the city. Sadek and I put our oxygen on and went out of the ship. We both had our shields up when we walked out and stood waiting at the end of the ramp.

Artarians have a natural shield that is formed by the energies of their bodies. Nothing can penetrate it and is formed automatically when they sense danger, or they can activate it at will. I have a mechanical shield that activates by command. It uses the same energies but they are supplied by embedded devices that produce them.

The group of creatures stopped and one continued toward us. We approached him meeting halfway. He stood about seven feet high and three feet wide, made me feel like a shrimp and I'm almost six foot.

"I'm Captain Packard of the Planet Artara," I said.

He just stood looking at us and didn't answer. He moved up a little closer and reached out with one of his tentacles and tried to touch Sadek, but his shield prevented contact. He had two fingers at the end of each tentacle. The creature withdrew from Sadek and made circling motions as he reached toward me. I turned off my shield.

Mike, you could be in danger! I received from Sadek.

But we won't know that if we don't allow contact, I transmitted back.

The being touched my symbol of Artara and tapped it then continued making circling motions.

Do you think he's telepathic, too? I thought to Sadek.

Could be, but I'm not getting anything, he answered.

His tentacle lifted while circling to my head and touched my forehead. I felt the presence of an extremely powerful mind and became so dizzy I stumbled forward losing my balance. He reached out with another tentacle that wrapped around my arms and chest giving me support.

Mike! I received from Sadek.

I'm all right, I answered.

*I - - - am - - - - Tol - kal - - - - need - - - - to - - - touch - - - - to - - - -
com - mun - i - cate - - - must - - - - know - - - - wave - - - -length.*

I waited, the dizziness subsided and it released me.

We can communicate now, I received, *I am adjusted.*

You mean you can change your brain waves to match mine? I asked.

Yes, don't you?

No, I didn't know that was possible.

*The others will be joining us and will adjust through me, then we can all
talk.*

The other nine came up touching each other and one touched Tolkal's
head and soon I was aware of all of them as they joined.

*I am Mike and this is Sadek. We represent the planet Artara. Did you
receive our transmissions before we landed?*

*No, but we knew there were two ships orbiting our planet. We could see
the beings in your ships, but could not communicate until now. We call our
planet Vulgarb. You are different from the rest.*

Yes, I come from another planet and I live on Artara now.

Why have you come here?

*We are searching to meet other people and worlds. We want to be friends
and exchange information and perhaps trade.*

What do you have to trade?

We would have to compare what we have with what you need or want.

Why do you wear this? One of the others touched the tubes on my face.

Your air lacks oxygen. I must have oxygen to live, so I carry tanks of it on my back.

Perhaps we can build a chamber to contain this oxygen so you will be comfortable while we meet together with the council.

You should find out first if oxygen will harm you. If not, we can use our ship as a meeting place if you want. It would save you from the trouble of building a place. Sadek, remove one of the tanks from my back and give it to them. Be very careful with it Tolkal. If it is near heat or fire, or just sparks, it will explode.

They took the tank. *If it is not dangerous to us, we will meet you here tomorrow at this same time with the council and we will use your ship. If we cannot, then you will have to come to our council.*

Agreed, I answered.

A warning before we part, he continued, *do not leave your ship during the night. There are animals that will eat you. You should be safe inside your ship.* He took his tentacle away from my head and they went back to the city while Sadek and I returned to the ship.

"That was an interesting meeting," Dalcamy said as we spoke through our screens in control, "but you took a chance letting down your shield. By the looks of them they could have over-powered you."

"We wouldn't have been able to communicate if I didn't, and they didn't act like they were a threat," I explained. "They have extremely strong minds."

"They would have to if they could actually see us in our ships while orbiting. It's strange we didn't sense them."

"They must be on a completely different wavelength from ours. At least now we know why the huge walls. I'm going to monitor for those animals tonight, I'd like to see what they look like."

"What emotions did you pick up from them, Weather Man?"

"Interest, curiosity, nothing hostile. We'll learn more about them tomorrow. I should make a report to the Commodore now."

We signed off and I called the Commodore. There was a five minute delay and he appeared on screen. I gave a complete report then waited for his reply. He was concerned about my dropping my shield, but agreed it was the only way.

"Be careful, Captain Packard, we still don't know these creatures. If they are as strong as you say, they could present a very dangerous threat to all of you."

I kept the exterior monitors on all night and set them to awaken me if anything appeared, nothing happened.

CHAPTER 2

The following morning Sadek and I readied the conference room for the meeting. Since we didn't know if they could use tables or chairs, we just set them in the room to one side to let them make the choice. We went back to control and watched the screen. Soon we saw fifteen Vulgarbs approaching.

They must be bringing the council, I said.

We lowered the ramp and Sadek and I met them. They didn't hesitate at all and came right up and into the airlock. Only five and I could fit at once, so Sadek stayed outside until they were all in with us. Then we led them to our meeting room. They formed a circle around Sadek and me. Tolkal entered the circle with us and stepped up to me. He made the same circling movements and wrapped another tentacle around me before making contact this time. He touched my forehead and the dizziness started again. When my head cleared he said, *all join.*

The circle touched one another and ended touching Tolkal. I felt them as they tuned in with us. Tolkal still held me and I waited. I felt a strong remorse from them.

We are sorry you have to go through the dizziness, but there is no other way for us to communicate. As soon as we break away our waves change back and we lose communication with you.

I don't mind, I answered, *it's only for a little while.*

We receive thoughts from you that don't seem to be yours, are you in communication with others?

Yes, the Captain of the other ship can hear and feel what I experience, also Sadek and the others on this ship.

But they are of different wavelengths than you. How is this possible without adjusting to them?

I can't explain it to you. I only know I can receive them, but we cannot receive you without contact.

You are the leader of this vessel?

Yes, do you have spaceships?

No, we explore space with our minds, but have not found anyone yet. When you came we were happy. You are so different from us we would like to know more about you.

We would like to know about you, also, I answered.

May we examine your mind to know you?

If their minds are as strong as I think, Mike, they could damage you. Sadek said.

We will be careful not to damage him.

It would simplify things, I said.

I felt them close in on me. The circle moved in as their minds pressed me. My whole life began to flash before me. Everything I ever thought, felt and heard came forward in my mind. I was glad Tolkal still held me, I didn't think I could stand up under the pressure of their minds, he gave me good support. I relaxed and watched as my life continued. It was like living it all over again, only speeded up. I felt concern coming from Sadek as he received my life as well. They had just reached the point of my life when I was being taken aboard Borkalami's spaceship for the first time when I became very weary.

We must stop, he is getting too tired, Tolkal said, he is not as strong as us.

I felt their minds back away as Tolkal still held me. I looked at Tolkal and said, *but you still don't know why we came or what we have to offer.*

Tomorrow we can continue, he answered. *You are unable to stand, you need rest.* He was right my legs weren't able to hold me up when I tried to stand. Tolkal was taking all my weight. *There is a place for him to rest?* He asked Sadek through me. Sadek led him to my sleeping room and Tolkal literally carried me. I fell asleep as soon as he released me on my bed.

The following morning I awoke completely refreshed and found Caltomacoe had the computer monitoring me while I slept.

This could be very dangerous for you, Caltomacoe said as I ate breakfast. *We don't know how they will use the information they will get from you if they continue.*

You're right, I said. *I didn't realize they would be that thorough when I agreed to this. It's early, perhaps we can meet them at the city and ask to know more about them. I hope we can do it without offending them.*

Sadek and I put on our tanks and walked to the city. We met them just as we entered. Tolkal approached me and we joined minds again.

We wish to know more about you before continuing.

You want to know if we would misuse the information we will receive from you.

I do not wish to offend, but I did not expect this.

We will show you our lives.

I started receiving pictures and was pressed too hard. *No!* I said, *this is too much.*

They stopped. *We will take you into our city then and answer your questions.* They showed us around and explained that they did not need buildings.

We draw our subsistence from the ground and atmosphere of our planet. We only need protection from extremely bad storms and the animals.

Then, you don't eat.

Eat, you mean like the animals do?

Yes.

No, you do?

Yes, we are animals. I felt alarm from them and confusion. *We don't eat intelligent life forms. We aren't like the wild animals here. You have read me; you should know that.*

They calmed down and began to think logically again. *Yes, we remember now. We saw you eat in your mind. You are very different from us.*

Are there other cities and nations on your world?

Yes.

Do you have to touch each other to communicate?

No, we are all the same wavelength. We can always be in communication with each other.

How do you get along with each other?

You are concerned if we will destroy others with your information because your world would have.

Yes.

Do you think all worlds are like yours?

I don't know about all the other worlds, so I want to be careful not to contribute to problems.

You need not be concerned; we do not destroy ourselves or others.

We're running low on oxygen, Mike, I received from Sadek, *we only have an hour left.*

We will return to your ship with you.

Entering the ship, I started removing my tanks. *Sadek will report to our Commodore before continuing,* I said.

You need permission before telling us more about you.

Yes, I answered smiling, they felt and enjoyed my humor. *Do you know each other's minds the way you know mine?*

Yes.

If I were to record your wavelength into our computer, you would be able to tell my superior all about yourselves. Would you be willing to do that?

Yes.

I took them into medical and showed them the opercule. One of you would have to lie there. One released from the others and laid on the table. I lowered the arm and started the computer. As the monitors came to life I explained them, but I didn't understand the readings. Finally the brain waves appeared and began to record. After the recordings were complete the computer made a recommendation of a complete analysis of the subject.

What would that be? Asked Tolkal.

It would examine him and take tissue and chemical samples, I explained as I raised the arm. *I would not do that unless you all agreed.*

You have done that to others?

I haven't, but it was done to me.

We went to control as I explained the cap and how we transmit.

Commodore Mackalie was on screen with Sadek as we entered. Sadek transmitted to me that they were ready to receive. Sadek and the Commodore removed their caps and we set the computer to receive the information from Tolkal.

Please do not go faster than our computer can handle. Just take the cap off when you're finished.

Tolkal took his tentacle from my head and I placed the cap on his. They began to transmit as I sat in the captain's chair. Bocha brought me lunch, a quick snack. An hour passed and Tolkal was finished. An hour later Commodore Mackalie began to vocalize in Artarian.

"The computer states that they are mostly intellectual and have no conflict with others on their world. They cannot leave their planet because they draw subsistence from it and would die if they left. You may continue to give them information, we may find something that will establish mutual benefits between us."

"Thank you, Sir."

The Commodore signed off and Tolkal approached me with his tentacle circling. This time he didn't have to hold me since I was in the captain's chair. They circled me and I agreed for them to finish examining me. They started exactly where they had left off yesterday. I was back in Avery, California almost five years ago.

The night was clear with luminous specks covering the sky. I stepped off the road and walked into a small meadow, part of Clyde's property. I stretched out on the sweet smelling grass just to stare at the sky and watch for shooting stars. A long one came along and as I watched, it changed direction! It did a complete reversal! That's no shooting star! I thought. It grew larger as I watched, seeming to come right at me. As it came down, I could see it was a spaceship.

I moved behind a tree thinking it was going to land right here in this meadow, but it veered off over the tops of the pines. There was another larger meadow about a quarter mile in, Clyde had shown me last year. I started heading toward it through the forest.

It had already landed when I arrived. I hid behind a row of manzanita that was between the ship and I. An opening appeared under the metal giant and a ramp lowered to the ground. Two beings descended the ramp and began walking in my direction. I stooped low behind the bushes and watched as they approached. They moved at an easy pace, not seeming to be in any hurry, yet decisive as though they knew exactly where they were going.

Their skin texture and features belied their human form. I could see them clearly because of the full moon. They were around six feet and slender. They wore silver tunics and pants that had a metallic glitter in the light. Their skin had a grayish tint and appear to be rough with small lumps. Their heads were round, similar to ours and hairless.

They reached the bush I was hiding behind and about to pass me when I stood up and revealed myself quite to my astonishment. I had no intention of doing that, but my body just stood up and turned to face them on its own accord. I was completely out of control! The two people looked at me and didn't seem the least bit surprised. They walked up to me and I looked them in the eyes that were large and dark with no white areas like Humans have. No nose and the mouth was small. Their ears were lobeless, round like ours and also small. There was a sweet fragrance about them that was rather pleasant. One stepped behind me and I just stood there like an idiot completely defenseless. The alien in front of me took hold of my left arm just below the shoulder. I could feel a gentle, but firm push on the back of my right shoulder and I started walking with them. They led me like a blind man toward the spaceship.

I tried to resist, stiffen my legs, push back against them, anything! My body just wouldn't respond to me, all I could do was watch. I could feel my heart beating hard from the heavy adrenaline my fear was producing. To be completely defenseless against alien beings was more alarming than if they physically attacked me. Even with my fear, I was still curious and questions kept running through my mind; who are they? Where did they come from? What do they want with me? Damn, now I can't go hunting with Clyde! I began to feel anger because they were interrupting my life. They led me toward and up the ramp at the same pace they had come down.

We entered the spacecraft and they guided me to a chair, turned me around and gently pushed me down into it. The chair was a recliner with thin metal arms. Once in it, they pushed it back until I was almost flat. Then they strapped my arms to the arms of the chair and my legs to the footrest. All during this I could not move of my own accord or mutter a sound. When they finished, one stood staring at me, my eyes closed and I slept.

CHAPTER 3

I wasn't as tired this time when they finished. They had sensed certain areas where I resisted their probing and backed away from them. One was my memory of the secret code that operates the ship. Others, Tomiya and I making love. They did not question my desire to keep those memories from them and passed over them quickly. I expressed my appreciation for their sensitivity.

There are some things we can use from you, but our world is so much different from yours we would never be able to go there.

We understand that, what can we share with you?

Your computers. You have given us much information, but your computers have more?

Yes, do you need medical also?

Possibly, I will submit to its examination and see if it can be of any use to us. We went to medical. Another Vulgarb touched my forehead and Tolkal removed himself and laid down on the table.

I am Mollow.

I will explain as the opercule works, I said.

The monitors came to life. They did not have organs as we. They are of a vegetable origin and survived on photosynthesis. The computer reported that the sterilizing rays would be fatal to them. They understood this as I read.

The computer would have to extract samples of his fluids to analyze for an anesthetic, I don't know how sensitive he is to injections.

Not as sensitive as you, answered Mollow, *you may proceed.*

Samples were extracted and analyzed, an anesthetic could be made.

Are you in communication with him? I asked.

Corbow is. If Tolkal has discomfort, Corbow will let us know.

The opercule looked deeper and found typical plant structure. They propelled themselves with small tentacles underneath them much like a millipede. They were neither male nor female and propagated from cuttings just like a plant. Their heads were mostly brain tissue, but still vegetable. Eyes were present, but they sensed more than actually seeing.

You see more with your minds than you do with your eyes, I said.

Yes, some of us have no eyes.

You don't understand these readings, another said.

No, I don't. Your systems are completely different from ours.

What is yours like?

I can show you when this is finished.

The computer wanted chemical samples from three areas. They understood as I read the message. The areas lit up on the screen.

He would feel that one, Mollow said, *the others are insensitive.*

I took two and then anesthetized for the third. Tolkal awoke one hour later and joined us. I had finished showing them a human body on the screen. They were surprised at the intricacies of our systems.

You can have much go wrong with you, we are simpler. You need this machine much more than we.

You don't think it can help you then?

Not enough to have, it would not be used much.

You said you searched planets with your minds. If you did find another planet with people, how would you communicate with them if you couldn't touch them?

We send a box. It will record the person and come back to us.

They would have to touch it then.

Yes.

Interesting, how many worlds have you searched?

All the ones in our solar system. We were going to start on our neighboring solar system when we saw you approaching. We hoped you were coming here. We saw you once before, but you left and we thought you would not come back.

How far out can you reach with your minds?

Only to the surrounding solar systems.

So you would not be able to leave your galaxy.

No.

Perhaps as we meet more worlds we can tell them of you and they will come.

That would help us.

Now that we have your wavelength we can feed you information from our computer, I said as I led them into the library.

I placed a cap on Tolkal and explained how to set the speed on the computer and to load it with the files they wanted. I loaded in the Artarian language first. They all tuned into Tolkal and I was released. I watched as he kept turning the speed up until it reached maximum.

Dalcamy, I transmitted, *they're using maximum and they're all receiving!*

I went to control and reported what happened and showed the Commodore the monitors as they searched through our files and received the information.

"Their minds are very quick as well as strong," Commodore Mackalie said.

"They are absorbing the information as though they were starving."

After reporting, I went to the kitchen and had dinner with Caltomacoe.

I don't know how we can help them much, Caltomacoe transmitted, *most of the information we have is useless to them.*

They seem to be enjoying it though. I think just the fact that they are learning will be satisfying to them.

Night came and I returned to the library. When I entered they all responded to me with circling tentacles. The nearest one touched me and I began to stagger. Another grabbed me to keep me from falling. Someone was yelling. Easy! Easy! Don't hurt him! It was Tolkal, he was the one that caught me. Caltomacoe became alarmed and tried to push them away from me with his mind, but he wasn't strong enough. There was a little tussle. I was too dizzy to keep track of what was happening. It happened so quickly I was taken by surprise. Soon the dizziness was gone.

We are sorry, Mike, we were excited. We have read half your library and would like to come back tomorrow to finish.

Yes, of course. You read fast.

Your computer makes it easy for us. We are sorry you were treated so roughly, it will not happen again. We have never had so much information available to us before.

We will bring you more the next time we come. Don't you need to store it?

We have already stored it in our minds it will not be lost.

They left and we watched as they hurried back to their city. Caltomacoe turned to me. *You could have been hurt by them. We have no power over them to protect ourselves.*

I felt you trying to push them, what happened?

I had no effect, it was like trying to push against a shield. I don't like this, we are too vulnerable.

Caltomacoe, we can't expect to be superior over everyone.

CHAPTER 4

The Vulgarbs arrived the following morning and I accompanied them into the library. They continued from where they left off yesterday. I continued to monitor the terrain hoping to see the animals the Vulgarbs told us about, but nothing showed. Every couple hours I would go to the library and check on them in case they had any questions. They would acknowledge me by waving a tentacle and then go back to their studies. About noon I entered the library, walked up to Tolkal and pointed to my insignia. He got the message and made contact.

Where are the animals you told me about? I've been monitoring for them, but I haven't seen them yet.

They roam at night. If any of us are out of the city after dark we're never seen again.

Have you ever seen them?

Yes, once, I was on the wall and one tried to get into the city after me. They are very vicious.

Can you show me what they look like?

The first thing I received was blazing red eyes. They walked on two legs and had long arms ending in claws. Tolkal couldn't show much detail on the face. It was a dark night and could just barely see its form, but he would never forget those eyes.

Was it larger than you?

About the same height, but smaller around.

Since you are telepathic, don't you have any protection powers?

Like what? He asked.

Pushing things away from you or mind control.

How do you do that?

I'll see if I can show you. We left the library and went into the meeting room where I set up a portable stool and concentrated on pushing it. It slid away from me with a scrapping sound against the floor. *I'm not as strong as the Artarians. They can do it better and with larger items, but you have such strong minds you should be able to do it.*

I didn't know that was possible, let me try. I could feel his concentration and the stool was picked up and thrown against the wall. He got so excited he broke contact with me and all the Vulgarbs came crowding in the room alarmed. Tolkal showed them what he learned by throwing the stool again. Caltomacoe heard the noise and came to investigate. I touched Tolkal's tentacle and pointed to my insignia and we joined again.

We can go outside and Caltomacoe can show all of you how he can move larger things. We donned our oxygen tanks and went outside where Caltomacoe gave a demonstration by moving the largest boulder we could find. They took turns at it until they were picking up and throwing it. I was amazed at their strength.

Mike, you have done a great thing for us, Tolkal said. *Now we don't need to fear those monsters, anymore.*

I'm surprised you didn't know about it before.

You said there was 'mind control' what is that?

I'll show you first by having Caltomacoe take control of me. Your mind is so strong, I don't think it would affect you, but you would know what it feels like to be controlled. Caltomacoe, take control of me. He did immediately while all the Vulgarbs were tuned in. I could feel their awe as Caltomacoe led me around and then released me.

Now I'll take control of Caltomacoe to show you how and you can practice on each other. Do I have your permission, Caltomacoe?

Yes.

I took control and led Caltomacoe around and then released him.

Would you mind doing that once more? Tolkal asked.

I did it again. The other Vulgarbs broke communication with Tolkal and me to practice on each other. Within an hour they had it down pat.

Will this work on all minds? They asked.

It's worked on all I've tried, Caltomacoe answered. *If you would permit me, I could see if I can control one of you.*

Corcar stepped up, *control me.* He broke contact with the others.

I could feel Caltomacoe's concentration, but nothing happened. He could not control Corcar. Finally Corcar joined us again.

You are not strong enough to control us, he said. *We could probably control you, but I don't want to hurt you by trying. We will teach our people. Now we have some protection. Is there anything else that can be done that we don't know about?*

I looked at Caltomacoe, Tolkal understood. *You are afraid to show us that.*

Caltomacoe looked at the large boulder that they had been throwing around; it exploded. The Vulgarbs panicked and ran away except for Tolkal. They slowly came back and stared at the pieces and then just looked at us. *They are frightened,* Tolkal said. *You have great powers.*

We have never used that power on life-forms, I answered.

The Vulgarbs stood around conversing with each other then they tuned in again. *This power you have is very dangerous. If it was used in fear or anger it could be devastating.*

We are much disciplined people, Caltomacoe answered. *We would not misuse it. We were merely demonstrating to you what could be done with the mind. We would not recommend it to life-forms that are not disciplined enough to control it.* They broke connection and discussed amongst themselves again.

I hope we haven't ruined things, I thought.

It's a shock to them, Tolkal answered, *they will adjust.*

It didn't seem to be a shock to you.

I know your mind better than they; I have first contact. We will go back to the city now and discuss this with others, we will return.

Caltomacoe and I returned to the ship and I called up Dalcamy. "Hope I didn't blow it."

"I don't think so, Weather Man. Once they think about it they'll realize what you've given them. It will probably strengthen our relationship with them, and I think it was good for them to see something of strength from you. It will keep their respect of us. I thought Corcar was getting a little cocky on the mind control lesson."

"I know it sounded like that," I laughed, "but I don't think he meant it that way. They aren't the most tactful, they just say what needs saying."

"They are not very disciplined for such powerful minds," Dalcamy said.

"Perhaps that's because they haven't had much exposure. I wonder how old their civilization is. I'm also curious about those animals. I wish we had some type of vehicle for ground exploration. We might think about designing something when we get back to Artara. In fact, I might start working on it while we're here."

"Maybe they need bait to come to," suggested Dalcamy.

"I'll think of something," I said as we signed off.

CHAPTER 5

The Vulgarbs came back just as I finished up lunch and we went into the meeting room. Tolkal and I joined.

We have discussed these powers you have and we understand you probably have more that you haven't shown us. We do not wish to be ungrateful for what you have shared with us, but we do not wish for any of our people to know about such destructive forces. Our people would not harm anyone deliberately, but as Caltomacoe pointed out, it takes a disciplined mind to control such power. Our minds may be stronger than yours, but not as disciplined.

Tolkal knows more about you than we because he has first contact with you. He explained that you are not a threat to us with these powers. If you are willing, we would like to continue to learn from you.

I felt so relieved I grinned from ear to ear. *Of course,* I answered. I asked Tolkal to stay with me as the rest went into the library. *I want to see these animals. Do you know anything of their habits?*

They live in caves in the mountains. I could take you there, but it would be too late to start today we wouldn't get back in time. I will meet with you tomorrow morning as the sun comes up and we will go.

Thank you, Tolkal.

Mike, there is something I would like to know. His curiosity grew strong along with feelings of embarrassment.

Why are you embarrassed? What do you want to know? I started laughing.

In your memory, you were doing something with another of your kind. I understood it was what you call a female of your species. You are much different from us. What were you doing?

Show me what you saw and I'll try to explain it to you. I saw Tomiya's face. She was smiling at me. She seemed to be moving slowly, first one direction then another. I could see other people behind her. *Dancing! I was dancing with Tomiya.*

What is dancing?

Well, you do it with music. You step to the rhythm.

What is music?

It's sound. It can be pleasing or exciting depending on the rhythm. Come with me, I'll play some for you. We went into the conference room and I had the computer play some soft slow Earth music. Tolkal listened to every note. It didn't impress him much. I played some rock and roll, then I felt his pleasure. He stood very quiet, but I could feel his enjoyment building.

The music makes me feel a sensation I have never felt before.

You like it. Music is a conveyance of feelings. You can use it to change your mood, or to heighten your mood. Dancing is a way of becoming part of the music. Dancing can also be a way to convey feelings for another person, if it's done right.

How do you dance?

This is rock and roll. I started dancing to the beat. *I twirled around and broke contact with him.* Just as well, he started swinging his tentacles to the beat. He twirled to my amazement, I had to duck his tentacles. I came up laughing. We danced until the music ended.

I like that. Tolkal said after we joined again.

We have all different types of music. Classical, operas, patriotic, ballads. Ballads tell stories, I'll play one. I played "Cowboy Bill" by Garth Brooks. As it played I visualized it in my mind so Tolkal would understand.

There are such animals as horses on your planet?

Yes, we still ride them today. A lot of the ballads are true. Some tell of legends and heroes of our past, and give accounts of our history.

Was that story true?

I don't know, it could have been. Other countries of Earth have their own types of music. I played Spanish, Japanese, and Hawaiian to show the extreme differences. I saved Artara for last, playing several of my favorites.

How do they make this music?

With instruments, the library would have them in the files.

Let's dance more. I smiled and played more rock and roll.

I bet your people would like square dancing. I said while we rested.

Tolkal saw the dance in my mind as I thought. *Could you teach us?*

I think so. We can do it outside. I'll set it up and teach you while we're here. Let's go to control, I want to show something to you. I programmed a heavy metal show into the computer and directed it to show on screen. Tolkal started enjoying the show. Caltomacoe sat back with us and watched. About half way through, I started feeling deep feelings of regret from Tolkal. *What's wrong, Tolkal?*

We can't move like that.

You don't have to. Make up your own moves. That's what's so good about this type of music, you can move the way you want. That brightened him up and he enjoyed the rest of the show.

* * * * *

Tolkal met me the following morning just as the sun was rising. I had my tanks on and he took two more.

Is this as fast as you can go? He asked as we walked.

This is about as fast as I can go, I answered as I ran.

He stopped and looked at me. I felt humor from him, but there was no physical reflection of his mental gaiety. *We will never get there at this speed,* he said. *I will carry you.* He picked me up and set me on his shoulders with my legs straddling his neck and held my ankles. *Hold on.* I grabbed his shoulders and we began again at about thirty miles an hour, if not more.

Won't you get tired carrying me?

You're light, I hardly feel you. I could go like this all day.

If you can run this fast, how can a two legged animal catch you? You should be able to out run them easily.

Maybe they can run faster.

I've never known a two legged creature to run this fast. Maybe a four legged one, but not two.

Then how do they catch my people and eat them?

Tell me what you know about them. How do you know they are being eaten?

When I was little, we found Morga partially eaten after being out all night. Then many of us disappeared, so we built walls around our homes and it stopped for a while.

When was the last time anyone disappeared?

Eight sunrises before you came.

Are these animals all over your planet?

No, just the Continent of Malgar. No one else has problems with them.

When did this all start?

When I was little. He felt my frustration to his answer. *Twenty summers ago,* he said.

And it started with Morga, I stated.

Yes.

We reached the base of a mountain and went around to the south side and found a large cave. Tolkal set me down. I examined the walls of the cave and found they were not formed naturally. The walls looked as though they were melted and fused.

Wild animals didn't do this, Tolkal. I had brought a light and we entered. The cave continued level for a while and then began to sloop down steeply. We kept following the passageway. There were no other corridors like natural caves have. We entered a large room with torches burning. I stooped and looked at the ground. There were tracks like Tolkal had made in the ground on our way here and many clawed looking foot prints. They resembled bear feet with long claws.

Listen to me Tolkal, we are in extreme danger here. I'm going to turn on my shield. No matter what happens don't lose contact with me. My shield will cover you so long as we touch, do you understand?

That is what Sadek had when I first touched him.

Yes, you may feel a tingling from my shield, but it won't hurt you. I thought the code and my shield activated.

I don't feel anything, he said.

That's good, I do.

We stayed close to the walls and walked around the room. There was another passageway on the other side. We followed it as it went steeply down and made a sharp right turn. When we were half way through the turn we could see a bright light. We continued very carefully and came out on a ledge overlooking another huge chamber built like a pit. Tolkal became very excited.

My people!

They were in the chamber with large lights shining on them. There was a pool of water, some were soaking. Others stood in smaller pools of a dark substance. I didn't understand what the darker pools were, but I did understand that they were being held prisoners. The only way out was a draw bridge that lowered to them from the cliff were we stood.

I will talk to them.

No! I said, *don't get them excited. It might bring the ones that are keeping them here. We don't want to join them. Let's get back and get some help.* We crept back into the rocks of the cliff and I sensed another person. We hid behind some large boulders that were in the dark. A two legged being stepped out onto the ledge and I felt cold fear coming from Tolkal. *Easy Tolkal, he doesn't know we're here.* He stood looking down at the Vulgarbs and I sensed a feeling of disgust from him. Tolkal's description matched this being. He stood about seven feet with claws on his feet and hands. His eyes glowed deep red just as Tolkal pictured. He had a ray gun strapped to his waist and a probe in his hand. His skin was brown and scaly with a smooth plate for a chest. He wore no garments, just a harness that crossed his chest and back. A cap, like a beret, covered the top of his head.

Tolkal, I want him alive to take back with us. You practiced mind control, control his.

What if I kill him?

You won't, go ahead. I felt Tolkal concentrate. The being turned toward us and stared, Tolkal got scared again. *You have him Tolkal, come on.* We walked up to him and removed his weapons. The harness was leather and had several metal loops, a small pouch hung from one.

Can you carry us both, Tolkal?

Yes.

Keep control of him. Tolkal swung me up on his shoulders again and wrapped a tentacle around the being lifting him. Once we were outside again, Tolkal went as fast as he could, he doubled his speed. We went to medical with this strange creature. I remove his harness and secured him in the opercule. *Okay, Tolkal, you can release him now.*

Once he was released he screamed and struggled and screamed some more. We just stood around watching him. I went through his pouch. There were papers inside with unreadable writing. A picture of him and two others. Finally he stopped screaming and laid still.

Who is he, Mike? Caltomacoe asked.

This is one of the animals that the Vulgarbs thought was eating their people. They are not eating them, they are keeping them prisoners in a cave deep in the ground.

Why?

That's what I'm going to find out.

I set the pouch down and walked over to the control panel. The being watched me while yelling unrecognizable words. I did a preliminary examination of him and recorded his brain waves. I took just enough samples for the computer to come up with an anesthetic and he yelled out at everything I did, more from fear and anger than pain.

What I thought was skin was not, it was like the exoskeleton that insects have. His head was solid exoskeleton shaped in an oblong bulbous form. Four small openings could be seen on the sides of the head. The computer said these openings were sound sensitive organs, ears. Three small round holes positioned above the mouth, about where our nose would be. These were spiracles like insects have to breathe through. A neck of pliable hide held his head and connected to his chest plate. The exoskeleton stopped at the sides. The chest and back plates ended in thick rounded edges leaving a soft space between. It was also covered with pliable hide. The arms extended from between the plates, forming shoulders. There was a similar opening at his waist. Another smaller pair of plates acted as hips, his legs protruded from the lower part of these. His arms and legs had coverings and joints similar to crabs.

Okay, I said, *someone touch him so we can talk to him.* No one moved. I looked at the Vulgarbs. *Tolkal, what's the matter?*

They don't want to touch him, they are afraid.

Have them join with us, Tolkal. They all touched and tuned in. *Listen to me,* I said. *They have not been eating your people. They have been keeping them prisoners. Morga must have escaped and they killed him to keep him from warning you. I want to find out why they are keeping your people prisoners. I can't do that without your help. One of you must touch him so I can question him.*

I will touch him. Corcar stepped forward.

Thank you, Corcar.

The being started screaming again when Corcar approached him. He struggled and tried to turn his head away from Corcar, but it was strapped down. Corcar made contact. I walked up to the other side of the table and looked at this strange scared creature. When his eyes rolled to me they glistened with facets. The lower part of his face moved when he spoke like it was a separate piece connected with hinges. I could see sharp pointed teeth inside as he yelled at me.

He called you a soft skinned monster, Tolkal related to me.

"I'm a monster!" I laughed. "You're the one doing the kidnapping. Why are you holding the Vulgarbs prisoners?" My comment and question was transmitted to him. He spat a disgusting brown liquid at me, staining my uniform. "Okay, you want to play rough? I'll oblige you." I walked back to the control panel and he started yelling and screaming again.

He doesn't want you to hurt him, he's scared.

Tell him if he cooperates I won't hurt him.

He says 'go to caltock'.

What's that? I asked. They transmitted the picture of his thought to me. *Tell him I don't have to, he's lying in hell right now.* When I was sure he got the message I pushed a button and a tube for an anesthetic inserted into him and he screamed again.

He says he will kill you.

I went over to him and said, "On my world, we cover insects with chocolate and eat them." I made a very vivid picture of him being covered in thick gooey chocolate and being bitten in half. Transmit all of that to him. He looked at me and struggled and a different sound came from him.

He's really scared, Mike, Tolkal said. *He's so scared his thoughts are all mixed up.*

Good, that's the way I want him. I pushed the button to anesthetize, he went out cold.

I looked over at Caltomacoe. He stood back, quietly watching.

What did you give him, Mike?

Something I saw Borkalami do on Earth, it was very effective, X42.

CHAPTER 6

You put him to sleep, Tolkal said a little surprised.

Yes, tell Corcar to break contact, he won't enjoy the dreams our prisoner is going to have.

We could have examined his mind to get the information, Tolkal stated.

Would you want to know his mind? I felt disgust coming from him. *I didn't think so,* I laughed.

I would, to help my people.

This is a better way, when he wakes up he'll tell us everything.

Ten minutes later he woke up screaming. I went over to him and he looked at me with horror. His face had the same hard leathery surface with no movable expressions. I could feel his terror of me as I approached. Corcar made contact again.

"Where do you come from?"

"Trok! I come from Trok. We need the ore from here to run our ships!" He spoke and yelled at intervals as his fear shifted to different degrees while he fought to control himself. Tolkal translated everything to me.

"So you're making the Vulgarbs mine it for you."

"Yes! They're strong and we don't have to feed them."

"Is there only one mine?"

"No, we have more. We took cuttings and grew more Vulgarbs to work them. The new ones don't resist; they don't know any difference! We keep them away from the ones we caught so they won't tell the young ones anything!"

"What's this for?" I held up the probe.

"It makes them behave, it causes pain. Poking them in the center, it hurts them. They do what we want."

"Where are these other mines and how many?"

"Three others! Further on down the mountain range."

"How do you get the ore off the planet?"

"Our ships come every seven nights, one is due tonight!"

"How many Troks in each cave?"

He hesitated, he rolled his eyes trying to decide if he would answer me. I started to walk back to the control panel.

"Twenty!"

"You've been very cooperative, I'm going to put you back to sleep."

"No!" he screamed and began writhing in his bindings.

"You won't dream this time, it'll be a good sleep for about eight hours. When you wake, you will feel good."

He laid quiet and watched me, but his breathing came in quick gasps. I put him to sleep with a regular anesthetic and let the opercule do a complete examination.

He's not an insect. He has organs, a circulatory and a nervous system as complex as Humans, but the organs were completely different. I didn't recognize anything. The Vulgarbs were fascinated by the examination and watched every detail as I explained. I ran an analysis to see if he could eat Artarian food and found he could. We put him in a sleeping room and locked the door. I set the computer to monitor him and sound when he awakes. Then we all went into the conference room to make plans.

First thing we should do is locate the other three mines. We have the advantage, they don't know we're here, I explained.

Mike, Dalcamy's calling, transmitted Caltomacoe from control. Tolkal and I went to control.

"I'm coming down to help, Weather Man. I've already reported the situation to Commodore Mackalie."

"Good," I answered, "see if you can scan the mountain range and find those mines while you're coming."

I felt wonder and amazement coming from Tolkal. *You're doing all this for us. Putting your own lives in danger and not even hesitating to do it.*

Tolkal, I come from a world full of danger, but I can't stand slavery and murder on any planet.

They should have come and asked us. We wouldn't have stopped them from taking the ore, we have no use for it. But they didn't even want to do the work!

Why didn't you know they were here? You knew when we came.

We've only been searching the sky for the last five summers. But we still should have seen the spaceships, I don't understand either.

When our prisoner wakes up we'll ask him a few more questions.

I've located the mines. Dalcamy reported an hour later as he joined us. *You were lucky to get as far as you did without detection, Weather Man.*

Did you find any type of radar?

They have receiving and transmitting equipment in one of the mines, but it wasn't in use while I was scanning. Evidently they only use it when their ships come. That's probably why they didn't detect our arrival. They are very lax on their security. Let's analyze those weapons you took from your prisoner.

We set them in the opercule. The ray gun was a blasting ray. Our shields will protect us. The probe was an energy releasing probe. It makes cells expand and rupture while causing them to vibrate. If it were applied to nerve endings it would prove very painful even though the amount of energy being released was very low, not enough to kill. The center of the Vulgarb's body is the most sensitive.

They are animals! Lacron, one of the council members, exclaimed. He became very angry. *What you did to our prisoner was nothing compared to this!* I began receiving pictures of what he would like to do to them. He would line them up and jab each one until they collapsed in screaming agony. I started laughing, to Caltomacoe's shock.

Dalcamy grinned at me and started explaining his plans. *We have five crewmen on each of our ships. That gives us twelve to fight counting Mike and me. Our second-in-commands, Mocki and Caltomacoe, will stay on board as guards for the prisoners with two Vulgarbs to help them. We can take twelve Vulgarbs with us. Twenty-four against seventy-nine should be just right.* He paused and I could feel his anticipation. I expected him to rub his hands together like a little kid just before sticking them into some joyful mischief. *We will release the Vulgarbs after we capture all the Troks. They will be safer where they are until we have things under control.*

We will watch the sky tonight for the ship, Lacron said.

Also, get more help from our village, stated another council member.

We should meet here at sunrise tomorrow, said Dalcamy.

I could still feel Dalcamy's excitement as we watched the Vulgarbs leave. Tolkal and Corcar stayed with us.

You're really enjoying this. I said to Dalcamy.

I haven't had a good fight in years.

I don't think they stand much of a chance against us. His enthusiasm was contagious.

Ahh, but we can still have our little games.

We can carry you to the mines and carry extra oxygen for you, Tolkal suggested. *My people can also bring the prisoners back to the ship leaving us free for more.*

Remember to keep contact with us while we're in the mines so our shields will cover you, Dalcamy said. *You and Weather Man work together, Corcar and I will be together. We will take the same mine you went to today first.* Dalcamy became very serious as he looked at the Vulgarbs and me. *Be careful tomorrow. Mistakes are fatal when you're dealing with beings like these. No mistakes.*

We talked and planned late into the night. The following morning we breakfasted early, the sun hadn't risen yet. The computer sounded that the Trok was awake. We went in to see him with a tray of food. He backed away from us with fear so strong I could almost smell it in the air as well as feeling it from him.

"I brought you some food," I said.

He doesn't understand, Tolkal said.

I set the tray down and stepped back motioning for him to eat. He looked at me and then the tray, but wouldn't go near it. I walked over to his bed and motioned for him to sit. He understood, but wouldn't. I took control of him and led him to the bed and made him sit. Corcar went up to him and made contact. I released him and he tried to get up, but we wouldn't let him.

"Why can't the Vulgarbs see your ships?" I asked.

"I don't know."

"Do you have any special protection for your ships?"

"No, just a shield against meteors and ray blasts."

"How does it work?" asked Dalcamy.

"I don't know, I only saw it a couple times. I'm a soldier, I don't know about the ships."

Dalcamy read him while he spoke and saw pictures of the device in his mind which he transmitted to me. *That could be the reason*, Dalcamy told me.

"Do you have this thing on all the time?" I asked.

"Yes, it's automatic with the engines. What are you going to do to me?"

"Nothing," I answered. "We will release you eventually. Have some food, it's safe for you to eat."

"What did you do to me?" He had discovered the sealed punctures about his body, probably had some soreness like I did after I was examined.

"I made some tests while you slept. That's how I know our food is safe for you to eat. You aren't harmed, the soreness will be gone in a couple days." We left him and locked the door.

CHAPTER 7

Fifty Vulgarbs met us as the sun rose.

We can't protect all these people, I said to Tolkal.

They are going to set up a line to transport the prisoners quickly.

The Vulgarbs carried extra tanks and lifted the Artarians up on their shoulders making contact with them. Dalcamy and I led as we headed for the mines.

Did anyone see the ships last night? I asked.

No.

We arrived at the first mine and were set down. Dalcamy and I led with our shields on and our Vulgarbs covered. We walked quietly. Two Troks came toward us and went for their weapons. We took control of them examining their minds. They were only guards, we sent them to the ship after disarming them. We reached the large chamber. There were about fourteen Troks standing around listening to one speaking.

He must be an officer, I transmitted to Dalcamy.

Yes, we'll keep him with us.

We walked boldly into the chamber. The Troks turned toward us and were seized with mind control before they could draw their weapons. We walked up and disarmed them. Dalcamy examined the one that was speaking and found he was the one in charge of this mine. His name was Bok Crall, he wore an insignia on his cap. Bok is their term for his rank, it's about equal to an Earth lieutenant. *He will stay with us, the rest will go to the ship.*

A Vulgarb made contact with Crall. "How did you do that?" he asked.

"We will ask the questions," I said, "and you will answer. Do you have communication between the mines?" He wouldn't reply, but the answer came to his mind.

They do, Dalcamy said, *a radio on his belt.*

I took the radio off his belt. He couldn't understand how I knew. He didn't seem to be frightened of us, he kept watching for a chance to escape.

"Where are the other three guards?"

He looked at us and started thinking about his "General Orders".

He's caught on Dalcamy, he knows we're telepathic. "You can answer, or we will take the information from you. You won't enjoy it I guarantee you," I said.

He still concentrated on his "General Orders".

Dalcamy walked up to him and touched his head. He flinched and staggered back. The Vulgarb caught him for balance. I received confused thoughts from him.

What did you do? I asked.

I zapped him, Dalcamy said with humor. *Won't damage him, but it'll give him something to think about.*

He recovered quickly and concentrated harder on his "General Orders". We told the Vulgarb to examine him only for the information pertaining to the mines. He fought valiantly, but lost the battle. We soon had all the information we needed.

"You can make it easier on your men by telling them to surrender," I said.

"I will not betray them."

Take him to the ship, Dalcamy ordered.

We continued into the cave were the Vulgarbs were being held. The remaining three were guarding them. We walked up behind one and took control. We could see another directly across the chamber and the third halfway around to our right. We started around staying in the shadows as we followed the path. The guard spotted us, but too late. Dalcamy took him. The third guard was more watchful. He spotted us when we were halfway to him and drew his ray gun. Dalcamy stepped out and advanced. The guard drew a bead and fired. The blast exploded against Dalcamy's shield and he continued to advance. The guard fired again and Dalcamy walked up and grabbed the ray gun out of his hand. He took his arm and came back with him. The soldier was too frightened to know what to do. When he saw us he started to struggle, but Dalcamy was stronger. We were ready for the second mine. Three hours had passed and we needed new tanks. We changed and the empties were sent back to the ship to be refilled.

This is taking longer than I expected, Dalcamy said, *three hours gone and three mines left, we must move faster.*

We went to the second mine. A guard spotted us as we entered. He yelled out once before we took control. We sent him out and continued. Five guards came running and had their ray guns in hand, they fired when they saw us. I was knocked down and heard Dalcamy call my name. I answered with a quick "okay" as the five were taken.

What happened? Dalcamy asked.

It just knocked me down, that's all.

We'll have to increase your shield, it shouldn't have done that.

Let's go on and get finished, I said. *Someone must have heard those shots.*

We were met by ten more with guns drawn, but this time we had them before they could fire.

None of these are leaders, we must hurry, Dalcamy said.

We arrived at the first large chamber, it was empty. We went on into the second chamber and found more Vulgarbs in the pit. We scanned the area, there were no guards.

There must be another passage on the other side, I said.

The passage was narrow. We followed it down and saw the other four crouched down. They started blasting as we approached. I didn't have Tolkal with me this time. He had to help take the prisoners out. My shield held up better as we took control and found the leader. He had radioed to the next mine there was trouble.

We'll meet them in the first chamber, Dalcamy said, *come on.* We stayed on the opposite side and spread out. *Wait until they all enter then take control.*

We waited about ten minutes. They came in very quietly and stayed to the boulders for cover. One spoke on his radio. We counted ten men after taking control and gathering them up.

He's not a leader, Dalcamy said as we removed the radio from the soldier. A Vulgarb made contact with him.

"Who were you talking to on this?"

"The others, they'll get you. They know you're here, you don't stand a chance. You know that don't you?"

"Good, you will tell them you need help in this first chamber. You have two prisoners and there are more to get," Dalcamy ordered.

"No, I won't."

Dalcamy touched his head. "Here's the radio," he offered when the soldier recovered. The Trok looked at Dalcamy and took the radio.

"Bok Posh! I need help in the meeting chamber. I have two prisoners, but there's more."

Posh acknowledged and the radio was silent.

"Good," Dalcamy said. "Weather Man and I will be your prisoners." *The rest of you scatter and wait until they're all around us then take control.*

But you may be taken control of, too, said one of the Vulgarbs.

Doesn't matter, Dalcamy answered as I stepped up beside him. He took control of the soldier and put a blaster in his hand. Then we waited. The other ten came, the leader came in first and the soldiers spread out searching the chamber. Dalcamy and I stood still, watching them advance.

"These are the two, Dak?"

Dak couldn't answer.

"Where are the rest of the men?" The soldiers were almost to us now. "Dak! What's the matter with you?" He pulled on his shoulder and Dak turned around and stared at him with the blaster pointing at his middle. Posh snatched the blaster from his hand and covered us. "Dak!" He shook him.

The soldiers came over when they heard Posh yelling at Dak. One of them tried to grab my arm and pulled his hand away shaking it like something was stuck to his hand. He starred at me then poked me with a claw. "He tingles," he said. Then his eyes just stared. Everyone stared, me too. Our people came to us and I turned my shield off so they could lead me away from the rest. Sadek started laughing at us. *Think we should keep them like that? I think it's an improvement.*

I'd laugh too if I could, I received from Dalcamy.

We were released with giggles. Dalcamy and I let them enjoy their joke and then we herded everyone out and regrouped with fresh tanks for the last mine.

There were three sentries posted outside the entrance. One on each side and one on an outcrop over the opening. The cave was facing us as Dalcamy crept up to the last large boulder and observed them.

They have different weapons, he transmitted.

I sneaked up behind him and took a look. *They look similar to rifle*s, I said. *They probably have a longer range.* The guard on top lifted what looked like binoculars to his eyes and turned in all directions. When he faced us he yelled out and began firing. There were explosions all around us. Dalcamy stepped out and took control of all three. We started to approach and shots came from inside. I fell with a stinging blow on my right arm about midway between my shoulder and elbow. It burned and I rolled on it thinking I would smother any flames. Dalcamy and Sadek immediately ran to me covering me with their shields. *Your shield is not strong enough, Mike,* Sadek said. He checked my arm and found a burned crease. He wrapped it to stop the bleeding. Better go back to the ship, he said.

And miss all the fun? I answered. *Not on your life!* I got up and continued with Sadek. We ran to the side of the cave and led the three away. I examined the binoculars the guard was using, they registered body heat. They could detect animal temperatures from natural surroundings. *Hmm, that could come in handy,* I thought as I hung them around my neck.

I crept up to the side of the entrance of the mine with Sadek and Dalcamy behind me. As I peeked around I came face to face with a muzzle and took control of its owner before he could pull the trigger. We took three more. I had the Vulgarbs make contact with them. "Which one shot me?" I asked. They stood looking at me.

That one did. Said Dalcamy. *He pointed to the center soldier.*

"What's your name?"

"Morck. I'm sorry I missed!"

"I bet you are. Who taught you to shoot?" I took a blaster from the Vulgarb. "This yours?" I looked at it, then lifted it to my shoulder. "Well? Is it?" I aimed it out the cave at a boulder. It had sights just like an Earth rifle. I turned to the soldier and he stiffened.

"Yes!"

He thinks you're going to kill him. Dalcamy said.

Yeah. "How's your eyesight?"

"My eyesight?"

"Better have it checked." I gave the blaster back to the Vulgarb and ordered the prisoners taken to the ship. We walked down the tunnel.

They were waiting for us as we entered the first chamber. They were using their hand guns. Six more were taken, but one got away running down another passage before we could gain control of him. We could hear him yelling as we ran to the passage. Shots rang out and boulders began to drop from the ceiling blocking our exit. We continued and more fell as our passage was blocked. *We walked into a trap,* Dalcamy said.

There were six of us sealed in a ten foot section of the tunnel. Sadek, Dalcamy and I with our three Vulgarbs.

Are you all right? We received from Bocha on the other side.

Yes, Dalcamy answered. *Stand back I'm going to get us out.*

We moved as far away from Dalcamy as we could. He turned toward the boulders and they started exploding. Pieces were deflected by our shields and soon the passage was cleared.

Some ran that way, Bocha transmitted as he pointed to the passageway on the other side.

We better split up. Half go that way, Dalcamy ordered. *Weather Man and the rest come with me.*

We headed back into the passage and Dalcamy cleared our way. We followed it and came to an opening on the side. We could hear voices as we approached. We moved closely to the wall and Dalcamy looked around the corner, he was met with shots. Someone started yelling and I could hear static. I ran to the other side of the entrance as more shots hit the opposite wall of the tunnel and Dalcamy took control of the shooter. I entered and found another screaming into the radio, I took control and examined him.

He's already called their planet, they're sending ships.

CHAPTER 8

As we entered the first chamber with our prisoners Bocha and the others met us with theirs and we started back to our ships.

We have forty prisoners on each ship, Caltomacoe explained.

We led our officer prisoner into the library of my ship after Dalcamy told Caltomacoe to get the other officers. We had the Vulgarbs make contact with all of them.

"Gentlemen," Dalcamy started, "now we will talk. You want the ore on this planet. The Vulgarbs are taking their people back."

A large Vulgarb walked in holding a probe in his tentacle. *I understand you are attempting to communicate with these . . . things*, he said with hatred so strong you could almost see it in the air around him. The officers caught it and faced him with pride and bravery.

They're certainly not cowards, I transmitted to Dalcamy.

Dalcamy continued, "The Vulgarbs do not mind you taking the ore, they have no use for it. They don't like you making slaves of them and neither do we." I read one of the officer's mind as he thought about his argument against slavery, but the others wouldn't listen. His name was Sepulved.

"You have more ships coming to help you," I stated.

There was relief, thoughts of 'they got through, good, things will change, we'll be free soon.'

"We will wait for them," Dalcamy said. "Meanwhile, we will learn your language and radio frequency from you so we can communicate with them."

"Why do you want to communicate with them?" Bok Micon asked.

"We do not intend to have a war with you over ore. None of your Troks have been harmed and we have the Vulgarbs back. We intend to negotiate with your kind for a mutual arrangement between you and the Vulgarbs."

"We are called Chikes when referred to as a group."

Dalcamy smiled. "Thank you."

First I want to know who killed Morga, the large Vulgarb said.

"Who's Morga?" asked Bok Crall.

He was killed by you twenty summers ago, he was of me."

I understood he meant they were brothers. The officers looked at each other. "Do you know anything about this?" asked Bok Crall of them.

"I do," answered Sepulved. "He was the first capture. We approached him as friends and tricked him into coming to the cave where we asked him questions. He figured out what we were up to and escaped. We chased him, but he was too fast and one of the soldiers shot him."

"Where is that soldier now?" I asked.

"I don't know. He's no longer in the fleet."

Was he punished? The Vulgarb asked.

"No."

The Vulgarb stepped forward pointing the probe at the officer. *Then you will take his place.*

The officer faced him and would not back away. "You think that will change anything?" he asked.

It will give me satisfaction. The Vulgarb answered as he jabbed with the probe intending to zap him. Sparks flew as Dalcamy stepped between them and took the probe with his shield.

"We do not torture life forms. There will be another way to appease your anger," Dalcamy said.

The Vulgarb looked down at Dalcamy. *Your plan better be good.*

"One of you will sit here," Dalcamy ordered pointing to a chair in front of one of the computers. "We will record your language."

The officers looked at each other and refused to cooperate. Dalcamy took control of Posh and made him sit. I set the computer to record his brain waves as Dalcamy placed the cap on his head and released him. The officers were concerned for Posh and objected.

"It won't hurt him," I said. I explained as we proceeded. His brain waves appeared on the screen and were recorded. Dalcamy set the computer to receive. The officer concentrated on his "General Orders" it was recorded with everything else he knew. When the computer finished recording, it began to sort the information and analyze the language with the understanding of the Trok. Once the meaning of the words was deciphered, they were compared with the Artarian language. When the language was organized the computer signaled and Dalcamy sat down placing the cap on his head. An hour later he was speaking their language. The Troks were very impressed.

"Your shields on your ship turns it invisible," Dalcamy said.

"You got that from Posh?"

"I know everything he does now, and Mike does too from my mind."

"You are telepathic then, I thought so!" said Crall.

"Your ships will be here in seven days, I hope they have someone of authority on them."

"They won't stop to talk once they find out what you've done." We received pictures of an immediate attack from Micon.

"They will risk killing all of you?" Caltomacoe asked.

"We do not allow hostages."

Same as Earth, I transmitted, *but they still negotiate.*

"We will contact them before they arrive," Dalcamy said. We all went to control and Dalcamy proceeded to call their ships. "Attention Trok Military Fleet. You are in route to Vulgarb. I am Captain Dalcamy of the planet Artara. We have captured all eighty of your chikes, none have been harmed. They will be released to you when you land."

"Why did you attack our chikes?"

"To free the Vulgarb slaves."

"This is none of your business. You will surrender when we land or be destroyed."

"If you think you can destroy us, you're welcome to try. Just consider; twenty-four of us captured all eighty of your chikes in one day with no casualties." Dalcamy broke contact.

Do they have weapons installed in their ships? I asked Dalcamy.

Yes, blasting rays. We will set the shields on our ships.

"They will come in shooting," Sepulved said.

"Fine, they will be shooting at you as well," Dalcamy answered.

"It won't make any difference."

Dalcamy set the shields.

So soon? I asked.

I don't want any surprises. Especially since we won't see them coming and they may be closer than we think. Tolkal, tell your people we will be moving our ships closer to the mines. We don't want your city to be in any danger. Also, they may want some representatives to stay with us when we make contact. Weather Man, you will go to medical with me.

He handed me a gown as we entered, I changed and laid in the opercule.

"What is this thing?" Micon asked.

"Our medical computer," answered Dalcamy. Dalcamy cleaned and sealed my arm, "I'm going to increase your shield, Weather Man."

"Okay." I felt three injections and a probe entered my side after it numbed to make the adjustment. When he was finished I put a fresh uniform on and rejoined Dalcamy and the others in the kitchen. I poured myself a cup of asil and sat. Tolkal had left to talk with his council so we had no communication going between us and the Vulgarbs that remained. I motioned to the large Vulgarb for him to make contact with me.

What are you called? I asked after the dizziness went away.

Hagankol.

You will stay with us?

Yes.

Good.

"When your ships start shooting at us you will all leave the ship and stand outside around it." Dalcamy said to the officers.

"Those will be full blasters! You're going to make us walk out in that?" said Posh.

"Mike and five of my men will lead you out. Your chikes will be safe, the shields of the ship will protect you. When your chikes see that their weapons have no effect on us, they may be willing to talk. I will stay in control and Mike will speak to them when they are ready."

"What if the chikes start to run?" asked Crall.

"They will not be able to go through the shields. However, they may harm themselves if they run into them. It would be like running into a metal wall. You might warn them before we take them out, they will not be able to see our shields."

He will stay with me, Hagankol said motioning to Sepulved.

I transmitted his message to Dalcamy.

"I cannot promise you that, Hagankol," Dalcamy answered. He is not guilty of the murder."

He was in charge! I will take him now! Hagankol wrapped a tentacle around Sepulved's chest, lifted him out of his seat and held him in the air in front of him. The officers became alarmed and tried to grab their comrade, but Hagankol was too fast for anyone to stop him. *I can crush him like the animal he is!*

Dalcamy stood up. "Go ahead! Kill him! If that's really what you want. But remember, your people will be living here after we leave. They will not have the protection of our shields. You kill him, his chikes will take revenge on your people. You want that? If you're willing to live with that, then go ahead and kill him."

Hagankol held Sepulved aloft and stared at him for a long time. The officer stared back and waited. Hagankol wanted to kill him, to tear him apart like Morga was torn. He shook Sepulved and dropped him. Sepulved picked himself up off the floor and went back to his seat. Hagankol left the room.

"I'm sorry his brother was killed," Sepulved said.

"Why?" Micon said, "They're just plants!"

"They are intelligent life! We had no right to do what we did! You know that!"

"Shut-up!" Crall yelled. "Remember where you are!"

The two officers glared at each other.

CHAPTER 9

Bocha entered and announced that several Vulgarbs had arrived to stay with us and negotiate with the Troks. Dalcamy went back to his ship after they boarded. We went to control and prepared to move our ships. We lifted and followed Dalcamy to an area central to the mines and settled down again. Two officers were taken to Dalcamy's ship to explain the situation to the soldiers while the other two remained on my ship and spoke to their chikes. The soldiers were kept in eight sleeping rooms, five to each room. We had nineteen meet with one officer in the meeting room and nineteen in the library with the other officer while we monitored the conversations in control. I had learned enough of their language to understand most of what was being said, and Caltomacoe translated when I had trouble.

"Why don't we jump them when we get out?" one of the soldiers said.

"It wouldn't do any good, we can't get through the barrier around the ship."

"We could threaten them into releasing us."

"These creatures will not break under threats, and with their mental powers we wouldn't be able to jump them. Just cooperate with them for your own safety. They won't be asking anything from you."

We gathered the food from the mines for the Troks and allowed their cooks to prepare it for them. We also took samples of each food for analysis. The computer reported the food was safe for Artarians and Humans.

I continued to learn the Trok language. The third day I took Morck outside the ship. I carried his blaster as I directed him out away from the ships. Tolkal and Corcar accompanied us. Morck was scared and figured I was still going to kill him with his own blaster. "Look up there." I pointed to a large boulder. On the very top were three twelve-inch rocks. I had an Artarian put them up there with his mind earlier. "I want you to shoot them. One at a time." I handed him the blaster.

What's keeping him from shooting you? Tolkal asked.

Me.

Morck took the blaster and looked at me. I looked right back at him.

"Don't waste any shots. Three rocks, three shots." He shouldered the blaster and took aim. He hit the first two and missed the last one. *Tolkal, put two more rocks up there.* Two rocks floated up and settled in the same places. "Again."

Dalcamy came up behind us as Morck took aim. He missed the first rock. I walked up behind him. "Take a deep breath and hold it. Now squeeze the trigger gently, like a caress."

He exhaled with a high-pitched squeal. "I can't believe this! You're my enemy and you're giving me shooting lessons!"

"I may be your enemy right now, but I'm not a deadly enemy. Go on, do as I tell you." He took a deep breath, held it and squeezed the trigger. The rock blew to pieces, he aimed at the second, it exploded. "Don't let yourself get winded, breathe between shots." The third rock disappeared. *Tolkal, three more rocks, please?* The rocks floated up and settled down. "Again, Morck." All three rocks disappeared. He hit each one dead center. "Good. Now we can go back." I took the blaster and we walked back to the ship.

"You just taught him how to kill you the first time." Dalcamy said laughing.

"Exactly, the next time he aims a blaster his life may depend on his accuracy." I couldn't resist watching on the monitor as Morck told the other soldiers about his shooting lesson.

"Why didn't you shoot him and get away?"

"Don't you remember how they took us? Do you really think I could have escaped? It would have been stupid to try. He would have only gotten angry, then he might have killed me."

"He's right, Sarg, we are no match for them. They can paralyze us without touching us."

"How can they do that?"

I turned off the monitor. We had no trouble with any of the prisoners. Some of them began looking at their captivity as a vacation from their duties. There was no doubt in their minds that their ships would free them and destroy their captors.

I saw Hagankol outside one afternoon; he had been avoiding us. I went out to him and he made contact with me. I could feel his depression and anger as the dizziness subsided.

I'm sorry Hagankol, I said.

I know, he answered. *I can feel you. It angers me to think they are going to get away with it.*

Maybe not, sometimes on my planet restitution is made through the governments. On our world they usually pay with gold or something valuable. Isn't there anything that would help pay back to you what you've lost?

How can you put a value on a life? He asked.

Well, you can't, but no matter what is done that life won't come back. Even if the guilty person is punished, your brother's life was still wasted and nothing can change that. But there must be some way for their government to show you they're sorry about it, and also give you a chance to release the bad feelings you have.

I will think about it, Mike.

Five days passed since we spoke to the Trok fleet and we had no word from them since. The prisoners were getting restless expecting them to come anytime now. We double-checked all our power sources and reserves to be ready for the worst. On the sixth day I was talking with Hagankol outside the ship again.

What would you think of a memorial for your brother? I asked.

What is that?

Well, the mines could be named after him with a plaque that would tell the whole story how he was killed and by whom. Earth does it for men that have done great things or even lost their lives for their countries. It would make a hero of your brother and he would never be forgotten by your planet or any other that sees the monument. We could call it the Morga Mines Memorial. And the Troks would have to honor him every year by closing down the mines for seven days. Three days before his death and three days after.

Hagankol looked at me. *That would show him honor. You could get them to do that?*

If they want to keep these mines, it would be stipulated in the agreement or else we'll seal those mines up so deep they'll never get to the ore again. Do you remember exactly what he looked like?

Of course.

Come with me. Caltomacoe, I transmitted, *I would like you to install a computer beaming rod on the exterior of the ship.* I received his acknowledgment as we went into the library. I had Hagankol put on a cap. *I'm going to set the computer to draw a picture of your brother. Picture in your mind his whole image front and back.*

Why?

Don't ask me why, just do it for me, I smiled. I loaded the program and ran it. When the instruction to transmit was given I nodded. Hagankol started to think of his brother from the head down. The computer began drawing; two images appeared front and back along with measurements of depth and height.

We went over and over the images until every detail was recorded. It took all the rest of the afternoon and into the evening. When it was finally finished we sat together and looked at it.

That's him.

The date, I said.

We discovered him the morning following the passing of the Sakitt Comet in the three thousand eighty-sixth summer.

You don't number your days, or name your months?

No, we keep track by what happens in the sky and how the climate changes.

Okay. I recorded the information into the computer under the picture. *How many summers did he live?*

Thirty.

I put it in. *How long is your average life span here?*

Around three hundred summers.

Three hundred! Do you keep growing all that time?

I felt humor coming from him although he didn't have any external expression of humor. I didn't think they could laugh, but the humor felt good and strong. *Yes, but slower. How long do you live?*

Eighty, ninety, lucky if we reach a hundred.

And do you keep growing? He asked.

Not after twenty-one. We even shrink a little when we get old, the bones settle.

If it was at all possible he would have laughed into hysteria his humor became so strong. I started laughing for him and couldn't stop as tears rolled down my cheeks.

What is this? He asked as he touched my tears.

Tears, I said trying to gain control again. *Our eyes release them under strong emotions, usually sadness or laughter.*

Laughter, it must be good to do that.

The humor is triggered by our minds. The body responds as laughter. It's mostly uncontrollable. There was a time after an operation when my body couldn't respond in laughter, but I still felt the humor in my mind like you do. It's just as good.

CHAPTER 10

I woke early the morning of the seventh day, had breakfast with Caltomacoe then went to control and checked our energies and power again for the thousandth time within the last seven days. Everything was in readiness. At ten in the morning there was an explosion outside the ship. I viewed the landscape to see where it was, a crater appeared ten feet away. I turned the radio on and tuned to their frequency.

"Welcome! Are we having fun yet?"

I thought Caltomacoe was going to fall off his chair with laughter. There were a series of explosions all around the exterior of both ships. They weren't even coming close to hitting us. Dalcamy came on screen.

"I think they're bluffing, Weather Man. They're trying to see what we're made of. Wait until it really gets heavy and then go out."

It was quiet for fifteen minutes. I turned the monitors on the prisoners to see their reaction to this. They were sitting quietly, waiting. A second blast of five shots came, they moved up a little closer. There were five minutes of silence, then five more shots, closer. I caught their plan; they're going to move closer every five minutes.

Caltomacoe, I transmitted, *in about twenty minutes they will be hitting our shields. That's when we go out with the prisoners in the middle of the blasts.*

The five Artarians to go out with me were waiting by the airlock with their tanks. I put mine on and we went to get the prisoners.

"Come out and wait at the airlock." They were very cooperative. Everyone lined up in ten minutes with the officers and us in front. "Remember," I said, "just stand by the ship, you'll be safe there."

Ten minutes later the first shot hit dead center on top of us. We opened the airlock and started exiting the ship. Explosions flashed all over the ship as our shields deflected the blasts. The prisoners followed us out dodging and cringing under the explosions until they realized they were safe. The shooting stopped and when the dust cleared away we were all visible. We could hear the roar of the engines of invisible ships. I looked over at Dalcamy's ship and saw his ring of chikes.

A soldier in my group made a break for it running as fast as he could. Sadek took control of him before he hit the shield. I walked up to him and Sadek released him. I took him by the arm and walked further out with him. "Look," I said as I pounded on the shield. "Touch it." He reached out and felt the shield. "Hit it!" I ordered. He hit it with his open hand. "If you had run into that you would have been hurt. Don't be stupid, you're almost home now." We walked back to the others.

More blasts came at us. They were low and parallel with the ground as though they were shooting directly at us. "Come on!" I yelled as I motioned with my arm for them to follow and started walking to the shield toward the explosions. They became more intense as we walked. We stopped a foot away from the shield and waited.

Finally they stopped. The soldiers all stood around looking at each other and were silent. A ship appeared ten feet away.

It looked like a large plane. There was a circular opening underneath that protruded from the main body about three feet. The craft stood on landing gears very much like a jet. I wondered how it would take off without a runway. The wings held blasters, three on each wing.

Mike, I received from Dalcamy, *go out and meet them.*

I walked toward the shield as Caltomacoe opened the section in front of me. As I approached, the alien ship opened and a Trok exited. We met half way.

"I'm Lor Sham." I understood he was the equivalent of a General.

"I'm Captain Packard," I responded.

"I was monitoring your lesson to that soldier, Captain Packard. You fight a war strangely."

"I don't consider this a war, just a mistake that can be corrected. Where shall we talk, your ship or mine?"

"You would enter my ship voluntarily?" I felt his surprise. This soft skinned creature is either very brave, or he has defenses I can't see. He looked me over as he thought.

"You are a Lor, correct?"

"Yes."

"On my planet Lors are honorable. When they sit down to talk, that's what they do. I believe you are honorable."

"My ship then." I followed him. Several soldiers stood at attention fully armed.

The Captain of the ship approached us. "Shall I search him for weapons, Sir?"

"No, you will see to it that we are not disturbed."

"Yes, Sir."

He led me to his office and motioned to a chair. I sat as he filled two cups with a hot black liquid and sat on the other side of the desk.

"Now," he started as he handed me a cup. "What is the mistake that you say can be corrected?"

"You have been mining here for twenty years, correct?"

"Yes."

"And you have been using the Vulgarbs as slaves."

"I understand that's so. I was not aware of that until I received your transmission."

"Then it isn't a standard procedure to take slaves?"

"No, we need the ore for our ships. Our planet is depleted and we found it is very difficult to locate. We knew there was intelligent life here, but they didn't seem to care about us mining the ore. At least they made no effort to contact us and we tried to transmit to them, but received no answer.

"When our mining crew started working they had no resistance from them so they were left to handle the mining their own way. We had no idea they were taking slaves."

"I was hoping that was the case," I said.

"The Vulgarbs don't care about the ore, but they do care about their people and they want to meet with you. One of them was killed when this first started. His name was Morga, restitution will have to be made for that. Then I don't think you will have any trouble continuing to mine here."

"And what might that 'restitution' be?"

"Making the mines a memorial to the dead Vulgarb. Then honoring him by closing down the mines for the week of his death. Also a plaque displayed telling the story."

"How did he die?"

I told him the story. When I finished the General stood up and turned toward a screen on his wall that was tuned to my ship and the chikes.

"Why didn't they answer us when we tried to make contact?"

"They didn't hear you. They didn't hear us either when we transmitted. They never saw your ships. They only learned of you since we've been here."

"We've been mining here for twenty years and they didn't know it?"

"Right, they thought their people were being eaten by wild animals and that accounted for their disappearance."

"Incredible!" He sat again and pushed a button on his desk. I heard the door open behind me as I took a sip from my cup, I didn't turn around. Coffee! It was coffee, strong and rich.

"Sir!"

"I want to know who the first officers in charge of setting up the mines were."

"Yes, Sir!" I heard the door close again.

"One of the officers is on my ship," I said. "He was against the slavery, but the others out ruled him. This is very good. We have a beverage just like it on Earth."

"We grow it in the mountains. What is the officer's name?"

"Bok Sepulved, he was the one that told me the story about Morga."

"You don't want him punished?"

"He wasn't responsible."

There was a knock on the door. "Enter!" The soldier came in with a file and left. The General read the file. "There were two others besides Bok Sepulved, they're dead now. I would like to talk to Bok Sepulved."

I transmitted to Sadek to send him. "He's on his way."

The General looked at me.

"Watch your monitor," I said nodding to his screen.

He watched as Sadek accompanied Sepulved to the shield. Just before they reached it, Hagankol moved up to Sepulved and made contact with him making him stagger.

"What is that Vulgarb doing?"

"That's how they communicate, it makes you a little dizzy at first. He's the brother of Morga."

"He's not angry?"

"Yes, very, he wanted to kill Sepulved, literally tear him to pieces. You have brave chikes General they were just out matched."

"You are telepathic," the General said as he came back to his desk.

"Yes." I finished my drink and stood up. "I'll go back to my ship so you can talk to him. When the other two ships land, we will release your chikes. You understand we are only holding them now for their protection. We don't want anyone getting hurt because of an accident."

"I understand."

The General opened the door and as I left the ship I met Sepulved on my way back.

"Goodbye, Bok Sepulved, perhaps we'll meet again sometime."

"I hope we do, goodbye, Captain Packard."

I returned to my ship and joined Caltomacoe in control. Dalcamy came on screen.

"That was a good meeting, Weather Man."

"I think things will work out," I answered.

An hour later two more ships landed. We released the prisoners by turning off our shields. I saw General Sham approaching my ship on the screen and went to the air lock to meet him.

"Welcome, Lor Sham."

"Thank you, I came to meet with the Vulgarbs."

"Fine." I led him to the meeting room that we reorganized with a small table and five chairs.

"It would be better if you were sitting down when they make contact. One will make contact with you and the others will join through him. They make circular motions as a sign of intentions." I transmitted to Sadek to have them come in as the General took a seat. They entered and moved up to the table towering over the General. I could feel his intimidation and stood beside him. Tolkal moved forward making circular motions toward the General and touched his forehead. The others joined in and they began to communicate. I took a chair and waited. After a couple of hours Corcar came toward me with circular motions and made contact. *We are about finished, is there anything you want to say before we leave?*

There is one more thing. I would like them to set up a round pillar in about the same position as my ship thirty feet high and ten feet in diameter. Made out of a non-corrosive metal all one piece.

The message was relayed and the General nodded. After the Vulgarbs left the General turned to me. "They are remarkable creatures."

"And very excitable," I said. "They are curious about everyone and seek knowledge about anything."

"I'll have a different crew sent in to do the mining. One that will get along with the Vulgarbs and I will personally make a yearly inspection to make sure this doesn't happen again."

CHAPTER 11

Two ships left for home with the eighty chikes the following morning. Lor Sham and I met with Dalcamy aboard his ship for breakfast.

"A new mining crew is on their way." Sham said as we ate. "How long have you been here?"

"About a month now," Dalcamy answered. "Where is your planet?"

"On the other side of the sun. It keeps the same orbit as this one so it's never seen from here."

"The Vulgarbs would never have discovered it," I said.

"That's an interesting shielding device you have on your ship," Dalcamy commented. "Did you design it purposely to make you invisible?"

"No, actually that was a bonus. It's the combination of the metals and energies used that causes it. We've only had it for the past eight years. We had to make a tracking system to be able to see our own ships in space. It was quite a problem in the beginning; we almost threw it out. Where are your planets?"

"We come from two different systems, Mike comes from Earth. Our map references are probably different from yours, it would be better to show you on our screen. We've been searching for other planets with intelligent life. Perhaps we could establish a relationship with yours as well."

"That's possible, do you power your ships with ore?"

"No, we use only energies. I'll show you around when we finish eating. You may want to convert your ships eventually since your ore is so hard to find. I don't imagine these mines will last forever."

"We haven't tried to leave our solar system. It would take generations to get that far at the speed we travel and we couldn't carry enough ore to do it. How long did it take you to get here?"

"Six months. It only took three months to get to Mike's world, his is our neighboring system. His was our first contact with another planet."

"In fact," I said grinning, "I was their first contact period."

"Yes," Dalcamy laughed. "I forget that we kidnapped you."

"Kidnapped?" Lor Sham asked looking at me.

"Yes, just like in the movies. Creatures from outer space kidnapping Earthlings and carrying them away to fates unknown." We all enjoyed a good laugh over that. The Trok laughter is a high-pitched squeal. Not very loud, I could hear him exhaling with the squeal.

"Come, I'll show you around," Dalcamy said when we finished eating. Lor Sham enjoyed the tour and asked many questions. It was the first time I saw Dalcamy's ship. It was very similar to Borkalami's. We showed him the control room last. The walls were light gray like my ship. A deep blue carpet covered the floor. Dark gray padded chairs stood at each station; adjustable recliners that gave full body support and protection. Dalcamy sat at a station and worked the keyboard while we stood behind him. Lor Sham pointed out Trok when his system appeared on the screen. Dalcamy brought up the maps of our systems in smaller scale inserts and pointed out our planets. He charted the locations of both our planets in relationship to Trok.

"Just in case you want to pay us a visit," Dalcamy said as he handed him a hard copy of the maps.

"I don't advise you to go to Earth yet," I said. "They're not quite ready for a lot of visitors, they need more time."

"Would you like to take a ride?" Dalcamy asked. "Just to see what she'll do?"

"Yes, I would," he answered. He looked at me. "So long as you don't plan to kidnap me."

I grinned and Dalcamy laughed. "That's Captain Borkalami's specialty, not mine."

"Perhaps you'd like to tell your chikes so they won't think we are abducting you," I said.

He spoke with the Captain of his ship and fifteen minutes later Dalcamy was starting the engines as we strapped into our seats. We lifted slowly and climbed steadily then picked up speed as we rose. We broke out into space like we were shot out of a cannon.

"How long would it take for you to get to my planet?" Sham asked.

"Let's take an estimate. I'll angle the sun and you tell me when you can see your planet."

Two hours later he spotted Trok. Dalcamy turned on the computer to recommend a path and time needed for arrival.

"Three days," said Dalcamy.

"Three days," he marveled. "This is a fine ship."

"Mine's better," I said, "bigger."

"I noticed," laughed Sham. "That's not all that's bigger."

Dalcamy laughed until he cried. "Well, Weather Man, he got you. When things are settled on Vulgarb, why don't we pay your planet a visit? We'll take you home."

"Yes, I think my Melcon would like to meet you." We turned around and went back to Vulgarb.

Dalcamy and I made a full report to Commodore Mackalie after Lor Sham left. "I think this is going to be a very interesting planet, Sir."

"Perhaps the most favorable. You may have found what we've been looking for," the Commodore agreed.

Three weeks later a ship landed with new Troks to run the mines. The pillar I had requested was installed. I moved the ship to about ten yards from it and had everyone clear out of the area. I set the programming and with the engines running to boost the computer power I pushed the button to activate.

The pillar came alive with sparks and bolts of energy, pieces flew and some areas melted. It glowed so brightly it was painful to look at it. The computer filtered the brightness as I watched the progress on screen. After an hour the computer shut down. Then I had the computer cover it with the same type of material our medical gowns are made of. I transmitted to Dalcamy to have everyone come back. When they arrived I set the computer for remote operation and went outside.

Everyone was standing around the covered pillar, the whole population of the Vulgarb city and all the Troks. I walked up to Hagankol and motioned for him to make contact with me. I told everyone to move back and stand next to my ship. Hagankol and I stood in front of everyone and I handed him the remote control. *Push this button*, I instructed.

He pushed the button and a blue flash from the ship lit up the pillar as the cover disintegrated and revealed a thirty-foot likeness of Morga with a plaque at his base telling the whole story. The statue stood gleaming in the afternoon sun.

Hagankol dropped the control, picked me up and circled the statue. He stopped at the plaque, set me down and read.

MORGA

First captive of the Troks to work as a slave mining ore to power their space ships. He was killed at the age of thirty while escaping to warn his people in the summer of 3086 following the passing of Sakitt Comet. These mines are named in honor of this Vulgarb hero.

THE MORGA MINES MEMORIAL

Mike, I don't know what to say to you.

You don't need to say it, Hagankol; I can feel it.

The others moved up and joined us with exclamations of wonder and appreciation as they read the plaque. Lor Sham came up and stood beside me. Yes, he thought, not only does this make a good restitution, but it also will serve as a good reminder to our chikes.

"I'm glad you approve, Lor Sham," I said. "I look forward to a lasting friendship between all our worlds."

"Tell me about your planet," he said as we walked.

"Earth or Artara?"

"Which one do you favor?"

"Artara."

"All right, tell me about Artara."

"Come into my ship, I'll show you." I took him to control.

"I don't blame you for being proud of your ship." He stood in the center of the room and looked at everything. The red carpeting and light gray, thickly padded chairs at each station. He lightly touched the concave keys on the control panels. "You mind?" He motioned to the Captain's Chair.

"Go ahead." He sat down and swung the command console over his lap. I watched him look up at the screen and envision the universe. "Mine is the latest model. On Earth, Borkalami or Dalcamy would have her before me. I'm a new Captain. Artara does things differently," I shrugged. "I am proud of her."

Music started outside. Dalcamy broadcasted square dancing music and the party began. The Vulgarbs took to square dancing like fish to water. We watched them for a while on the monitor.

"Is that some kind of ritual dancing?" Lor Sham asked.

"No. We taught the dance to them. It originated on Earth." We sat at a station together and shared the caps as I visualized Artara.

"That seems like a pretty mild group of people for you to have the talent you show in military tactics."

"Military tactics?"

"Yes, I heard the stories from my chikes of how they were captured. Especially the first one you caught, Heise. What did you do to him?"

"I scared him."

"You certainly did, he's leaving the fleet because of it. Say's he never wants to see another planet as long as he lives. You know that soldier starts shaking if your name is just mentioned."

"Hmm, I didn't intend that. I figured he'd get over it when he found he wasn't hurt. How long will it take him to get out of the fleet?"

"About a month, why?"

"Was he a good soldier before? One you'd want to keep?"

"Yes."

"Things should be wrapped up here in another couple of days. Maybe I can have a talk with him when we go to your planet."

"You think you can change his mind?"

"Well, maybe I can find out what he's really afraid of and help him get over it. You see, I didn't really do anything but talk. I gave him a drug that made him dream about what he feared the most at the time."

"Then his fear is all in his mind."

"Yes, maybe I can read him and find out what it is."

"He said you stuffed him in some kind of machine and threatened to eat him."

"I put him in the medical opercule, you saw it. I'll run the memory on it, you can see for yourself." I handed him a cap and explained what it was for. Then I searched the files and loaded the report then ran it up to the episode with our first prisoner and turned on his cap. I shared it with him and switched it off when it was finished. He just sat and thought quietly after removing his cap. I respected his privacy and didn't read him.

"I want to show you one more thing." Again I searched through the files and found the episode when Hagankol picked up Bok Sepulved and shook him. I ran it from the beginning of the conversation. "Now you tell me which one could have been more devastating." I said when he finished listening.

"Obviously Bok Sepulved, his threat was real and immediate. Captain Dalcamy handled it quite well, but why didn't he just control the Vulgarb like you did with our chikes?"

"We can't control the Vulgarbs, their minds are too strong. In fact, there's not much we can do against them except destroy them and we won't do that."

"Well? Where did you get your tactics?"

"From Earth. Want a cup of asil?"

"What's that?"

"It's an Artarian hot drink. Takes the place of Earth coffee." He looked at me and wasn't sure what I meant. "Coffee is an Earth name for the drink you gave me on your ship." I explained as we went into the kitchen. I fixed two cups and handed him one. "It's safe for you, I ran an analysis of our food from the information we recorded from Heise."

He took a sip. "Good." We sat at a table.

"Earth is a violent world. Always warring with each other. I guess certain 'tactics' come natural to Earthlings. Others like Dalcamy, Borkalami, Caltomacoe and Komi learn from training and experience. What about you? You're in the military, surely you've used certain 'tactics' to get information."

"Yes, but more on the physical side."

I got up to refill our cups when something wrapped around my chest and I was picked up off my feet as a tentacle touched my head.

"Hagankol!" I said as my head cleared. "I'm not a rag doll to be picked up at will!"

I'm sorry, Mike, he said as he put me down. *Bocha has been hurt.*

Where is he?

I'll take you to him.

"One of my men is hurt," I explained to the Lor. "I'll be back."

I'm sorry I yelled at you, Hagankol. I need to get a first aid bag from medical first. I went into medical and got the first aid kit. *Now you can take me to him.* He picked me up and out we went.

CHAPTER 12

Hagankol went as fast as he could and set me down next to Bocha. He had intense pain as I scanned his body. He had a crushed leg. I pulled out the numbing disk and held it to different areas of his leg until it was completely numb. *How did this happen?* I asked Hagankol as I worked.

We were demonstrating to the Troks and one of our small ones threw a boulder without looking and it hit Bocha.

I grabbed Bocha's arm to reassure him, "you'll be all right." *Look, Hagankol, I'm not strong enough to lift him with my mind, but you are. Think of him lying on an invisible board and lift him keeping him in the same position he's in and bring him to my ship.* I watched as Hagankol lifted Bocha. He picked me up and we quickly returned to the ship with Bocha floating beside us. Lor Sham met us at the airlock. We set Bocha in the opercule and it examined him after disintegrating his clothes. Lor Sham watched as Bocha was anesthetized and the procedure began. When the opercule finished, Caltomacoe took Bocha to his room. I set a numbing disk by his bed and went to control to have the computer monitor him and let me know when he wakes.

"Will he be all right?" asked Lor Sham.

"Yes, we'll have to give him physical therapy when he's healed enough, the computer says eight weeks." *Why don't you let your people know he's going to be all right, Hagankol, and thanks for your help.*

Dalcamy appeared with all the other Artarians following him. "How's Bocha?" he asked.

"Sleeping now, he'll be all right."

I stayed in control to watch the monitor. Lor Sham stayed with me. "Have you found many inhabited planets in this system?" I asked.

"No, there is one I should warn you about. There's life there, but it's very primitive. I lost five chikes. They attacked as soon as we set down, didn't even give us a chance to talk to them."

"What kind of weapons did they have?"

"Spears mostly and arrows." I brought up the solar system on the screen and he pointed to the fifth planet from the sun. "Don't go there," he said.

"Okay, I won't." I smiled as I turned back to the monitor. "Tell me about your ship. How do you take off and land? From the looks of it, I would think you needed a runway."

"We used to have runways until we developed this design. We can leave the ground straight up then fly parallel if we want. Or leave the planet in an angle and become a rocket in space."

"I see, then you would need two ports of propulsion."

"That's right. Tune your screen to my ship." I tuned it in as he directed. "There's one port underneath, to lift us. See it?"

"Yes."

"There's another just like it in the rear."

"The ground isn't scorched like rockets would cause. What do you emit?"

"Hot air. The force is quite strong. Once we are high enough, we have rockets to push us away from the gravity field. Then we use hot air to navigate space."

"When you return, you rely on the wings to slow you and navigate in atmosphere."

"That's right."

"It must take a tremendous amount of ore to keep your engines running."

"We planned to set space stations around the planet to store extra ore for ships to load from for long trips. Maybe even some of the neighboring planets further out. But, that's infeasible."

"Why?" It sounds like a good idea to me."

"There's only twenty years of ore left here, at our present rate of use. We would double that building the space stations and by the time we get them built, there won't be any ore to put into them."

"This is the only place you can get it?"

"Yes. We surveyed this whole planet. These mountains are the only source."

"Well, I guess you're going to have to come up with something else."

"They're working on it."

We talked for another two hours and the monitor sounded.

"He's waking up," I said as I started for Bocha's room. Caltomacoe met us there and we entered. I grabbed the numbing disk and was numbing his leg when he woke up. "Hi," I smiled.

"Still there?" he asked.

"Still there. You're going to be in bed for three weeks. Then we'll start working on walking again."

"I can catch up on my studies then," he said.

"What are you studying?" I asked.

"Captainship."

"Really! How long you been at it?"

"Just since we started this trip."

"You'll be good at it, Bocha. How's your leg feel?"

"Good now, thanks Mike."

I gave him the numbing disk and turned to Caltomacoe. "I want the computer to monitor him constantly for the next two weeks I don't want him having any more pain than necessary." Then I left with Lor Sham.

Lor Sham had one more meeting with the Vulgarb council and the next day we lifted for Trok with everyone waving goodbye. We stopped at orbiting level to watch the Trok ships rise and then Dalcamy came on screen.

"You lead the way, Weather Man."

I laid in the course and accelerated. "Why does he call you Weather Man?" Lor Sham asked. I laughed and told him the story. We landed three days later.

Melcon Kafka was not there; he had an emergency meeting and had to leave. Lor Sham led us to his office and introduced us to his staff and other Lors. Sham was upset about his Melcon, or President, not being available. "Never there when you need him!" he said.

"How long will he be gone?" I asked.

"A week."

"That's all right," Dalcamy said, "we'll wait. Meanwhile, we can show your mechanics our ship."

"Yes, and I can talk to Heise."

Dalcamy went out to the ships with the other Lors and Sham sent for Heise. Twenty minutes later there was a knock on the door. "Enter!" Heise walked in and stood at attention at Sham's desk. I was standing behind Heise so he didn't see me when he entered. "At ease Heise. There's someone I want you to talk to."

"Hello, Heise," I said.

He spun around and stepped back looking at me. Fear rose in his eyes. He glanced at the Lor and then watched me while trying to control himself. His hands began to shake and he clenched and opened them constantly at his sides.

"I understand you want to leave the fleet because of me," I said as I began to read him. He always had doubts about how he would react to alien imprisonment. When I called him an insect and would eat him, it broke all his defenses and his doubts turned into reality. His dreams showed him being torn up and eaten. Being completely defenseless physically clinched his insecurities. He needed to turn his fear into anger to get rid of his doubts about himself. I walked up to him and he stiffened, not wanting to run.

"Hit me, Heise," I said.

He looked at me surprised and glanced at Sham. Sham just sat on the edge of his desk and watched. He hit me square in the face and sent me flying against a wall and I slid down stunned. I heard a growl and Heise picked me up by my shoulders, digging in with his claws. He raised his right hand intending to rip my throat out with his claws. The Lor grabbed his arm and called him to attention. Heise looked at the Lor and obeyed.

"At ease, Heise." I said while straightening myself and wiping the blood off my face. "That's a hell of a punch you have." He glared at me.

I pulled up a chair and told him to sit down. "You're a Trok, be proud of that. No matter what anyone else says or thinks doesn't matter. If they don't like the way you look, that's their problem not yours. Don't let anyone take your pride. There may be times when that's all you'll have to hang on to. I don't think you should leave the fleet, Heise. I know you don't really want to, do you?"

"No, not really, but I could be a danger to the other chikes. I broke, I told you everything." His anger and fear was completely gone now.

"I don't think that will happen again, I was your first experience. You'll know how to fight back next time. You're not a coward, Heise. Only the stupid and the dead don't feel fear. I wouldn't hesitate to have you on my side, you've shown what you can do." I finished rubbing my face as we all laughed.

"I thought you had some kind of protection that wouldn't allow anyone to hit you," Lor Sham said later.

"I do, but I didn't turn it on."

"He could have killed you."

"He intended to rip my throat out, he pictured it plainly in his mind. I was counting on you. If I stopped him with mind control we would have been back to square one and his insecurities about himself."

Sham shook his head. "Well, it worked. I think I'm going to have a choact'av soldier there." I didn't understand the word he used and would have asked him, but we walked into a medical room. The unfamiliar word just slipped my mind. I hadn't realized where we were going and Lor Sham picked up on my surprise.

"Thought you were telepathic," he said laughing.

"I am, but I don't read constantly."

"Can't have you spurting all over the place. Besides, you might pick up an infection, can't have that." Lor Sham had them clean my face and check my shoulders. Blood was seeping through my shirt where Heise's nails dug into me. That looks like a blaster burn, Lor sham thought as I removed my shirt.

"It is. My shield wasn't set high enough to protect me from your long range blasters."

"I hope you rectified that."

I smiled and nodded.

The doctor didn't know how to stop the bleeding at my shoulders. "Our bandages won't work on him, Lor Sham." Their bandages were stiff with a coating on the underside. They wouldn't bend to the shape of my body or adhere to me.

"That's all right," I smiled. "Just press on the wounds for a few minutes, they'll stop bleeding. I'll seal them when I get back to my ship." They followed my instructions and cleaned the blood away.

I slipped my shirt back on and walked out with Lor Sham. Dalcamy and the others met us as we entered the Lor's lounge.

"What happened to you?" Dalcamy asked.

"It's all right," I answered.

"He straightened Heise out," explained Sham.

"Oh, really," answered one of the other Lors, "what does Heise look like?"

"He's fine now, he's staying in the fleet."

We had lunch together and then were shown around the base. We watched their soldiers at the firing range, I was impressed by their accuracy.

"Would you like to try it, Mike?" Sham asked.

"Yes, I would."

He had a fresh target set up for me and handed me a blaster. I cradled it in my arms like a rifle and took aim. I hit the target dead center.

"Good shot!" Sham said.

"No recoil, it feels good." I took another shot.

"This is rapid fire," Sham explained as he moved a lever.

I took aim again and squeezed. Steady blasts shot out as long as I held the trigger, the target was obliterated.

"Very impressive," I said as I handed it back to Sham. "That soldier should have killed me instead of just wounding me." I said to Dalcamy.

"You were lucky, Weather Man."

"Dalcamy is right," Lor Sham said, "you were lucky." I'll have to find out who that soldier was and make sure he gets more target practice.

"Morck." Sham looked at me. "The soldier's name was Morck, I gave him shooting lessons. He won't miss again." I said smiling.

He looked down the line of soldiers as they practiced. "Bok Lorka!"

"Sir!"

"I want to see Morck here." He turned back to me. "You've done a lot of shooting. Were you in the military on your planet?"

"I didn't serve, ours is voluntary. I used to hunt on my planet, I miss it at times."

"Maybe we can get some hunting in before you leave. We have a game reserve not far from here you may find challenging."

"That sounds good, but these things would blow them apart. Got anything smaller?"

"Everything you need, I'll arrange it."

"Sir!" Bok Lorka returned with Morck, they both stood at attention.

Lor Sham handed Morck the blaster I had fired. "I want to see you shoot."

I smiled at Morck and said, "Three shots, Morck, in a triangle dead center. You can do it."

A new target came up and Morck took his position. He fired once, breathed and fired again. Breathed once more and took his finale shot. The target lowered and rose with three stickers in a triangle in the bull's eye. Lor Sham nodded. "Very good, Morck. You're dismissed."

"Yes, Sir."

"How would you like to be our shooting instructor?" Lor Sham asked me with a laugh.

That evening I showered and checked my face. There was a large bruise where Heise hit me and scratches from his fist. I changed my shirt and disintegrated the bloody one. As I was leaving my quarters to see Bocha, Caltomacoe met me. *You sure you don't want something for you face, Mike?*

No, it doesn't even hurt anymore, I answered as I reached Bocha's room. *But I want you to check my shoulders when I finish with Bocha.* He nodded and walked away. *How you doing, Bocha?*

Hello Mike, what happened to your face?

I was giving a lesson on self-worth, I laughed.

Who won, you or the student?

Both. How's your leg?

It's doing all right.

I scanned his leg. *It's healing. We just have to give it time.*

When I left Bocha's room, I met Caltomacoe in medical. *They're almost two inches deep, Mike!* Caltomacoe said as the opercule examined the punctures on my shoulders. *That was a severe lesson you taught.*

I don't think I'll do that again. It was harder on me than the student. The opercule had to reopen the wounds and clean them. It registered some traces of bacteria deep inside.

Two days later I received a message that Lor Sham would pick me up the next morning to go hunting.

CHAPTER 13

Sham picked me up in a four-seat vehicle very similar to a jeep except it floated two feet off the ground. Two soldiers sat in front, one driving. I climbed in back with Sham.

"This is what we'll be hunting." he showed me a picture of an animal with four legs and a pointed head that ended in a snout. It stood about three feet from the ground shaped somewhat like a grizzly, it also had an exoskeleton. "It has two sets of eyes," Sham explained. "One set here," he pointed to the top of the head just where the snout starts, "and another set underneath his head where the mouth is. They eat anything, vegetable, insect and meat. If it grows or moves, it's edible. It's called a Macao. It can chase an animal down and literally run over it. Or if the animal is too big, it will raise up on its hind legs and come down on it. Three hundred pounds of crushing weight and tearing teeth. They're not afraid of anything, I've never seen one run away.

"There is only one spot that is soft enough to be fatal, the middle of his chest. You have to wait until he stands up to get a clear shot. You have to hold your ground to make him rear up. If you run he'll just chase you down and run over you."

"Is he good eating?" I asked.

"Not a delicacy, but yeah, he's pretty good eating. Makes a choact'av trophy." That word again. I understood it was the equivalent of our "helluva" as he explained. As we drove, the terrain became more wooded and after an hour we entered a gate into the reserve.

"Do you keep all your animals in reserves?"

"Yes, protects the chikes and the animals. Hunting is allowed with permission, that way we can control the animal population and keep the chikes happy."

We stopped under a large tree that would shade the vehicle and climbed out. The air was hot and dry. We were in the middle of their summer. Sham handed me a blaster as they took theirs. We walked along the dirt road for a while then cut in through the woods. I had already worked up a good sweat and my shirt stuck to me, but the material turned cool with the dampness and felt good. The undergrowth was thick and we had to push our way through at places. We came to a clearing and stood quietly, watching from the trees. The grass was purple and covered the ground like a blanket. A mound rose in the center of the meadow.

Forms that I took as birds flew overhead and we spotted a couple of small animals running about. We were too far away to see them in detail. They had four legs and ran jerkily. They didn't run for long distances at a time, just a few feet. The animals stood about a foot or so.

"Not here," Sham said, "everything leaves when there's a Macao around. They like fields like this, plenty of vegetables and if an animal is too stupid to leave, meat." We skirted the meadow and headed back into the forest. Finding a well-used animal trail to follow made the going a little easier and quieter. We began to climb as the ground sloped up steeply. At the top was another field much larger than the first. We surveyed the grassland, no Macao. We hunted until noon and took a lunch break, the soldiers carried everything in back packs.

"How large is this reserve?" I asked.

"About three thousand quadbas, we have them spotted all around the continent." A quadba is their form of measurement which is about equal to one and a half Earth acres. "A lot of the animals were in danger of extinction from hunters about a hundred years ago. We set these reserves up to save them. It worked out so well we decided to keep all wild animals in them and regulate the hunting. Since we have so many reserves just about everyone that wants to hunt can get permission."

We started following the trail again and came to an anthill that was crushed and clawed apart, ants scampering over it still upset. "There, a Macao has been through here," Sham said pointing at the rubble. "Not too long ago, either."

"That track is like a cat's track on Earth, I said as we examined the ground. "Does this Macao have retractable claws?"

"Yes." Very good! He thought.

We could see things gnawed as we followed the trail. A rotting log was torn apart, the Macao evidently looking for insect morsels. We continued to follow the prints. We were climbing again and the underbrush got thicker. At times we lost the trail and had to spread out looking. We thought the Macao would go straight up, but found he had skirted the steeper part, circled to the other side and headed back down. We followed for another hour and came to a pasture. We could see the Macao like a black spot in the center. Sham and I stepped out into the meadow and approached with our blasters at the ready. The Macao hadn't spotted us yet. He was busy tearing something up. When he did see us he growled, started to rise and swung a claw then came back down on all fours. He stood looking at us then broke out in a run toward us. I took the shooter's stance and raised the blaster as he came. When he was about three feet away he rose with a ferocious growl towering over me showing great pointed teeth still dripping with blood from his latest victim. I saw the white circle on his chest like a bull's eye and fired. He was knocked over backwards and crashed to the ground.

The soldiers behind me cheered and broke out cans of liquid that turned out to be very much like beer, but too sweet to my liking. We inspected my kill as we drank to the hunt. The Macao was six feet long and a fine specimen.

"He's young," Sham said. "He'll be tender, we'll have a feast tomorrow. Let's go see what he was so busy with."

We walked to the spot we first saw him while the soldiers prepared to dress out the Macao. We found another animal that was shredded almost unrecognizable.

"A Lerch, what's left of it.

They're good eating, too. Not much of a challenge though, new hunters start with them. Well, did you have fun?" he asked putting his hand on my shoulder as we walked back.

"Sure did, we don't have an animal like that on my planet. We have dangerous animals, but they don't have to be killed so dramatically. That was great."

"I thought you would enjoy it. I'll have the hide and head preserved for you."

"I have just the place for it."

One of the soldiers had gone back to get the vehicle while the other still worked on the Macao. As we approached we spotted another Macao charging the soldier.

"Ligh! Macao!" screamed Sham.

The soldier looked up and saw it coming. He scrambled for his blaster, but slipped on the guts and fell. I started running at an angle to draw the Macao's attention and it turned as it spotted me. When it was clear of the soldier I stopped running and waited for the right moment. He rose, I took aim and the blaster didn't fire. I turned on my shield as he came crashing down. I hit the ground with my face just under his teeth. His eyes were like the Troks, many faceted and red. He tried to bite my face with his teeth and got a mouth full of energy from my shield, it surprised him and he reared. I rolled away from him and saw Sham running to draw attention. I laid very still and the Macao charged Sham. Sham killed him, then came running to me as I stood up.

"You all right?" he said as he tried to grab me then yelled and jumped back.

"I'm sorry, I still have my shield on." I turned it off.

"No wonder he let you go, can you feel that?"

"Yes, it's a little uncomfortable, but when your life's at stake you can put up with anything."

The soldier joined us. "Thanks, Mike, it would have had me if you didn't distract him."

"It's okay, I'm just glad it worked." Sham looked at the soldier and was about to rebuke him for calling me by my first name.

"It's all right, Sham," I said as I touched his arm. "My own men call me by my first name."

He looked at me and decided to let it drop. "Why didn't you shoot the Macao?"

"My blaster wouldn't fire."

Sham picked it up and aimed it at a tree, it didn't fire. He opened it and found the energy pack dislodged from the chamber.

"I don't know how that happened." He pushed it back in and fired. When he opened the blaster it was dislodged again. He opened his blaster, it was all right. He checked the soldier's blaster and it operated fine. "It's defective. Here, you use mine."

"Looks like we're both going back with trophies," I said as we started to gut the second Macao while the soldier stood guard. It was dark by the time the other soldier returned with the vehicle. Needless to say, he was surprised to see two carcasses. We returned to base and Sham had his chikes unload.

"Come on over to the Lor's lounge after you clean up, we'll have dinner together." I went to my sleeping quarters and showered. Caltomacoe met me as I was on my way to see Bocha. *How's Bocha?* I asked.

He has to use the numbing disk quite a bit, but he's healing.

Hi Bocha, I transmitted as I entered his room. *How you feeling?*

It hurts at times, the numbing disk takes care of it.

Is there enough energy in it? I asked as I checked the disk. *Better get a fresh one.* I went to medical and then returned to Bocha's room. *Anything you want?* I asked as I set the disk next to his bed.

No, I have everything I need. Dalcamy was here, said you went hunting. How'd you do?

I got a trophy for my room, I said grinning. *Wait 'til you see it. I've never seen an animal like this before. We're going to have a feast tomorrow night, I'll bring you some so don't eat dinner.*

Sure it's safe to eat?

It's safe. I ran an analysis on a small piece. From the reports I've been getting from Sadek, all their food is safe.

We visited for a while and then I went to the Lor's lounge. By the time I got there Sham had told the day's adventure and I received pats on my back as I entered.

"To the mighty hunter!" they said as they raised their glasses after handing me a drink. Dalcamy grinned at me as he drank with us. We went in to dinner and discussed the arrival of Melcon Kafka.

"He's due in tomorrow," Sham stated. "He called me and said his meeting completed sooner than expected. Should be here about noon, just in time for our Macao feast."

"Your hide should be ready in a week, Mike," one of the other Lor's said. "My brother is good at preserving, he'll do a good job."

We talked and ate a delicious meal and then had more drinks and started talking politics.

"How is your government set up?" asked Dalcamy.

"Well, we're a military government as you probably have all ready surmised. The Melcon is elected by the chikes. He stays in office so long as the majority is satisfied with him. The terms run three years. All the military branches are under his direct control."

"Is the planet under his domain or are there other governments?"

"There are other governments."

"Do you war against each other?" I asked.

"Not anymore. We have spats once in a while, but there is too much respect between countries to have an outright war. Our powers are about equal. There are only four ruling governments on the planet and arguments are settled at meeting tables now."

"There was a time though," another Lor stated, "when we had some bloody battles. But that's past, now we go to other planets for mining and exploration."

"Have you thought of colonizing planets?" asked Dalcamy.

"Yes, but we haven't found anything suitable yet. And we don't travel far away, it takes too long."

"Maybe we can help you with that," Dalcamy said.

"Oh?"

"I've spoken with our Commodore, if you're willing to let a couple of your Captains and a crew of five for each come to Artara with us, we'll train them and send them back with a couple of our ships for you to have."

"Like yours?" asked Sham unbelievingly.

"Probably more like Mike's," Dalcamy laughed. "There won't be any weapons on them though, we don't have weapons."

"From what I've seen and heard, you don't need them," Sham observed. "How long would you need to train the chikes?"

"Couple of years. There's a lot of detail in computing and spaceship handling and a year in travel time."

"So you're talking three years. You say you spoke to your Commodore, you can transmit that far away?"

"There is a time delay, but we can get through clearly."

"Perhaps we can set up some kind of communication between our worlds, then," another Lor suggested.

"That's possible. We did it with Mike's world."

"I think a Lor should go back with them, too."

I looked at Sham. "How about Sham?" I asked.

"No, I've got too much to do, I can't take off for three years."

"Let Kafka decide," said another Lor. "We can spare the chikes, but the Lor would have to be chosen by Kafka, and his responsibilities taken on by the rest of us."

"Mike," started Sham, "you said something today that I've been wondering about."

"What?"

"You said your men call you by your first name."

"That's right."

"How do you maintain discipline?"

"I don't have to. The Artarians are self-disciplined people. They have to be, with the mental powers they have. I don't have to remind them I'm the Captain. We work together like a team; they know what they must do and they do it."

"What if one displeases you?"

"Then I tell him about it and it doesn't happen again."

"We should have it so easy," a Lor said and we all laughed.

CHAPTER 14

Dalcamy and I walked back to our ships together. The night was warm and a full moon lit the landing pad.

This has been quite a day for you, he transmitted.

It sure has, I don't think I'll ever forget it. I answered as I thought about the thrill of the kill, then the teeth gnashing at my face.

I'm glad I turned your shield up. Dalcamy replied to my thoughts.

Yeah, me too!

We said goodnight and I entered my ship. I've been setting the computer to wake me if anything turns up during the night with Bocha and I did the same that night. I had no trouble getting to sleep. I was awakened abruptly and sat up in bed about two hours later. Bocha's name was flashing on my screen. I jumped out of bed and ran to his room. As I opened the door I saw he had dropped the numbing disk on the floor and was trying to reach for it.

I'll get it Bocha, just lie back. I picked it up and started numbing his leg.

I woke and needed it, but it slipped out of my hand. Oh, that feels better all ready, thanks Mike.

I checked the energy level. *It's half full, think you'll need another one before morning?*

No, it'll be enough, I'll probably only need it once more tonight.

Why didn't you just get it with your mind?

That would have triggered it and wasted the energy.

Hmm, Then we should figure out something to keep it from falling on the floor or . . . I know. I ordered a strand of metallic thread from the computer about seven feet long. I tied one end to the top of Bocha's bed and the other end to the disk. *Now if you drop it, you can pull it back.*

Good, thanks, Mike.

Sleep well, Bocha. I went back to bed.

The following morning as I was exiting my ship a couple of soldiers were walking by and they saluted me. I smiled and nodded my acknowledgment and started checking the ports on the ship. Several other soldiers happened by and they all saluted. I thought it strange because they hadn't done that before and wondered why. When a lone soldier happened by and saluted, I motioned for him to come over.

"Why is everyone saluting me?"

"You don't know?" I shook my head. "Because of what you did for Ligh yesterday, they're paying you honor."

"The whole base?" I asked in surprise.

"The whole base, they will salute you from now on."

"Am I supposed to respond someway? Salute back or something?"

"No. Is that all, Mike?"

I grinned at him calling me Mike. "Yes, I guess so. Thank you." He saluted and left.

Dalcamy and I met Melcon Kafka with the Lors in our dress uniforms. We watched as his aircraft landed. It was a fuel burning aircraft and very streamlined. It looked as though it could travel as fast as an Earth jet. We were introduced to him and we all walked off the pad together.

"I'm sorry I wasn't here when you arrived, gentlemen. I trust my Lor's showed you around and kept you occupied."

"Yes, we have been very impressed," I said smiling.

"He shot a Macao, Kafka," Sham said, "and we plan to have it tonight."

"Very good, you'll have to tell me the story." He said as we entered his office. "I understand we had some problems on Vulgarb," he said as he sat behind his desk. "Have they been resolved?"

"Yes, the Vulgarbs are appeased and we have new crews running the mines."

"Good, I'll expect a written report."

"There's one in your Report File."

"Sit down, gentlemen." He motioned to the chairs in front of his desk. "Tell me about yourselves and how I can be of service to you."

"We come from Artara," Dalcamy began as the Lor's brought up chairs and sat with us. Dalcamy explained our search and made the same offer of the ships and technologies we had.

"That's very interesting and what do you want in return for all these things?"

"Friendship, exchange of information, perhaps trade between our worlds. We would like to be of help to you economically, socially, however we can."

"What you're saying then is that you want to be involved in our affairs."

"To the extent that it would be beneficial to both worlds."

"Interesting, and what do my Lors have to say about this?"

Sham spoke up first. "I have spent the most time with them, Melcon Kafka. Mike showed me Artara through his mind and it looks very good. They already know just about everything about us. I think we can benefit by their counsel and participation, and their world will benefit by the experience."

"You said 'through his mind,' are they telepathic?"

"Yes, we are," I answered. "You seem to know quite a bit about telepathy, although you are obviously not telepathic yourselves."

"We met a world of telepaths a few years ago."

"Yes," one of the Lors commented with grief.

"You had a bad experience." Dalcamy said.

"To say the least," Melcon Kafka answered. "I'm just glad they hadn't developed space flight at the time."

"They are in this solar system then?" I asked.

"No, a neighboring one. They held our first contact ship prisoner. We sent a fleet of six ships to search for them when they didn't return on time, they were too far away for any communication."

"There was quite a fight to get our chikes back and the losses were heavy on both sides." A Lor finished explaining.

"We haven't left our solar system since," Melcon Kafka continued, "and you're how many solar systems away?"

"We are three solar systems away." Dalcamy answered.

"And you're suggesting two Captains and ten chikes."

"And a Lor," Sham said, "that's our idea."

Melcon Kafka looked at Sham. "You realize those chikes would be completely stranded if anything went wrong."

"Yes, they would be, but remember they had eighty of our chikes on Vulgarb," Sham answered, "and I witnessed them showing as much concern for our chikes as they did for their own."

"Would you be willing to go with them, Lor Sham?"

"Without hesitation."

"Why don't you allow us to show you more of our nature before you decide?" Dalcamy suggested. "I can understand your concerns. If I could, I would set up a communication device for you now, but I don't have the materials with me. Your chikes will bring it with them when they return."

"How can you show me this?" asked Melcon Kafka.

"We can join minds aboard our ship. I'll show you whatever you want to know." We received a picture of a Trok with a blank stare from having his mind wiped clean of all memory by the other planet.

"No, that won't happen," I said. "We don't have anything that would do that."

"What are you talking about?" asked a Lor.

"Direna," answered Melcon Kafka.

"It's safe, Melcon Kafka," said Sham, "I've done it."

"Let me think about it. I'll give you my answer tomorrow."

"Fine, meanwhile, if you don't have anything pressing, would you like to tour our ship?" asked Dalcamy.

"Yes, I'd like that."

We'll show him your ship, Weather Man.

As we were walking to my ship Melcon Kafka noticed the soldiers saluting me.

"Whom are they saluting?" he asked Sham.

"Mike. He saved a soldier's life yesterday."

"Looks like you have much to tell me, Sham."

We entered my ship and I gave them the grand tour. Caltomacoe assisted me in explaining. I looked over at Dalcamy and thought. *You should have a ship like this, not me.*

Then I would have to give up mine. I'm not ready to do that.

"You should feel how smoothly she lifts, Kafka," Sham said. "She goes five times faster than ours."

"Would you like a test ride?" I asked.

The Melcon hesitated and then answered, "all right."

I could feel the Melcon's nervousness as we strapped ourselves in and started the engines. I checked with control for clearance then lifted off. We headed out and made some maneuvers in space. I explained the guidance system and handling. I came down to orbiting level, set the computer to maintain and led them to the engine room and showed them the rest of the equipment. We returned to control and landed back on Trok.

"This is all very impressive," Kafka said, "and you're willing to give us two ships like this?"

"Yes."

"And it's completely self-contained and powered."

"Yes."

"You realize we would copy it and make more."

"That is expected." Dalcamy said. "You won't be able to use yours when the ore gives out, these will replace them. We'll give you the instructions to build them and the chikes we train can train others."

He was almost convinced. He wondered how many chikes would be willing to go after their last experience. It would have to be on a voluntary basis, he would never force anyone in going that far away for three years knowing there could be no rescue. He turned to the Lors. "Which one of you would be willing to go?" They all responded by raising their hands.

I took them to medical and explained the opercule. "Do you think you could help Direna?" Melcon Kafka asked.

"You mean he's still a blank?" I asked in surprise.

"Yes, nothing we do helps him. It's been seven years now."

"Was he the only one affected that way?"

"Yes. They . . . examined him to get all the information they could about us. He was a Lor, a good one."

"We could take a look at him," Dalcamy answered.

"One of my chikes told me you did something like that to him, but he wasn't hurt. He said he didn't feel a thing," Sham said.

"We didn't force the information out of him," Dalcamy explained. "We wanted to record your language so we could talk to you. We recorded his brain waves and then set the computer to record anything he thought about. Eventually we had what we needed."

"How did you get him to think about things?"

"It's natural, your mind is always thinking, you can't really stop it. You can direct it on subjects, but as soon as you rest or relax your mind just functions on its own. We just recorded what his mind thought."

"If you can restore Direna, I'll agree to anything you ask," Kafka said. "Within reason." We laughed at the added comment.

"I wonder how he will react to us," I said as we were led to the infirmary.

"If his mind is truly a blank, there won't be any reaction. He won't remember his experience."

We waited in an examination room and soon Direna was led in like a child. Dalcamy and I read him.

"He's still in trauma!" Dalcamy said astonished. "He must have gone through extreme pain. His memory isn't all gone, just locked up."

"Can you help him?"

"I would have to force him out of trauma. That will cause more pain. It would be making him unlock his mind. I can try." Dalcamy had him sit and took a chair facing him. I withdrew and waited with the others as Dalcamy concentrated. A flash of fear went through Direna's eyes and he jumped in the chair, then went blank. Dalcamy concentrated again. Direna screamed and jumped back out of his chair knocking it over trying to get away from Dalcamy. The attendants went to grab him.

"No! Leave him alone," Dalcamy said. "It's better if he can get away from me."

"That's the first time we've had any reaction from him at all," the attendant said.

"It causes him extreme pain to have thought function. They were very cruel people."

"Can you cure him?"

"It will take time and several sessions. I can't go too fast, it would be too painful for him and he would regress. He'll have bad dreams. Someone will have to be with him all the time for reassurance. He may have dreams tonight. Make sure he has a lot of personal items around him to recognize so he knows he's home. I'll also have to have your chikes around when I'm working with him for him to see. If I work alone with him he'll become frightened. If you'll notice he's calmer now that the attendants are standing with him."

"Then he is aware of us."

"Yes. I don't know the level of his understanding, but he is aware of his kind around him."

"Is his memory intact?"

"I can't tell. If there is memory loss, he can be re-educated, but we have to unlock his mind before we'll know that." Dalcamy walked up to Direna. "Direna, I'm going to help you get rid of your pain." Direna didn't respond.

Dalcamy said he would see Direna twice a day, morning and afternoon. He stressed that Direna was not to be left alone for a moment. I went back to my ship to see Bocha. He was in the middle of a lesson when I entered his room. *Hi! How's your lessons coming?*

Pretty good, with all this rest I'm getting, the lessons are moving faster than before. I'm actually ahead of schedule.

Good, but I'm not going to like losing you. You're a good man to have around.

It won't be for a while yet, Mike. The physical stuff is going to slow me up.

I don't think you'll let it slow you up too much. How's your leg?

Better today, I didn't have to use the disk as much. Caltomacoe scanned it today and said it was healing well.

I'm glad. We should set up that therapy program pretty soon then and start as soon as your leg is ready.

You met the Melcon today. He has problems about sending his chikes, he read.

Yes, but I think he'll come around when he knows us better. I checked the energy level in his disk and found Caltomacoe had given him a fresh one. *I have to go now,* I transmitted, *but I'll come back with your dinner.*

CHAPTER 15

The Macao was delicious. I took Bocha a plate of food and watched as he took his first taste. *That's good, Mike, have you had any yet?*

No, I brought yours first.

Here, taste this, he said as he held up a fork full of meat. I tasted and found it very good and tender.

Yes, that is good. I'm going to get some before it's all gone.

There was enough to feed the whole base and they made it into quite a party. Sham had told Kafka the whole hunting adventure. After eating I mingled with the soldiers comparing worlds with them and exchanging some hunting experiences. A couple chikes mentioned that we were attempting to help Direna, they all knew about him. One chike, that joined us later, was on the planet with him.

"I hate those Things," he said, "They took delight in torture."

"Yes, we could see the damage they did to Direna. Dalcamy knows how to help him, he's stronger than I."

"Do you read our minds all the time?" one asked.

"No, I can feel your emotions most of the time if they're strong enough, but I don't read beings all the time. They have a right to privacy. I don't even read Artarians all the time."

A young soldier asked, "What does it feel like to be read?"

"You don't feel anything, you wouldn't even be aware of it."

"Then what hurt Direna?"

"They didn't just read him, they extracted information from him forcibly. There's a difference."

"Have you ever done that? Take information from someone?"

"Not in that manner. There is a way of doing it that won't cause pain or damage. It wasn't necessary for them to do what they did."

"Show us how you would do it," the young soldier said.

"Are you volunteering?" I asked.

"Yes."

"All right, you have General Orders memorized correct?"

"Yes."

"Don't think about the fifth order. Think about anything else you want to, but don't think about that and I'll find out what it is from you. When you're ready just nod."

He nodded. I started to read him. He thought about poetry, his girlfriend, his parents, his education in the service, a movie he went to last week, the General orders, his girlfriend, order number 5. I started quoting it.

"I didn't!"

"Yes, you did, you can't help it. It's there in your mind. All I have to do is wait until your mind brings it up. I told you not to think about it. You had to think about it in order to remember not to think about it."

"You can learn anything you want from us then," it was Melcon Kafka. He was standing behind me all along. I turned and faced him.

"Yes, I can, but I respect a person's privacy. The only time I read a person without their knowledge is when I sense danger from them."

"You have this power and yet you frightened Heise into talking. Why didn't you just read him?"

"I didn't know your language then. It took me a week to learn it."

"How did you learn our language?" Kafka asked.

"Through the computer. We had one of your Boks sit with a cap on and the computer recorded everything he thought the same way I just demonstrated. Then the information was fed to me as I put the cap on and reversed the process. That's how we can re-educate Direna if necessary."

"Can we see this computer work?" the young soldier asked.

"Are you volunteering again?" I asked laughing.

"Yes."

We went to my ship. There were seven soldiers and Kafka. I explained the procedure while placing the cap on the volunteer's head. "First, I have to record your brain waves. The computer will transmit to you through them." Three rows of straight lines appeared on the screen like an oscilloscope has. We waited a few moments and the lines changed into wavy lines. "That's your wavelength. What's your name?"

"Eroch."

"I'll record your name with the brain waves. Now we're ready. I have it set at my speed. If you feel dizzy, we'll stop and slow it down." I set it up for Artarian language and flipped the switch. Fifteen minutes later he was taking the test and did well. He became extremely excited.

"Melcon Kafka, I'd like to go to their planet if you decide to send us!"

Kafka looked at the young soldier and answered laughing, "I see the comline is alive and going strong." He took a notebook from his pocket and wrote his name. "If there is a list of volunteers asked for, yours will be the first on it."

"Me too, Melcon Kafka?" asked another.

"And me?" said another.

"I'd like to go, too." They all volunteered.

"Don't forget Ligh--I know he wants to go. He told me he did."

"You chikes realize you will be too far away for us to help you."

They all sobered and knew exactly what he meant. Then one of the volunteers spoke up. "Sir, if we run away from danger and other telepathic people because of one planet, we'll never learn anything about them. And, isn't that what the fleet's all about?" Melcon Kafka looked at him and nodded.

The next day I went with Dalcamy in the morning to see Direna. They brought him into the examination room and had him sit. When Dalcamy sat across from him, he jumped out of his chair and moved away from him.

"It's all right, Direna, I'm going to help you. You're aware of that aren't you?" He went blank again and Dalcamy led him back to his chair. This time when Dalcamy sat Direna didn't respond until contact was made. Pain and fear flashed in Direna's eyes. He squirmed in his seat, but didn't try to run again. Dalcamy withdrew from him.

"I'll visit with you again later," Dalcamy said.

"He's had some real bad dreams," one of the attendants said. "He woke up screaming three times last night."

"It's going to get worse, they hurt him very badly. He's a brave Trok to be responding this quickly. He's starting to work with me now."

The next morning Direna spoke while Dalcamy was in contact with him.

"Hurts!"

Dalcamy withdrew. "I know Direna, that's why I'm going slowly. It will hurt, but soon the pain will go away along with your bad dreams."

That afternoon Melcon Kafka accompanied us. "Direna," Dalcamy said, "the Melcon is here with us." He raised his head a little in recognition and pain flashed through his eyes.

"He knows!" Kafka said as he knelt beside Direna and took his arm. Dalcamy made contact.

"I--won't--help them!" he screamed.

"Good, Direna, you don't have to," Dalcamy answered.

He squirmed in his seat as Dalcamy continued. When Dalcamy withdrew, Direna continued to squirm.

"What's happening?" I asked. "You've broken contact."

"He's doing it on his own now. Talk to him Kafka, you're important to him. Sit here where he can see you." Dalcamy stood and Kafka took his seat, as Direna stared at Kafka.

"Home! I'm really home!"

"Yes, Direna, you're with us now, we want you to get well."

He struggled and squirmed for another twenty minutes then went blank again.

"He's gone back!" Kafka got upset.

"It's all right, Kafka," Dalcamy answered. "He's tired and resting now. Keep a close watch tonight. He may try on his own again and there should be someone there to talk to him."

The next morning when they brought Direna in the attendant was excited. "He tried twice last night on his own. He didn't talk, he just stared at us while we talked to him."

"Good," Dalcamy answered. "He's an exceptional fighter."

Direna sat down and started reacting without Dalcamy making contact. "I- - -can- - -do it!" he stared at Dalcamy.

"Good, Direna, I'll just sit here with you then and we'll talk. You have a wife, do you remember her?"

He squirmed and concentrated, "a little!" Everything he said came out in screams of pain.

"I can have her come see you this afternoon, would you like that?"

"Yes!"

"When we are finished here, don't try on your own until your wife is here this afternoon. I don't want you to be too tired to talk to her. Do you have children, Direna?"

More squirming, he fought for a long time. "Don't know! I can't- - -remember!"

"That's all right, it'll come to you eventually."

"Dalcamy!"

"Yes?"

"Thank you!"

"You're going to be all right, Direna."

Direna went blank again and the attendants took him back. That afternoon we met Direna's wife, Aga. Lor Sham brought her to the Lor's Lounge where we waited.

There didn't seem to be much difference between sexes except she had markings. Dark lines crossed her face and body. She wore a bright yellow harness with different colored pouches. They were all brightly colored. Lor Sham introduced us. She was frightened by us, but held her courage. She had never seen aliens before. "Melcon Kafka told me you were working with Direna, how is he?"

"He's coming along fine," Dalcamy said. "When he talks to you, he'll be screaming his words. It's the pain. It hurts him to think, but he's a fighter and he wants to be free."

"Does he have a lot of pain?"

"Yes, it will go away eventually and he knows that. Don't be alarmed when he goes blank again, he's just resting." Dalcamy asked her many questions about their lives together explaining it would help him to talk to Direna. They don't have any children; that's why Direna couldn't remember them.

"Do you have pictures?" I asked.

"Yes." She handed me some pictures of her and Direna. "Our shecotch time," she said. I understood it was similar to a honeymoon. "We were only joined six months when this happened to him."

Dalcamy looked at them. "These will help. I'll show them to him and have them put in his room."

When it was time to see Direna, Kafka joined us and we went to the infirmary together. Direna responded as soon as he saw Dalcamy.

"Wife?" he screamed.

"She's right here, Direna."

She walked up to him and he looked at her with recognition. "Aga!" She hugged him and their faces touched. I assumed it was their way of kissing. She stroked his side where the chest and back plates separate. He put his arms around her and responded by repeating her name.

"Sit here Aga," Dalcamy said, "and talk to him."

"I've missed you so much, Direna."

"Love! You!" he answered. "I!" then he let out a scream and grabbed his head.

"Easy, Direna, take your time," Dalcamy said. "Can you stay here, Aga?"

"Yes, of course."

"Direna, Aga is going to stay here and see you every day."

"Sorry! Didn't want upset her!"

"It's all right, Direna," she said. "I'm going to be here all the time now. You're going to get well and come home."

"Home! Home! Home!" he grabbed his head and screamed again.

Dalcamy and Aga worked with Direna for another week while I worked with Bocha on his therapy. Both showed improvement by the end of the week. Bocha started walking with a cane and growing stronger every day. Direna could talk in full sentences without screaming. At times while Dalcamy was in contact with him, his mind would open and Dalcamy would receive his experiences like a flood gate had opened. It was very painful for Direna to get to that point, but once it was reached the pain subsided and he was able to speak almost normally. Kafka and I were with

Dalcamy on one of these occasions. Aga sat beside Dalcamy and held Direna's hands.

"Direna," Dalcamy said before making contact, "Mike is going to join us today. He's not going to do anything, just listen, all right?"

He looked at me and then at Dalcamy. "All right."

"I'll make contact first, Mike and you join when I say." Dalcamy made contact and after a few minutes told me to join. I joined in and listened.

What do you want to think about? Asked Dalcamy.

What happened to the Others! PAIN.

There was a war over you and your chikes, many of them were killed.

Are all our chikes free?

I don't know, but I think so. I think they all came back.

Good.

I started receiving pictures of the beings that did this to him. I felt extreme pain as he thought. I had no chair, so I sat down on the floor next to them. I could see soft skinned beings like us with huge heads and very small piercing eyes. They were short and thin. The pain grew as he concentrated on them. They were staring at him and asking questions. Excruciating pain, I could hear someone moaning. They were laughing at me as I fought them. Bastards! I thought, won't tell them a thing even if they kill me.

"You're causing your own pain, Direna. You know that. We are stronger than you, we can take what we want. See?" Pain. My head felt like it was being ripped open. I heard more moaning. They bent over me and peered into my eyes as they ripped at me. I felt hands grabbing my arms and I swung out and buried my fist into something soft. It gave me great pleasure to think I hurt them back. I struck again at the eyes this time and I connected. Mike! Someone shook me. Who's Mike?

"Mike! Break contact!"

Dalcamy! I was looking at Dalcamy! "Direna! Is he all right?" I turned to him and he was calmly sitting there looking at me.

"He's all right, Mike, it was you that scared us."

"Those fucking bastards!" I yelled, "Did you see what they did to him?"

"Calm down, Mike, it's over."

I was fighting mad and it took me a long time to stop my anger. I looked at Kafka, he didn't say anything he just watched me.

"You were supposed to just listen, not take part," Dalcamy scolded.

"I got carried away."

"I was afraid I was going to have two patients on my hands. It did help him having you there with him, but I don't advise doing that again."

"Who did I hit?" I asked as I looked at Kafka and Dalcamy. Dalcamy looked at me and I saw a mark on his face from my blow. "Dalcamy! I'm sorry, I didn't know it was you. I thought I was hitting them."

"It's all right, Mike," he smiled.

We turned back to Direna. "Why didn't you leave when the pain started?" Direna asked me.

"I didn't want to desert you. How long did that go on?"

"I don't know, I can't remember when they stopped."

"You may never remember that," Dalcamy said. "Your mind was probably locked up by then and they didn't care, they had gotten what they wanted."

"How long would it take?" I asked Dalcamy.

"To do this kind of damage, not long, two, three hours perhaps."

"They would have had it faster if they used our method and he wouldn't have been harmed."

"They didn't care, Mike. They enjoyed it."

"The Bastards!" I started getting mad all over again. "Where is their world, anyway?"

"Mike," Kafka said, "why do you want to know?"

I looked at Kafka and realized I was thinking of vengeance. "Never mind, I guess I'm not quite thinking right."

"Why don't you go on back to your ship, Mike and rest," Dalcamy said. "You've been through too much. I'll come over when we're through."

I looked at the others and didn't feel right about leaving. "Go ahead, Mike," Kafka said and Aga nodded. When I got to my ship I had the computer produce a punching bag that resembled those monsters of Direna's. I hung it in the recreation room and tried to beat it to pieces. I was still at it and sweating hard when Dalcamy walked in with Caltomacoe.

"That's one way of releasing anger," Dalcamy laughed.

I swung around at the sound of his voice and he stopped laughing abruptly. "Mike! We'd better have a talk."

They followed me to my quarters and waited until I finished showering and put on a fresh uniform. I felt better, but I was still angry.

I'm going to read you, Mike, Dalcamy said as I came out to my sitting room where they waited.

I looked at him and realized he wasn't asking, he was telling. That angered me more. *All right.* I stood and looked at him in defiance.

Vengeance isn't going to help, he said.

It isn't right for a race of beings to commit such atrocities and not be punished for them.

How do you know they haven't been? It was seven years ago, and they still don't have space flight. Why do you think that is? Direna had all the information on Trok spaceships, so they must have had the knowledge about them.

Maybe they didn't have the physical strength to build them, I answered. *They didn't look very strong. How do we know they don't have space flight?*

We haven't seen them. Surly they would be looking for other planets if they did.

Why don't we find out for sure?

Do you think you could handle them if we went there?

I looked at Dalcamy and knew what he meant. I thought about it for a time. *I don't know.* I ran my hand through my hair and walked away from them. *Didn't it anger you when you found out what they did?*

Yes, it angered me, but I'm not about to start something with them. I think we should stay away from their planet and keep as many other beings away from it as we can. If they never develop space flight they can't harm anyone else.

Maybe we can set some kind of warning beacons around their planet.

What language would you have them transmit? Dalcamy asked grinning.

CHAPTER 16

Another two weeks went by and Direna had improved so much he left the infirmary and moved in with his wife. They lived at the officer's quarters which were set up like apartments. He had some memory loss in areas concerning spaceships, military maneuvers and tactical information. Kafka supplied information and we fed it into the computer. Several Lors volunteered to be read into the computer to add information for Direna. When the information was sorted Dalcamy ran an analysis to check for completeness. There were still some missing information and the computer put out questions. Technicians began to come after Kafka asked them to help. More information went in. Finally the files were complete.

"You know, Kafka," Dalcamy said. "When he finishes this, he'll know more than any other chike on your base."

"Then maybe he'll be the next Melcon," he answered.

Direna came in and looked at the computer. He was nervous, but he had complete trust in Dalcamy and would do anything he asked.

"Have a seat, Direna," Dalcamy said smiling.

He sat down and Dalcamy placed the cap on his head while Kafka, Aga and I with several Lors stood watching. He recorded Direna's brain waves then flipped the switch for transmission. Direna became intensely absorbed in what was being fed to him. He listened for fifteen minutes then the testing started. The chikes applauded him as he passed with no errors.

"This is amazing!" he said. "Do you realize how this could help our chikes? Have any of you tried this? We could restructure our whole training curriculum and do all our teaching through these. Our chikes would be---,"

"Direna," Kafka interrupted him laughing, "we are more concerned about you right now. First you learn. We'll think about helping the chikes later."

He went on to the next lesson and did equally well. "That's enough for today," Dalcamy said. "If you get too tired it won't transmit to you. You can start again tomorrow morning."

"We have thirty volunteers to go to your planet," Kafka said, "and more are signing up every day. But it's going to be hard to pick a Lor to go."

"I'd like to go," said Direna, "but it wouldn't be fair to Aga. We haven't been together for over seven years."

"Why can't she go with you?" I asked.

"We'll even give you a second shecotch," said Dalcamy.

"The Island?" I asked.

"The Island," Dalcamy said smiling.

"You'd love it, Direna. They do everything for you. If you just start to think of something you want, it's done or given to you."

"If you really want to go, you can," said Kafka. "You should take it easy for a while, anyway."

"I spoke with the Commodore last night," Dalcamy said. "He's sending a technician ship to set up communications between our worlds. By the time we get home Direna should be able to contact you."

I could feel Kafka's relief. Communications was his main concern in sending his chikes. "Would you mind taking thirty chikes and two Lors then?" he asked. "It would make a good technical force for the new ships."

"I agree," Dalcamy said. "There could be more specialization then. We could carry fifteen chikes and one Lor on each ship. We'll have to ask you for additional food supplies."

"I'll have Bok Crall assist you. And, Mike, Heise signed up to go. He was a little late, but I'm going to add him to your list. I think it will be good for him."

* * * * *

Lor Sham brought my trophy. One side had the thick plates of the exoskeleton and the other side was top quality leather hide where the plates attached. The head was intact and stuffed. It had glass replicas as eyes and looked life like, teeth and all.

"You'll have quite a story to go along with it, Mike."

"Yeah. Did you keep yours?"

"Think I'd turn down something like that? You bet I kept it."

Two weeks later we were ready to leave. Dalcamy and I were given packets that contained pictures and names of the chikes going with us. Heise was included among my passengers, along with Ligh and Lor Walrod. Direna and his wife were going with Dalcamy. The chikes lined up outside the ship on the morning of our departure. None of them carried weapons. Lor Walrod, Caltomacoe and I greeted them as they entered and my crewmen directed them to their quarters. We assigned two chikes to a room and Lor Walrod shared my quarters.

After takeoff the soldiers were given a tour and shown what to do if the warning for evasive maneuvers sounded. They were also shown how to use all the facilities. Then they were put to work learning the Artarian language.

One evening I was in the kitchen enjoying a cup of asil when I overheard part of a conversation. "Dak, that's crazy! Why would they go to all the trouble of teaching us their language?"

"Shh! They'll hear you."

I went over to them. "Mind if I join you?" I asked.

"Mike, we just had a crazy thought."

"Voss!"

"I think we ought to talk about it, Dak."

"Would you expect him to admit it if it were true? Besides, it's probably a crazy idea."

"Are you uneasy from the idea?" I asked not wanting to read him.

"Well, I had this thought. If a planet was cannibalistic, what better way than to make friends with another planet, promises and all just to entice them to go there and---,"

I started to laugh, he stopped talking and they both looked at me. I laughed so hard tears streamed from my eyes. "I'm sorry," I said. "When I was first taken to Artara I was plagued with a nightmare where I was being killed for their meal." They started laughing and I continued laughing. "It just struck me funny to hear the same thing coming from you."

"How did you first meet the Artarians?" I told them the story of my abduction.

"Do you miss your planet?"

"No, I just wish things could have worked out better with them that's all. I wish we were able to show them the things that will be shown to you."

"So we won't be eaten when we get there?" asked Voss.

"All right, rub it in," said Dak as we laughed.

It had been about twelve weeks since Bocha's accident and he improved so much he walked with barely a limp. We happened to be working out at the same time in the recreation room. A soldier called Kenkir noticed the punching bag I had made and recognized it one afternoon. He was surprised to see it.

"That looks just like a Dextarian!"

"Yeah, I made it one afternoon after a session with Direna. It angered me what they did to him and that's how I got rid of my anger, by beating on it."

He went over to it and took a few punches at it and then started seriously hitting it. I read him and found he was one of the chikes taken prisoner.

"You knew them," I said.

"Yes. They would play a game with us once in a while." He struck the bag harder as he remembered. "They'd stand in a circle around one of us and push him with their minds until he fell down. One side would push and the other side was supposed to catch him. Sometimes they did and sometimes they didn't. The soldier was always hurt somehow by the time they stopped.

"Another pastime they had was to make us see things that weren't really there. They made a contest out of it to see who could frighten us the most. They had very active imaginations and of course, being able to read us, they knew all our fears and used them against us. My fear was snakes. What's your fear, Mike?"

"Spiders," I answered.

"They'd have delight with that. A friend of mine had that fear. He killed himself after we got home. He couldn't forget, and he couldn't live with the memory."

"Could you feel the strength of their minds?" I asked.

"I don't know what you mean."

"Sometimes when a telepath makes contact, you can feel his strength. It's a power or presence that you can feel."

"I didn't feel anything, show me what you mean." We sat down together and I took control of him and then released him.

"Did you feel anything?"

"No, I just couldn't move."

"Did they ever do that to you?"

"No. They issued vocal orders and caused us pain if we didn't obey."

"Mental pain?"

"Yes."

"I just wonder how strong they really are."

"You're not thinking of going there are you?"

"No. Dalcamy said we shouldn't, and I guess he's right. How did they get you out?"

"We were all kept in one building in cells, six of us together. Our ships blasted the area for a week and one day Lor Sham walked in with forty soldiers. They blasted our cells open. I don't know what happened to all the Dextarians that were guarding us. They just disappeared when the shooting started, we didn't have any food at all while our people were blasting."

"Then they would have left you to starve if the war took that long."

"I guess so."

"Nice people."

"They didn't really care. I don't know why they bothered to take us prisoners, unless it was just for their own entertainment."

"They must have had a reason. Why else would they have examined Direna the way they did? They wanted something. Did they make any of you do any manual work for them? Or ever take everyone out of the cells?"

"No. They didn't even let us out of our cells to exercise. We did our exercises in our cells to keep from getting stiff and weak. When they did take anyone out it was only one chike at a time and they'd have their fun right in front of us."

"How did they get you in the cells in the first place?"

"They invited us to a banquet, they were real friendly when we first landed. At first we kept guards on the ship, but when they seemed so glad to have us there we eventually stopped guarding the ship. Then one day they invited all of us to a special banquet in our honor, they said. They must have drugged us, we woke up in the cells."

"Sounds like they don't know how to control people, that's good."

We finished working out together, Kenkir went back to his studies and I went to control.

"Do your people really eat insects?" Heise asked me in the middle of lunch one afternoon.

"Some do, it's kind of a joke with them. Chocolate-covered ants and grasshoppers. They don't make a meal of them. There are tribes in Africa that do when they don't have anything else to eat."

I taught Heise and a few others to play chess and we started a tournament going amongst them. The tournament lasted a month with

Dak winning. We had a victory party honoring him. Caltomacoe made a cake and decorated it with a drawing of the king in the center over Dak's name. It was their first experience with a cake and they thoroughly enjoyed it.

Some soldiers brought musical instruments with them and we had several times of entertainment. The time passed quickly with the enjoyable companionship of the chikes and the day came when Artara appeared on our screen.

"That's a beautiful planet," said Lor Walrod.

"It's an oxygen base atmosphere. Much more oxygen than your planet," I explained, "otherwise, you'll find the air breathable."

We landed and Commodore Mackalie and my wife met us as we disembarked.

"Welcome home, Captain Packard."

"Thank you, Sir. This is Lor Walrod."

"Welcome."

"Thank you."

We started walking to the buildings as Dalcamy and Lor Direna and his wife joined us.

"The first thing we should do is contact your Melcon Kafka to let him know you arrived safely," Commodore Mackalie said as he led us to Main. The Lors were shown how to operate the equipment and Kafka's face appeared on screen.

"Lor Direna! I see you have arrived."

"Yes, Sir." They spoke in their own language so Commodore Mackalie didn't understand what was being said. I transmitted to him the conversation. "It was a good trip, even my wife enjoyed it."

"Good, I'll be waiting to hear from you every week with progress reports. You should see the size of that technical ship. They have started sharing several teaching technologies with us, it's going to restructure our training programs completely."

"The chikes and I have experienced their teaching methods on our way here. We all speak Artarian fluently now and the chikes have picked their fields of specialization. These techniques can be used in our schools as well. I had another idea on the way here that I would like to discuss with the Commodore, but I thought perhaps we could join forces and explore together. Would you consider this, Kafka?"

There was a five minute pause because of the distance of our planets, finally his reply came. "It would be something worth looking into, both our planets would gain by it. Who knows what other contacts we may make?"

They signed off and Lor Direna turned to Commodore Mackalie, "Were you able to follow our conversation?" he asked in Artarian.

"Yes, Captain Packard translated for me. I think your idea is a good one, we'll have to discuss it in more detail. Right now I need to speak to Captain Packard and his wife in my office, if you would excuse us. We have provided living quarters for you and your chikes," he motioned to several Artarians who had been waiting. "They will show you. I'll join you again later. We have a celebration planned."

Tomiya and I followed the Commodore to his office. *Mike,* he began, *Bocha won't be on your ship anymore, he only has a few months of training left for his own Captainship so I have assigned a new crewman to you,* he handed me a file. *I'm sure you will find this person very qualified.*

I opened the file and read the name TOMIYA PACKARD. "Tomiya!"

I decided I didn't want to be separated from you like this again, Mike. I studied Bocha's position when I found out he was interested in being a Captain.

Tomiya, I said, *you know you could be exposed to danger. We don't know what can happen when we go to different worlds and I can't show favoritism toward you.*

I know that Mike, but we will be facing it together. I would rather have it that way than sit safely at home and wonder about you all the time. I want to be there with you.

I looked through the file and found she passed very highly on all the tests.

Your wife has opened a new career for our women. Fifteen more have started training for various positions.

Well, you know on Earth it's nothing unusual for men and women to be working hand in hand even in extremely hazardous jobs. I see no reason why a woman couldn't do any of the jobs on a spaceship. It's just that I wouldn't want to have to order her into a situation that may take her life. But then, I feel that way about all my personnel.

Then it's settled. She is assigned effective now. The Commodore signed the papers and handed her the assignment.

Thank you, Sir. Tomiya responded.

What about Earth, has anything new happened since I've been gone? I asked.

China opened up to us. We found out that concentrated exposure to Fargon energy has a temporary sterilizing effect on human reproductive organs. It only lasts for five years then wears off and they're fertile again.

I'll bet China loves that. Are there any side effects?

No. We set up stations all over China and our medical ships helped the sick. America and the other countries want them too, but America wants to run a ten-year test before making it available to everyone.

Yeah, that's just like America.

I like the idea that Direna brought up. Earth might be interested too, the Commodore continued. *It might even help them settle their differences to start thinking about something else.*

Let's see, Commodore Mackalie sat back and thought. *Larry Hendricks went back to Earth for a wife. He has joined Naygee's work force, he likes working on the ships. Tommy wants to be a Captain when he's old enough. I think he'll do well, and Vyacheslav has become a very good Medical Technician. He's working in Main now and he plans to work on Earth, but doesn't want to go back to Russia.*

They might want to kill him if he did, I said. *The Premier still thinks he's a spy for him. If he showed up on a medical ship, he'd be in deep trouble.*

I think Trok is going to work out well for us, Mike, but I don't like the idea of arming the ships. They expect them fully armed.

It would give the Troks more protection if we did. They don't have telepathic powers and if they don't have weapons, what defense would they have? You know, I don't think it's a bad idea to arm all our exploration ships. If you think about it, what would have happened if the Vulgarbs had been unfriendly toward us? Their minds were so strong, we wouldn't have had much chance against them. I think we should have an 'insurance policy' aboard ship.

I'll think about it, Mike. Dalcamy found out were the planet Dextra is. I've been giving it a lot of thought.

I have too, I wonder what they were after.

You want to go there don't you, Mike?

Yes, I guess I do. Does Dalcamy know more about it?

Only what he learned from Direna.

I spoke to one of the soldiers on my ship that was there. It occurred to me that they didn't have mind control. We would have the upper hand then.

Only until they learned it from us. Then they would have more power over other life forms. We don't have enough information about them to get a recommendation from the computer, so it's going to have to be our decision.

And what about the atrocities they did?

Are you suggesting we go there as avengers? We really don't know the whole story. We don't know why they interrogated Direna like that.

I think we ought to find out.

Well, we have plenty of time to decide. We have these thirty chikes to educate and two ships to build. We'll talk more about it later.

Speaking about ships. You know, my ship is so great and---.

Say no more, the Commodore laughed. *We are in the process of building replacements for everyone. Captain Dalcamy will be getting his tomorrow. Captain Borkalami already has his.*

Tomiya and I were on our way home when we met Allen. "Good to see you, Mike! Tomiya."

"Hi Allen, how you been?"

"Great, I'm half way through my training now and I'm developing telepathy."

"It's working! Good. I guess that means you'll be going back to Earth, then."

"Susan has to go back, anyway. The trial date is set four months from now. We'll go back together and I'll talk to the Captain of the Narcotics

Division then. I'm not quite ready yet, but they can start thinking about it. We figure another year."

"You've decided to go through with the idea of being a telepathic agent for the Narcotics Division?"

"I want to give it a try. If it doesn't work out, I'll come back and be a Captain."

"Do you think it's such a good idea to talk about it a whole year in advance?" Allen read me. *I don't think he's on the take, Mike. There's never been any indication of it.*

A lot can happen in a year.

I'll see when I get there, four more months may make a difference in how strong I am.

"I got to tell you about the Vulgarbs," I looked at Tomiya, "but not now. I have an appointment to keep."

Allen laughed and said, "Why don't you give me a call in a day or two," and he looked at Tomiya, "or three or four."

CHAPTER 17

Two weeks later I called Allen and after he arrived the three of us visited while I told him all my adventures. We went to my ship and I showed them my trophy.

"That doesn't look so vicious," Allen said as he looked at the top view.

"From the top view, no," I said, "but when he rears up," I lifted the head.

"Oh! Mike!" Tomiya exclaimed.

"Hey! That's something else!" Allen said, "And you were under one of these things?"

"Yes, it was just a good thing I had a shield."

"And his teeth were already bloody from a fresh kill," said Dalcamy as he came in.

"Dalcamy," said Tomiya, "I'm going with Mike on his next trip."

"Yes, I heard you were taking Bocha's place. It looks like we may be going to Dextra. You're in for some excitement," he grinned.

"Dextra, what made you change your mind?" I asked.

"I've been talking to some of the soldiers that were there. They made a few mistakes I think we can avoid and perhaps find out more of the story behind their actions. We will be working as a team again."

"I'll be monitoring you this time," I said.

"Yes, I'll keep my men on the ship and just take Raygar with me when we meet the Dextarians."

"When are we going?"

"Not for a couple of months. They want to check out your ship after our last trip. So we'll have a vacation, Weather Man. I'll be in touch, we'll have to plan our strategy."

That evening we double dated with Allen and Susan for dinner and then went to the Recreation Center. Two months with Tomiya was like paradise. She showed me the courses she took and we picked up on our daily exercises.

We visited the Coens and told them all my adventures. They had some adventures of their own. They went on several camping trips, did some fishing and explored the cave where I met the borak.

"You know, I never did explore that cave," I said, "I should go back there sometime."

"Yes, you should, Mike," said Henry, "that cave is worth the climb. There's one large chamber that is full of stalagmites and stalactites, some forming full columns."

"And tell them about the crystals we found, Henry," said Martha.

"Oh, yeah, just a minute I'll get one." Henry left and returned a few minutes later with a large crystal about two inches in diameter. "These were laying all over, some were still embedded in the walls. Isn't it beautiful?"

"It is," I said as I took it. It was a deep red. Henry had polished the crystal until its surface was smooth and shiny. "Why don't you make something out of it, jewelry or something?"

"I was thinking of that. I wonder what it is."

"It's Halite," said Tomiya.

We all looked at Tomiya. "You know about this stuff?" I asked.

"Of course, it's all over Artara. It's a mineral. Depending on the area, you can find it in all different colors."

"Has Larry come back from Earth yet?" I asked Henry.

"I don't think so, why?"

"Why don't you send it to him and have it appraised? You might be able to get an exclusive contract for them. You still have family on Earth, don't you?"

"Yes. They could use the money." Henry looked over at Martha and smiled. "I don't have to ask Larry, I could send it to our daughter, Cathy." Martha smiled back and nodded enthusiastically.

Several days later we received a dinner invitation from Tommy's family. Karen was glad they decided to stay permanently. Tommy has been doing very well in school. He's now fifteen and taking Captain Preparation courses. All the information we transmitted from Vulgarb and Trok was included in his studies. We had a long conversation about them.

"Corla, I wish I could go with you," he said when I told him we were going to Dextra.

"There will be plenty of planets to go to when you're ready Tommy," I said. "Have you heard from Larry?" I asked Karen, "I understand he went to Earth to find a wife."

"He's been gone six months now, and it looks like he found one. He plans to have the wedding on Earth. Our house on Earth was sold for us and with Richard's retirement, we should have enough money for his and Tommy's Earth wedding when the time comes."

"I'm not going to get married. I want to be a Captain like Borkalami."

"I'm a Captain and I'm married," I laughed.

"You're different, you married an Artarian. Larry wants to have kids. I don't think a Captain should."

"Well, you're young yet, Tommy. You may meet an Artarian to marry like I did."

"Yeah. That would be okay, she could be my Second-in-Command, too."

"That wouldn't be good, you'd never be together. She would be on duty when you're not. Better for her to be a crewman, that way her schedule could match yours."

"Yeah, that's right." I happened to glance at Richard and Karen. They looked as though they didn't approve of Tommy marrying an Artarian, but they didn't say anything.

"What's been happening with Borkalami? I haven't seen him since I've been back."

"He's looking for more planets like Dalcamy did. He'll be gone for a long time this time." Tommy grew very serious and I could see he was missing Borkalami. Again, I looked at Richard and Karen. They smiled mechanically. Hmm, I thought, looks like there are still a few problems. I got nosy and read Henry. He wanted to take Tommy fishing not long ago. Tommy turned him down; he wanted to be with Borkalami instead.

"Have you done any fishing lately, Tommy?"

"No."

"Why don't the three of us go while I'm here?"

"The three of us?"

"You, your father and I. We could go back to that lake where I had that fight with the borak. Maybe we can explore the cave, too. How about it, Richard?"

"I'd like that. Tommy and I haven't fished as much as I expected. He's been too wrapped up in . . . things."

"All the more reason to go." I looked at Richard and winked.

You know, don't you? He looked right at me as he concentrated.

I nodded and turned to Tommy. He was looking down at his plate and missed what transpired between his father and me. "You pick the day, Richard."

"School's out, we can go anytime. How about day after tomorrow? Would that give you enough time to be ready?"

"I'm always ready to go fishing. Day after tomorrow will be fine. I'll pick you up at eight forna."

Richard smiled broadly. "We'll be ready."

Tomiya and I spent the next day shopping. "I can't believe I got rid of all that stuff."

"Well, maybe it's around, Mike, but we don't have time to look for it now. We'll get a new set now, when we find the other equipment . . . it'll be mine."

"Right! And we'll put it to good use." I picked her up and kissed her passionately.

"Mmm, you better watch it. You keep that up and we'll never go shopping."

I met Richard and Tommy at eight sharp. Richard seemed more excited than Tommy as we loaded the skylift with their equipment. We were half way there when I remembered I didn't get any bait. "Bait! We don't have any bait."

"We don't need it." Richard said. "Had this little magneto made. It can put out about twelve hundred volts with no amperage."

"What's it for?"

"Worms. You find a nice damp spot, stick the leads down into the ground and tweak the crank. The worms crawl out right to you."

"I didn't know you had that, dad."

"I was saving it for a surprise when we planned that last fishing trip we didn't go on."

"Well, we'll christen it on this trip." I said.

It took about two hours to get to the lake. We set up camp, and then went swimming. Tommy kept diving under and coming up with little critters. Richard laughed and followed him under several times, but he didn't have the breath control Tommy had. He came up gasping and looked at me. "That kid's a fish!" then dove under again. Richard and I walked out of the lake and laid in the sun while Tommy back floated.

"This was a good idea, Mike."

"Are you sorry you came to Artara?"

"No. I like Artara. I just wish Tommy and I could be as close as we used to be. He's always thinking about Borkalami. Borkalami is good to Tommy and I can understand their attachment, but he shouldn't come before his father."

"Maybe I can have a talk with Tommy while we're here."

"He'll think I put you up to it. No, we have to work it out."

"I know he loves you, Richard."

"I know that, too. He just needs to reevaluate his relationship with Borkalami. Borkalami is a hero to him, and I have to say, I'm jealous."

"Maybe this assignment he's on will give you a chance to gain your relationship back with Tommy."

"That was Borkalami's thought when he asked for it."

"Borkalami asked for this assignment?"

"Yes. He saw the problem building in Tommy. Borkalami visited me while Tommy was in school. He said he thought if he was away long enough Tommy would look to me more. He said he loved Tommy, but he didn't want to come between Tommy and me."

"When did Borkalami leave?"

"Just last week."

"I'll do whatever I can to help, Richard."

"Thanks, Mike, you have already, just setting up this trip like you did. It's given me a place to start."

"Then you'll forgive me for reading you that night?"

"Are you kidding? I was hoping you'd see it. Tommy has a deep respect for you, too."

I shook my head. "You have too much competition, it shouldn't be. We'll have to make you a hero in Tommy's eyes."

"No, Mike. No acts, no phony stuff. He has to accept me as I am. I have ideas, don't worry, the next time you come back things will be different."

We woke at dawn and went fishing. Richard's magneto worked perfectly. The fish attacked the worms like they were starving. We caught the fish and fed our hunger.

"Where's that cave, Mike?" Richard asked as we cleaned up camp.

"Up there." I pointed to the mountain.

"What do you say we go see it? How about you, Tommy, want to go?"

"Yeah!"

"Better take bread crumbs." I said real seriously.

"Bread crumbs. Why?"

"To leave a trail. We might get lost."

"Aw, go on."

Richard laughed and ruffled Tommy's hair. "He's pulling your leg, Tommy."

We made the same climb Henalag and I had made five years ago. I couldn't help thinking about that first year on Artara. I was always full of wonder of this new world and the Artarians. Memories came flooding back.

"You're in deep thought, Mike." Richard said as we climbed.

"Just thinking about the beginning, Richard. You know, I was actually angry with Borkalami and Komi for interrupting my life on Earth. That seems so long ago now."

"I read the file about your first trip here. I don't know how I would have reacted if it were me."

"It would have been different for you. You have a wife and family, I didn't."

"I suppose, yet, space always fascinated me. I'm going to get one of those transceivers."

"You are? Wow! When?" Tommy's eyes sparkled with excitement as he looked at his father.

"Soon, they're making it for me. I thought I'd have your's and mom's patterns put in it."

"I'll show you how to read and do things, dad. We can have a lot of fun together!"

Richard smiled and ruffled Tommy's hair again. "I plan on it."

We reached the top and looked down at the cliff. "Is that the cliff you fell from, Mike?"

"Yeah." I took hold of a vine and started down. Tommy came next, then Richard. Tommy ran over to the edge and looked down.

"Wow, what a long ways to fall."

"It could have killed you, Mike."

"Lucky I guess," I shrugged. "Come on, let's go in the cave."

We lit our lights and entered. It was narrow at the entrance, only one of us could fit through at a time. Once inside it opened into a small chamber. We shined our lights around the walls and they sparkled back at us.

"Corla, this is neat." Tommy spoke barely above a whisper. We went further in passing through to another larger chamber. It was so large the beam of our lights faded before reaching the far wall. "Wow!" Tommy's exclamation echoed through the cave. Massive pillars reached to the high ceiling. Stalactites covered the ceiling.

"Careful where you step, Tommy." Richard explained. "The stalagmites are still growing. If you touch them, the salts and oils of your hands can change their properties and kill them."

"What are stalagmites?"

"The smaller columns on the floor, see?" Richard pointed to the closest one. "Above, directly over it is a stalactite." Richard lit up the ceiling. "They will eventually join, causing a full column like that one." He directed his beam to one of the massive columns.

"You know a lot about caves."

"It was my hobby when I was a boy."

We moved around looking at everything, being careful where we stepped.

"Dad, look here." He pointed at a group of clear protrusions on a natural shelf formed into the wall. They were oblong squares in various lengths. They reflected Tommy's light.

"Crystal. This place is a natural storehouse of minerals."

"Here's some halite." I said as I joined them with a large red crystal in my hand.

"Where did you find that?"

"On the floor over there. Henry showed it to me when I was visiting him. It polishes up real pretty."

"Can I keep it, dad?"

"Okay, Tommy, but lets not take too much. These caves are better left natural, we don't want to upset their balance."

We went further in, exploring everything. Tommy walked a little ahead of us in full amazement of the cave. I noticed Richard watching the floor very closely, especially where Tommy walked. I was about to ask him what he was looking for when he yelled out.

"Tommy, stop!"

Tommy stopped dead in his tracks. "What's wrong?"

"That floor won't hold you. See the cracks? There must be another cavern below this one." We shinned our lights together, lighting up large areas of the floor as we swept the beams in a half circle. A hole gaped where the floor had given way. Richard got down on his knees and tested the floor, moving slowly toward the hole. He reached the hole and shinned his light over the edge.

"It's a cliff. It's safe up to this point." We joined him and looked over the edge.

I heard Tommy gasp. Even he couldn't find words to express the beauty that lay beneath us. The walls lit up white from our beams and dazzled with sparkles.

"Some kind of florescence." Richard said. "Too bad we don't have a rope. We'll have to come back, Tommy, and do some serious exploring."

Tommy's excitement sprung out so strong it almost made me flinch.

"Really? Oh, man!"

"As soon as I get my transceiver, Tommy, we'll come back together. It could take days to explore this whole cave."

"We won't get lost? I mean, if it's as big as I think, we could."

"We'll mark our way, we won't get lost. I'll show you how to draw a map as we explore."

I read Tommy as they spoke together. His admiration and awe of his father was growing by the minute. Yes, I thought. They'll be all right.

* * * * *

"Mike! It's been a long time." I had called General Buyemsky in Russia. "What have you been doing?" I related my adventures and the trip coming up. "So there are many other planets with life out there. I wish our world could join you on these explorations."

"Perhaps in the future it will be possible," I answered. "We're thinking of forming an Interplanetary Fleet. Perhaps Earth will be able to join. There wouldn't be any competition between governments, it would be strictly scientific and exploration."

"That sounds good. I will mention the possibility to the Premier. Have any other Earth governments been informed of this?"

I knew he meant America. "No, we haven't organized it yet, we've just been talking about it. I have no idea when it would be started. But I'm sure it will come and Earth will be invited. The thirty men from Trok will set the pace and standards."

"Everyone would have to speak Artarian?"

"Yes, it will be Artarian based."

"So Artara will have all authority over the fleet."

"Yes, especially since some ships will be armed with blasters for the people that do not have telepathic powers. They have to be able to protect themselves."

"All the planets will receive information about the other planets?"

"Yes, it will be fed into the Main Computer and everyone will have access to it. In fact, I'll give you the address for our last trip before we sign off and you can bring it up. I'll make sure you are the first Earth government to be invited."

"Before America?" he said surprised.

I laughed and answered, "It's only fair, Artara came to America first in the beginning. It's your turn to be first now. I'll let the Commodore know in case it starts before I return. Does the Premier know you have a communicator in your home yet?"

"No."

"I hope it doesn't get you into trouble."

"Not when I tell him this news, he will think we have something over on the Americans." We laughed together.

"You know, General," I said seriously. "If you ever need asylum, you can get it on any medical ship."

"Thank you, Mike, but I don't think that will ever be necessary. We have known for a long time that your ships have been taking some of our people when we wanted them arrested. But they are not a threat to us if they are on another world."

"Do you really believe they were a threat to you?"

"Anyone that undermines our government is a threat."

"Do you think you will be able to come to Artara when the Fleet starts?"

"I don't know, I would like to, but the Premier will pick the men."

"Well, maybe I'll be able to come visit with you sometime."

"That would be good, I would like to see your trophy."

I gave Buyemsky the access code for the file of my last trip and we signed off.

CHAPTER 18

A couple of weeks before our scheduled departure Tomiya and I inspected the ship. She also brought a few personal things for our quarters. We found my quarters were enlarged for the two of us. I was surprised and was told by Caltomacoe that Dalcamy had suggested the changes. It was a very nice improvement. We also had a larger bed, king size by Earth standards.

Tomiya started inspecting the computer and preparing for her various duties while I went about mine. She handed me reports daily on her tests and findings they were complete and efficient. Bocha stopped by one day to wish us 'good journey'. He told us that he was scheduled for testing next month.

Tomiya spent the evening before take-off on board ship for some final tests to be run that night on the engines. I reported in early the following morning. We lifted off with Dalcamy leading.

The six months went by much quicker this time for some reason, couldn't possibly be because Tomiya was with me, and we were orbiting Dextra. We scanned the surface and only found higher life forms in one area of the planet.

"That's strange, Dalcamy." I said as we discussed our preparations on screen. "You be careful down there, and keep in contact. I'll have Caltomacoe monitoring you, he's stronger than I."

"All right, Weather Man, I'll report everything. Mocki will be monitoring us, also."

Dalcamy landed and scanned the area watching to see if anyone was going to meet him. No one appeared. Raygar and he left the ship and approached the one large building in the area.

"Looks like there's only one building," he transmitted. Caltomacoe relayed the information into the computer and I activated the screen to see what Dalcamy was seeing while Tomiya stood beside me.

"Inspect that building on the outside before you go in Dalcamy, I want to see how it's shaped."

I watched as Dalcamy and Raygar circled it. It was huge with many rectangular windows. There appeared to be a building within a building. The center being at least twelve stories high. Surrounding the center structure was a lower building with many sides as it made a complete circle somewhat like a castle. It was made of bricks with the same gray coloring as the ground. The top of the building ended with peaks at all the corners. He circled on around and came to a main gate that had a garden within. There was a large solid double door going into the central building.

"Dalcamy! It looks like a prison to me," I said.

"A prison? Where are the guards?"

He pulled on a rope that we assumed was some kind of bell. A very small man between four and five feet tall came out and approached the gate. He was humanoid shaped with long skinny arms and large head with small beady eyes. Completely hairless and had small ears that stuck out from his head. He stood in front of Dalcamy.

Who are you? He was telepathic and spoke directly to Dalcamy's mind.

Captain Dalcamy of Artara.

Do you have passengers to add?

No, I've come to learn of your planet.

Come in, Captain Dalcamy.

He stepped in with Raygar and the little man closed the gate and locked it, then led him through the double doors. The screen went blank when the doors where closed.

Caltomacoe, what happened?

I lost contact there must be some kind of barrier around that building.

I called Dalcamy's ship to see if they could pick up anything. "Snatches, we'll transmit them to you." The screen showed lots of interference like snow on a television screen. I could see a large foyer and a staircase that turned slightly as it ascended. Dalcamy was in conversation with three people now, but I couldn't make out what was being said. He was following them and started down a stairwell then we lost him completely.

What do you want to do? Asked Caltomacoe.

"Have his ship lift and hover over the building and see if we can pick him up again."

Reception started again with Dalcamy's ship hovering, but I still couldn't hear anything. Cells appeared on screen and there were small people locked inside like the one that answered the door.

"Captain Packard," came loudly over screen, "this is Captain Dalcamy. Come down, it's safe for you to land. It was all a misunderstanding."

"That's not Dalcamy," I said. "He's never called me by that name." We watched the screen closely, he was still moving and looking around. *Caltomacoe, see if you can talk to him.*

Dalcamy can you hear me?

"Of course I can hear you, what's wrong, Captain Packard? Come on down."

"Damn, I wish we had blasters!" *Caltomacoe, tell who ever that is to bring Captain Dalcamy back upstairs.* There was laughter as a response.

Mike, we don't know if we're actually receiving Dalcamy or someone else.

If he's not out of there in twenty minutes we're going to get him out. Transmit that as a threat. The screen showed much activity. The cells came back as though Dalcamy was retracing his steps. Voice contact started again although broken up. They were back upstairs now in the foyer. They stepped outside.

"Please tell your other ship you're all right, Captain Dalcamy. We don't want any trouble."

"We'll return to my ship first and then tell him," he answered. Dalcamy's ship settled outside the gate and Dalcamy and Raygar boarded and lifted.

"Weather Man," Dalcamy came on screen, "thanks."

"What happened?"

"You're right. It's a prison, and there are more than just Dextarians in the cells. I want to scan the area for metal."

"You think they've taken more prisoners like Trok?"

"Could be, some of those prisoners looked hurt. Let's find out if there are any spaceships around." We scanned the area and found two spaceships hidden under camouflage. We left the area and headed for Trok to make plans without being overheard by the Dextarians.

"Dalcamy, Mike! What's wrong?" asked Kafka as we walked out of our ships and met him. "I didn't expect to see you again for at least three years."

"We need your planet to plan on," Dalcamy explained, "we just came from Dextra."

"You went there? Why?"

"We wanted to find out what's happening there and why they tricked your men. We found they've tricked some more space travelers and are holding them prisoners."

Kafka came out with some words I never heard before and didn't understand. I assumed he was swearing. "Come to my office, I'll have my Lors meet with us and we'll decide together how to help them."

We explained the situation to the Lors, and they told us how they attacked the prison last time. "Our ships are too slow, it would take over a year for them to get there, but we could arm your ships and use them."

"That might be a good idea," Dalcamy said. "Now I can see the need for weapons. There's a force field around the prison that prevents anyone from leaving."

"That's why our reception was so poor," I said. "What was happening downstairs?"

"The caretaker was showing us around. He's insane himself, he had made up his mind to add us to his prisoners. He wasn't going to turn the force field off to let us go, but your threat scared him. He remembered the last time. I'm glad you didn't fall for the invitation that was sent out."

"You heard it?"

"Yes, I could hear everything. I don't know where the transmission came from. You evidently couldn't hear me."

"No, we could only see broken pictures and then we couldn't be sure if it was you, that's why the threat. Would you have been able to get out?"

"Yes. They are not very strong, but I would have had to hurt someone. I'm glad it didn't come to that. This is what we'll do." Dalcamy explained we would have blasters installed on both ships outside the shields. My ship would be relatively emptied of personnel to be able to handle all the prisoners after we get them out and bring them back to Trok. Dalcamy would go to the prison and tell them to release the prisoners to us or we would blast them out.

"What if they threaten to kill the prisoners?" I asked.

"Then we will threaten to annihilate them."

It took two days to install the blasters on our ships. I left four crewmen on Trok and took Caltomacoe and Tomiya with me. Dalcamy took a force of forty Trok soldiers and Lor Sham.

Three months later I was orbiting Dextra as Dalcamy and Raygar approached the prison that was surrounded by Dextarian soldiers with weapons. One Dextarian approached Dalcamy and Raygar in the open as I monitored them. Again, they communicated mentally and Caltomacoe projected what he received on screen for me.

We were expecting you this time, the Dextarian said.

Good, perhaps you'll tell me why you are holding so many men prisoners.

You weren't supposed to go in there.

I did and I want to know why.

What happens on our planet is no business of yours. You will take your ships and leave.

When you start making prisoners of space travelers, it becomes our business. You will release them all to us or we will take them by force.

You are greatly outnumbered and you stand there issuing me orders? He laughed.

I'm giving you a chance to settle peacefully. However, if you want to fight I can oblige you. Dalcamy turned to walk back to his ship.

Wait! I'll release the travelers, but not our own.

All.

As Dalcamy stood facing the Dextarian, he motioned to one of his men. "Go get them." As the soldier walked toward the prison the Dextarian thought, they are of no use to us, anyway. Why should I fight over them?

Dalcamy and Raygar waited patiently. The gates opened and the prisoners began to come out. They came one by one, slowly. When they saw what was happening they ran toward Dalcamy. Raygar stopped the first two prisoners while Dalcamy told me to land. As I was landing, Dalcamy's ship lifted and hovered over the prison guarding them. One prisoner stayed with Raygar and the second directed the men to my ship. They came running as Tomiya lowered the ramp and directed them in. There were fifty prisoners, not all were capable of running and were being helped by their comrades. I noticed Dalcamy making some Dextarians turn back.

Those are soldiers acting as prisoners to get on board, Caltomacoe explained to me.

This seems too easy, I said to Caltomacoe. *They hardly fought us with all that army.*

We'll find out more when we talk to their prisoners.

Raygar had covered the prisoner that was with him with his shield. As they turned to enter Dalcamy's ship a shot fired at the prisoner deflected by the shield. Dalcamy stopped and turned to face the Dextarians as Raygar continued with the prisoner.

Do you want something?

No! Not at all. It was one of my soldiers, he fired out of place.

Dalcamy entered his ship and lifted. We headed for Trok. I inspected the men and found several of them injured and two staring into space like Direna had. The Dextarian prisoners seemed to be in better shape I surmised they had better defenses against the abuse. There seemed to be two different peoples from separate planets. They were humanoid people with coloration differences one race was green with large lips and eyes the other were very red with green eyes much like humans with white areas. They all wore uniforms and looked disheveled and dirty. I wondered how long they had been in that jail. I examined their wounds and found the only medical help they had was from their companions. Tomiya helped me communicate with them and we took the injured ones into medical with their companions supporting them.

The first injured man fought to keep from lying on the table. I motioned for the next one and he cooperated. I scanned him and took basic chemical samples for the computer to analyze and make recommendations. He was frightened and I tried to explain to him what I was doing. He had deep bruises around his bones and a couple of organs were bruised, but healing. He had a broken arm that was healing also, but wasn't quite in place. It needed to be broken and set.

"Your arm is placed badly," I said.

He looked at me and didn't understand. I raised the opercule and went over to him. I drew a rough picture of a broken bone placed wrong and pointed to his arm. He understood and so did his companions. I pointed to the opercule and drew a slash through the bone and drew another broken bone set correctly. Again they understood. Then I pointed to him and imitated sleep. He nodded and laid back down. After helping the first prisoner, I had no more problems with any of them cooperating even though they didn't understand what I was trying to say.

I had the opercule run a chemical analysis on one of each race to determine if Artarian food was safe for them to eat. One of the races had a problem with the same foods as Humans, Borko, Horgonon, Magnax and Caylif. These four vegetables are poisonous to Humans, Caylif being the most lethal. The information sparked my curiosity, but I didn't have the opercule go any further. The other race had no problem with any of our foods. I had all the injured persons treated and comfortable by the time we reached Trok, except for the two men that continued to stare blankly.

CHAPTER 19

Dalcamy came over to my ship as we lowered the ramp after landing. The prisoners came out and stood around the ship not sure what to do next. Kafka came up to us looking at the confused men as he approached.

"This can't go on any longer, look at those men," he complained. He directed them all taken to the infirmary. He noticed the two that stood staring blankly and shook his head.

We waited a couple of days before trying to question them. We picked two healthy men from each race and brought them into Dalcamy's ship one morning when we decided it was time to talk. Dalcamy motioned for one of them to sit. He sat down and Dalcamy placed a cap on his head and recorded his brain waves. Then he sat and placed another cap on his own head. He set the computer to dual communication. As he flipped the switch and started to concentrate the man jumped out of the chair and pulled off the cap. He talked to his companion very excitedly. I read him, he was comparing the communication with Dextra and didn't trust it. Only on Dextra he was strapped down to a table. No wonder the first soldier fought laying on the table! I thought.

Dalcamy just sat quietly and waited while they discussed it. Finally he sat down again and replaced the cap. Dalcamy started communicating again. Shortly Dalcamy switched the computer to record and removed his cap. Dalcamy repeated the procedure with one of each of the pairs we brought until we had a recording of each of their languages. Caltomacoe and Mocki took caps at different stations learning one language each while Dalcamy learned one of the languages. After about four hours we were able to communicate with all of them as Dalcamy, Caltomacoe and

Mocki translated. We invited them to the kitchen where we had lunch while introducing ourselves.

"My name is Toy Bannin from the planet Thrae and this is Habiton Corca." They were the humanoids with red colorations and green eyes.

"Thrae!" I said. "That's Earth spelt backwards. I'm from Earth, Mike Packard. Where is Thrae located?"

"Three solar systems away."

"I'm Calla Banto from Boro."

"And I'm Mebnia Finera."

"We know you're from Dextra", Dalcamy said, "what are your names?"

"Cosca Ogie."

"Haben Quess."

"Good, now that we know who everyone is let's find out why you were imprisoned on Dextra."

"We were taken first," Toy said, "and I guess it was stupid of us. We landed and half of us went to that building and met the same little man that brought you down stairs. Once we were inside, we couldn't get out again. Then the rest of our men walked in! They said they got an invitation. Our captain, Captain Kyal Corger was with us and they took him into another room. When we saw him again he was . . . like he is now. I don't know what they did to him, he won't talk or anything."

"We know what's wrong with him and we can help him," Dalcamy said. Calla's story was similar. The mistreatment of the rest of the men was evident from their physical conditions and they went into some details of the horror stories of their experiences.

"Do you have any idea what they were looking for?" I asked.

"They wanted to know how to fly our spaceships, and they wanted to know about us, physically."

"What do you mean physically? They wanted to know you inside?"

"Yes, they said they were going to run some tests. That was just before you came back. You scared them the first time, what did you do?"

"We threatened to attack them," I answered, "that's how we got you out."

The two Dextarians didn't speak at all and Dalcamy addressed them. "They are your people, do you know what this is all about?"

"Yes," answered Cosca. He seemed ashamed of what has been happening. "Our women only have male children. Our race is dying out. We haven't had a female born for fifteen years. Our scientists say if we can find another planet that we could interbreed with, we may be able to save our race."

"Why all this cruelty then?" I asked.

"It's the military," answered Haben. "When this started the military took over to 'preserve' the race and to find ways to go to other planets. But they didn't know how to build the ships. Then they got prisoners like them. They tried to find out how to fly their ships. But they wouldn't tell and the methods used to get the information blocked them when they examined too long. They're getting desperate now. We haven't much time left."

"You mean they still didn't get the information they wanted?" I asked.

"No, their minds locked up too soon."

I became extremely angry and looked at Dalcamy, I knew he felt my anger as he returned my gaze. I decided to remain silent for a while.

"What caused this to happen to your race?" Caltomacoe asked.

"A long time ago we had a disaster that caused us to go underground to live. The world was literally wiped out, the surface was unlivable. We survived by making a life underground. Over a period of time the air purifiers and chemicals used to sustain us caused our reproductive problems. We discovered it thirteen years ago and tried to live on the surface again, but it didn't do any good. It was too late to change the course. The only hope we have is for new blood. So the military took over saying it was stronger than the rest of us. Actually none of us are very strong, physically. Our strength seems to have gone over the years, too."

"Why were you prisoners?" asked Dalcamy.

"We're with a group that are trying to get rid of the three Generals in charge. They think they can force other people into cooperating with us and all they are doing is making things worse. They want to use their spaceships," pointing to the others, "and invade other planets. Our scientists are against them, but they have no say. They're not even allowed to talk to the people that are taken."

"That's what the tests were going to be," said Cosca. "They were finally going to let the scientists and doctors find out if they would be compatible with our people. They wouldn't have hurt them, it's the military that's been hurting people."

"Would you submit to such an examination, Cosca?" I asked. I had regained control of my emotions again.

"If it would help my people, yes."

"Good, I will have our opercule examine you after lunch and run an analysis to see if we know any life forms that are compatible to yours."

The other four looked at me and beamed their approval. Haben caught the implications. "And what of them?" he asked. "They may be compatible. Does your opercule know of them?"

"We will ask for volunteers," I answered. "Where can we find these three Generals?"

"Underground and very well guarded, we can't get to them ourselves. The soldiers like them being in charge."

"Sounds like the soldiers don't care what happens to your people." said Mocki,

"They are soldiers," answered Cosca with a shrug.

When we completed lunch I went to medical with Cosca and started the examination. The others followed and watched. I put Cosca to sleep for the final phase, and as he was sleeping ran the analysis and found Artarians to be compatible.

"Interesting," Dalcamy replied.

"What about you, gentlemen? I asked the other four. "Would you submit to save a dying world?" They looked at each other negatively. "What if it were your world being threatened by extinction? How would your people react?" I asked.

Calla picked up a gown. After he was finished, Toy laid on the table. Toy was compatible with Dextra. Calla was compatible with Earth.

"They were so close and didn't know it," Caltomacoe said. "If they were just more caring."

"Now we have grounds for negotiation," I said.

CHAPTER 20

Dalcamy and Caltomacoe began working with the two officers. "They are going to take a little longer than Direna did," Dalcamy told me a week later. "I don't want to wait that long to get back to Dextra. I think we should go back now."

Three months later Dalcamy landed on Dextra while I stayed in orbit.

You again! The little man responded. He shot thoughts of pain at Dalcamy and he mirrored them back at him. The Dextarian screamed and grabbed his head.

If you are willing to listen now, we can help you solve your reproductive problem. But if you don't want our help we will simply leave and put a barrier around your planet so that no one will come here again.

You can help us? How?

I know a planet that is compatible. We can help you negotiate with them.

Why don't you come in then, and we'll talk. He was so sweet if you looked hard enough, you might see honey dripping from his evil little mouth.

No. You will have your Generals, Scientists and Doctors meet with me on my ship tomorrow morning two couts after sunrise. I'll be waiting for them. If they don't come, we will leave and no one will ever come here again. Do you understand?

Yes, I understand, he said sarcastically.

The following morning there were nine people outside the spaceship with armed soldiers standing guard. There was no mistaking the Generals. They wore brown uniforms as the soldiers, but had insignias on their arms, epaulets on their shoulders and medals weighted their chests. They produced a very showy demeanor. The others dressed simple, shirts and pants. Dalcamy lowered the ramp. The soldiers started in with them and Dalcamy stopped them.

"You are in no danger from us, your soldiers can wait outside." The Generals started to protest, but the Scientists and Doctors continued into the ship. Dalcamy led them to the meeting room where Toy, Habiton, Cosca, Haben and Mocki waited.

"Sit down and make yourselves comfortable. I am Captain Dalcamy from Artara. My Second-in-Command, Mocki. This is Toy and Habiton of the planet Thrae. I think you know Cosca and Haben."

"I'm General Alma. This is General Norie and General Daggany."

"I'm Doctor Bella. I was the director of our Science Department. Now there are only the six of us left. "Doctors Mortez, Borgami and Gelvez are medical doctors. Each one nodded as they were introduced. Doctor Kalmatore, Biologist. Doctor Salavine, Chemist."

"I understand you three Generals are in charge of your planet," Dalcamy said. "That's correct," said General Alma. "Generals Norie and Daggany are under me."

"I see," said Dalcamy. "You will take orders from these men from now on." Dalcamy said motioning to the Doctors and Scientists. "They will be in charge collectively and have to agree on all decisions."

"They are scientists! They know nothing about military defense!"

"You don't need military defense now, you need people. We will help bring people to you and also take you to them. But there will be no more harm done. You have hurt enough people with your cruelty and 'examinations'. These are the conditions:

"First. You will disband your soldiers. We will furnish your protection from now on.

"Second. You will destroy that prison.

"Third. These six men will be a ruling panel for your planet. And finally, you will begin living on the surface of your planet again.

"We will assist you in building new cities to live in. We will give consultation on ruling matters to help you establish a new government. Eventually you will be governing yourselves and have space flight."

"You can't just walk in and take over like this!" said General Alma.

"How long do you estimate the life of your people?" Dalcamy asked Doctor Bella.

"About another forty, fifty years. When this last generation expires."

Dalcamy turned back to General Alma. "Your men have caused enough mental damage to other beings to warrant us sealing your planet until extinction. We can do anything we want."

"Why are they here?" General Norie asked motioning to Toy and Habiton.

"They are compatible with your race. If you agree to our terms we will present you to their planet."

"What if they turn us down?" asked General Daggany.

"We will not consider the 'what if' until we face it, but we will continue to help you."

General Alma became extremely angry. He looked Dalcamy in the eye, drew a weapon and pointed it at him. "You will do as I say or I'll blow you to pieces and take your ship."

"You would not be able to take this ship anywhere without me. I advise you to put that away or I will be forced to take it from you."

"Alma! This is crazy! He's offering to help us and you sit there threatening him!" Doctor Bella said.

General Alma had taken control from the beginning. He had visions of ruling the whole planet when he solved their problems. Now he saw all that slipping away because of an alien. He decided to shoot Dalcamy. Mocki took control of him and Dalcamy reached across the table and removed the weapon from his hand.

"You are not General material." Dalcamy said as Mocki released General Alma. "You are no longer in charge of anything. You will join the soldiers outside while we continue our discussion." Raygar led him out as the other two Generals stared.

"The men that were examined---," Doctor Kalmatore started to ask.

"They will be all right, we can help them," Dalcamy answered. There was an explosion outside. Raygar came back and explained that Alma grabbed a weapon from a soldier and shot at him.

"We are going to have trouble with him," General Norie said. "He's extremely violent."

"I'll be right back." Dalcamy turned on his shield and went outside.

Alma stood amongst the soldiers with a long-range blaster and raised it at Dalcamy as he walked out of the ship. He fired and the force was deflected by Dalcamy's shield. The soldiers all backed away from Alma, he fired again as Dalcamy approached. Dalcamy took the weapon and threw it on the ground.

"Alma, you don't want power, anymore, do you? You could care less who has power over this planet. Fighting and weapons abhor you. General? Why would you want to be a General?"

"I don't know why I would want to be a General, who suggested I should be?" he walked away.

Dalcamy, I transmitted, *you have to show me how to do that.*

You haven't learned that yet, Weather Man?

The soldiers watched Alma walk away and then looked at Dalcamy. "What did you do to him?" They were too far away to hear the conversation. The telepathic power of the Dextarians didn't seem to be very strong. Most of them didn't try to use it.

"Nothing. Soldiers aren't needed anymore, you can leave anytime you want."

They looked at each other, "we'll wait until we hear that from the Generals."

"Very well." Dalcamy went back into the ship. "We won't have anymore trouble from Alma," he said as he entered the conference room.

"What did you do to him?" asked Cosca.

"I just talked to him, and he decided I was right." Dalcamy picked up on the emotions and thoughts of the two remaining Generals. They feared General Alma. They didn't believe just talking to him would change anything.

He must have done something, what powers do these people have?

Can they truly seal our planet to extinction? It would be good if Alma is out of this, but I don't believe it.

I wish I could see what this Dalcamy is thinking, he's not like all the others.

"Now, let's get down to business." Dalcamy said as he sat down again. "Are our terms acceptable to you? Or do you need more time to think about them?"

"If there is no military, why do you still need Generals?" asked General Norie.

"Actually, you won't be Generals, but you will be needed to keep work details and business in order. You will probably have to increase your number, perhaps these two can join you," Dalcamy motioned to Cosca and Haben. "There will be plenty of work to be done and organization will be important. That's why you will always be needed. You could call yourselves Work Force Managers or something like that.

"We will send technical ships here with technicians to show you what has to be done and workers to help when physical strength is needed. Our medical ships will also come and help you to strengthen yourselves. However, it will be six months before any of them will arrive. Meanwhile, you will pick young healthy men, with the correct attitudes, to go to Thrae and, hopefully, meet some women to bring back here. What would be your estimate in numbers necessary to start with, Dr. Bella?"

"Fifty would be good, and once they give birth, perhaps another fifty. If just half gave birth to female babies we would be saved."

"The men of your species determine the sex?"

"Well, that's the way it's supposed to work. We ran tests and found the male and female sperms are strong, but our women's systems are killing the female sperms and only the males are surviving."

"Then when we have the women from Thrae you can inseminate female sperms to produce one hundred percent female babies for the first year."

"Yes, that should work, then we can let nature take its course and eventually we should be back to normal."

"Do you think your planet would be willing to cooperate?" Dalcamy asked Toy and Habiton.

"We have some under populated areas were the women out number the men. It may be possible." Toy said.

"It would depend on how they are approached. If they know about Captain Corger they may not help just out of anger." Habiton added. He still had hatred against the Dextarians.

"We can't keep his condition from them. He would be the first person they would ask about. Perhaps we can get him back to normal before we get there," Dalcamy answered. "You said you were three solar systems away, how long did it take you to get to Dextra?"

"About nine months," answered Toy.

"That's probably how long it will take us.

"I see no reason why we can't agree to your terms," started Dr. Borgami, "how do you two Generals feel about this?"

They looked at each other. "It seems we have no choice," said General Daggany.

"You have a choice," Dalcamy said. "You can be a part of this or not. Remember, we are only offering our help," Dalcamy addressed everyone as he spoke. "If you would rather we stay out of it, fine. However, no one else will ever come here again."

There were a few moments of silence as they thought about Dalcamy's last comment.

How could he seal our planet?

What does it matter who does the helping so long as our people are saved?

It matters because an alien world will have control over us.

We will die without them. General Alma had the answer in his hands and he destroyed the opportunity with cruelty.

Even if these Artarians didn't come, we would never be able to save our world through General Alma's methods and you know he would step in again as soon as they left. To refuse Dalcamy's help would be condemning us all.

Daggany! Alma would kill us both, you know that!

Ha! Not only us, he would kill everyone in this room! He was humiliated in front of everyone, he would have to. We must agree to save our own skins, if nothing else. Let's face it, could control from these Artarians be any worse than Alma's? You can only die once.

General Daggany spoke up. "We will have all the available and willing young men report to us. The four of us will pick them?" General Daggany asked the other two Dextarians who were to be part of the managing unit and they nodded their approval. "Then we are no longer Generals, but Work Force Managers," all agreed.

"Good," said Dalcamy smiling. "You will disband the soldiers and organize the young men. We will leave for Thrae in about ten days."

They left the conference room and went outside to meet a crowd of people, military and civilians. They had been gathering while the meeting was taking place. The two Generals stood halfway up the ramp for everyone to see them and they announced the disbandment of the soldiers. There were some disgruntles from the soldiers as they threw their weapons down. Most of the civilians cheered when they heard the scientists and doctors were going to be in charge. Everyone cheered and danced and jumped when it was announced that a planet had been found and was going to be approached for help.

* * * * *

"Weather Man, ready to head for Trok?" Dalcamy's face appeared on screen. Ten days had passed and fifty Dextarian men were chosen.

"All set," I answered. We lifted with twenty-five Dextarian passengers on each of our ships. Dalcamy made a full report to Commodore Mackalie. One technical ship, a freighter and one medical ship was dispatched with orders that the ships were to be manned at all times. They are to contact Borkalami on the planet Trok if there is any sign of trouble. Captain Borkalami had been dispatched for Trok a week ago, I requested his co-ordinance.

We landed on Trok early in the morning, Kafka met us. The Dextarians followed us out of the ships. Trok soldiers kept their distance from them, not trusting the Dextarians.

"Looks like everything went well," Kafka said as he observed the Dextarians.

"There were a few objections," Dalcamy said smiling.

"But they saw the error of their ways," I said laughing.

"Lor Sham will see to their housing until you're ready to leave again. Let's go to my office and discuss what you need for your journey."

We spent the day with Kafka and I invited him aboard my ship that evening. "I want to introduce you to Captain Borkalami."

Borkalami's smiling face came on screen. "Good to see you, Mike."

"Borkalami, have you found anything?"

"No, looks like you and Dalcamy have been getting all the action."

"Just lucky, I guess. We won't be here when you arrive. I want to introduce you to Melcon Kafka. He's in charge of things here."

"I'm happy to meet you, Melcon Kafka."

"I'm looking forward to your arrival."

"Melcon Kafka will supervise the installation of blasters on your ship, Borkalami."

"Blasters? We're carrying weapons now?"

"We have found them to come in handy as persuasive tools. Just the sight of them on our ships draws attention."

"So you haven't used them."

"No, so far they've only been for show."

"What about the telepathic defenses? They should be sufficient."

"Yes, but suppose you don't want telepaths to know about certain powers? Like the people on Dextra."

"I get your point. Very well then, blasters it is. Good journey to you, Weather Man. Perhaps we'll meet soon."

"Good journey, Borkalami."

"One question, Mike," Kafka said as we signed off. "How would you have sealed off their planet?"

"We couldn't, it was a bluff." I grinned and we laughed together.

CHAPTER 21

We continued to make plans with Toy and Habiton for our trip to Thrae.

"Can anyone else command your ship besides Captain Corger?" I asked.

"No."

"You don't travel with a Second-in-Command?"

"Why? The Captain knows it all."

"Yes, but now you're without him," said Caltomacoe. "You would be stranded."

"I guess we'll have to change that. We never had a problem before."

"We can't carry fifty Dextarians and your men, too," Dalcamy said. "We will have to leave the men here and bring back a Captain that can take them home. We'll take Captain Corger with us and I'll work with him on the way. We should also take about five of his men to be with Corger when he comes back to reality. You two and three others. You pick them Toy."

"I can do the same with Captain Bruno," I said. "Caltomacoe has already started working with him."

Lor Sham supervised the loading of the food supplies. Two weeks after landing on Trok, we lifted for Thrae. I was gratified to see Lor Sham ordered five cases of coffee loaded on my ship. They called it feaka. We pushed our ships to the limit. We had thirty-one passengers and were wishing for more room. Caltomacoe used my quarters for privacy while treating Captain Bruno.

He's not co-operating, Mike. He tries to escape every time I make contact.

Maybe you'll have to force him to listen to you to make him know you're trying to help him. Let me come with you next time.

I joined with Captain Bruno as I had with Direna as the five Boros watched. Our pain was intense as Caltomacoe moved in. We wanted to run and started to rise, but my stubbornness gave us strength to fight back. No! Damn it! I heard moaning.

Captain Bruno, I'm trying to help you, but you must work with me.

Who's that? Your eyes are different....PAIN.

I'm Caltomacoe. You are safe now, we got you away from Dextra and will be taking you home.

Boro?...PAIN...Home?...PAIN...I could hear more moaning. Someone else is here, who?

Mike, he has joined you to give you strength. He shares your thoughts and pain. Listen to me. We will talk many times until your pain goes away, but you must concentrate.

PAIN...PAIN...It hurts too much!

I'm going now, but I will be back to help you. Mike! Come out!

I'm Captain Bruno. Why are you calling me Mi---Caltomacoe. I realized who I was as Caltomacoe slapped me. "You don't need to get violent." I said rubbing my face.

"I'm sorry, Mike, I was having a hard time getting you back again."

"Its okay, Caltomacoe," I said smiling.

"That was the best session we've had since I started. Do you think you can help for a while?"

"Yes, but we should do something that would trigger my return easier. Do you know how to hypnotize?"

"I don't know what that is."

"I bet the computer does, lets go to medical." It took me an hour of questions and explanations before the computer acknowledged hypnotism. I set it to make Tomiya the key word and told everyone to leave medical while I ran it. I also informed Dalcamy what I was about to do so there would be no accidents. If he were to come on screen while I was using it, no telling what might happen.

"That's a good idea, Weather Man. Thanks for letting me know, but I don't think it would affect me. I wouldn't be able to see what your screen is projecting to you. I'm having trouble with Corger, I think I'll have Mocki join with him."

When all was clear I sat in front of the screen and turned on the program. I awoke an hour later fully refreshed and feeling great. I couldn't remember any of the hypnosis, but I wasn't supposed to. All I could remember was turning it on. When I left medical Caltomacoe and the others were waiting.

"Did it work?" Caltomacoe asked.

"I don't know, we won't know until I join with Bruno again."

Caltomacoe met me at breakfast after my sleeping period and we went in to see Bruno with his men. Caltomacoe made contact and I joined again. Captain Bruno, do you remember me? I'm Caltomacoe.

Caltomacoe, we talked before - - - I can't remember...PAIN... what you wanted.

I'm trying to help you. We will take you home when you're well.

Home! Yes,...PAIN...you said you were taking me home. How long?

About six months, but I want to get you well before then. I took my eyes from Caltomacoe and saw Calla. Calla! He's here too!...PAIN

Caltomacoe told Calla I recognized him. He took my hand and smiled. "There are five of us here with you."

Only five?...PAIN...I could hear someone moaning. Who's moaning? Who's hurt?

Mike's moaning because you are hurt.

I don't...PAIN...understand!

You will in time, Caltomacoe answered. You are confused because of what the Dextarians did to you.

Dextarians! I - - - re-member. Extreme pain shot through my head. I screamed and grabbed my head. I don't want to think about that--go away! I must think about it. No!

Captain Bruno, it was Caltomacoe again. We must think about it. But we will go slowly so the pain won't get too bad. The only way you can be free is to remember everything. Do you understand?

Yes.

Do you remember going to Dextra?

I remember landing. There was a big building...PAIN...a little man... PAIN...welcomed me. Asked us in. It hurts! I screamed.

Yes, Bruno, I know. We'll stop for now and rest. I will see you later. "Tomiya."

I looked at Caltomacoe and the others and withdrew from Bruno. "It worked," I said. "He has a lot of pain, but I think he's going to work with you now."

"Are you all right, Mike?" Caltomacoe seemed really worried about me.

"Yeah, why?"

I could feel Caltomacoe join me. He was looking for something. I started daydreaming. *Are you practicing being a Vulgarb?* I felt his humor and my visions continued. It seemed like a long time, but when Caltomacoe broke contact it was only for a few minutes.

"You're all right," he said with a sigh of relief.

"I didn't know you could do that."

"I was concerned about this affecting you. The computer explained this type of examination to me. If you had been harmed, it would have been painful for you."

"Interesting, so you just learned about it yourself."

"Yes," he smiled, "while you were hypnotizing yourself."

We had one more session with Bruno and Caltomacoe said he wouldn't need me anymore because he was starting to work with him now.

"He missed you, Mike." Caltomacoe said the following day after his first session. "He said your strength helped him. You are a very determined person."

I laughed, "Yes, I guess I am. Tell him I look forward to being able to exchange adventures with him when he's well again. He has been to a lot of planets and I want to hear about them."

Captain Bruno's men were staying with him constantly. I had reports of Bruno working on his own and talking to his men periodically. Four weeks later Bruno walked into control with Caltomacoe.

"Captain Packard," he said. "We finally meet in person."

"Captain Bruno! I'm glad to see you so much better," I grabbed his arms in friendship.

"You and Caltomacoe have helped me, I don't think I would have been able to be normal on my own. Even my men have been a tremendous help to me."

"You must be a good Captain to them, they really care about you. We should be at Thrae in about five months now. Do you know what's happening?"

"We are going to Thrae to get women for them. I don't want to see them get anything after this."

"I can understand that, but the ones that did this to you are not in power anymore. Would you hold a whole world accountable for the actions of a few?"

"Well, since you put it that way, I guess not."

A Dextarian entered control to view the screen and Bruno's head tipped as pain flashed across his face from the sight of him.

"Still hurts, doesn't it?" I said.

"Yes, I'm looking forward to the time when I can think and remember without pain."

"It'll come, you're over the worst part now."

"Show me your ship, Captain?" he asked.

"Very well, Captain," I answered. I gave him the grand tour. He told me of some 'extras' they had on their ships that would fit in on ours.

"I miss showering with water," he said.

"I did, too, at first," I laughed. "But these showers are more practical in space."

"Mmm. Do they shower with water on Artara?"

"Fraid not. You can go swimming on Artara that makes up."

"Let's have some of that coffee you've been bragging about."

"All right." We went to the kitchen where I brewed a pot of good rich coffee. We sat at a table and I watched his face as he took his first sip. He slowly sat back and began to smile. His eyes sparkled his satisfaction. "Thought you'd like it."

"You have this drink on Artara?"

"Earth. It has quite a bit of caffeine in it. If you're not used to it, you might feel a little hyper."

He took another sip and relaxed. "I like your ship, Mike."

"Do you remember everything about your ship? Or do you think you'll need some re-education?"

"So far I remember, but I wouldn't know what I've forgotten."

I smiled, "No, I guess you wouldn't know what you've forgotten. We can find out when we reach your planet and our computer can re-educate you if necessary."

"How does that work?" he asked.

"It can feed information into you."

"Hmm. The Dextarians take information out, and you put information in. Interesting."

CHAPTER 22

Everyone on board started learning the language of Thrae. They had to work in shifts and in about two months we were speaking it exclusively. Bruno continued to improve and the day came when Caltomacoe told me his pain was gone. Even when Caltomacoe examined him as he did me, Bruno had no pain. I threw a party for him. Several of the Dextarians congratulated him and apologized at the same time. It was a good time for establishing a rapport between them.

We were four months into the trip and tension was building from being so crowded. Squabbles started once in a while, but broke up before anything got too serious. I wasn't sleeping well at night and Tomiya had to awaken me several times telling me I was moaning in my sleep. I actually began to dread going to bed.

What's happening to you, Mike? Asked Caltomacoe, *you don't look good.*

I don't know; I don't sleep well. I have bad dreams and when I wake up I can't remember them.

Caltomacoe examined me. I started daydreaming again and was rudely awakened by a terrific banging pain in my head. He pushed on it and I concentrated. I saw blackness and then Dextarian eyes staring at me. I could hear voices, but the words didn't make any sense. Caltomacoe withdrew and I found I had bent the arms of the chair I was sitting in.

Someone's been interrogating you while you're sleeping! Anger blazed in his eyes and radiated from his being. The anger I had felt from Borkalami when we were on Earth was nothing in comparison to what Caltomacoe was displaying. *Go to bed at the regular time. I'm going to find out who it is while you're asleep.*

I was extremely tired when I went to bed and fell asleep almost instantly. I saw Caltomacoe's eyes burning with anger and fear filled me as I jumped awake. I was sitting up with sweat pouring down my face. My heart felt like it was going to fly out of my chest; it was beating so hard. Tomiya woke up startled as I sat there breathing hard trying to control myself. I realized that Caltomacoe had found the intruder and I was experiencing the Dextarian's fear. *Don't kill him, Caltomacoe!* I transmitted.

Tomiya caught my thought and asked what was happening. I transmitted the whole thing to her as I dressed. She came with me to meet Caltomacoe in medical. He was strapping the Dextarian called Formald Molinick to the table as we arrived. *What are you doing, Caltomacoe?* He didn't answer me, he continued working.

The computer lowered and covered the Dextarian's head as he struggled in the straps. Formald was so frightened he reached out to me with his mind. *Please stop him! What is he going to do to me? His mind is so angry I can't understand his thoughts; please do something!*

I looked at Caltomacoe and tried to read him, but his anger blocked me, too. I couldn't read him. "Are you going to kill him, Caltomacoe?" I asked very calmly.

Caltomacoe looked at me. "Don't you think I should?" He flipped a switch and walked away from the control panel. "We will leave him here for a while and let him think about what he's done." He walked over to Formald and stared at him.

I tried to read Caltomacoe again, but he had his thoughts concentrated on Formald and deliberately blocked me. Formald reached out to me again. *Help me! Help me! Don't let him!*

Caltomacoe turned to me and said, "Come, Mike, Tomiya, let's have some asil." I looked at the computer and saw it was busy with the Dextarian, but I didn't know what it was doing. I was surprised that

Caltomacoe would leave someone in it with no supervision. Caltomacoe took my arm and walked toward the door.

Don't leave me! Captain Packard, don't leave me!

"Caltomacoe, what is the computer doing to him?" I asked again as we went to the kitchen.

"It's just recording him. I want to find out if anyone else is involved in this."

"Then what is he so frightened of?"

"He thinks it's going to interrogate him. He's going to be waiting for it to rip his mind apart. We can monitor him in control while we have our asil."

An hour later the computer shut down and we went back to medical. "Your machine failed! I felt nothing!" he screamed at Caltomacoe as we entered.

"You think so," answered Caltomacoe as he put a cap on and received the information. We waited and watched Formald struggling in his bindings. "So, you are a friend of Alma. You were in on the interrogations."

"How do you know that?" Formald asked as he looked at Caltomacoe.

"Our machine didn't fail. You see, we don't torture people and we still get all the information."

We left him again for Caltomacoe to tell us what he learned. *Alma is back to his normal, sweet self. He has ten faithful followers. He's planted one on each of our ships to sabotage our efforts and learn the control of our ships from the Captains. Dalcamy is probably having bad dreams, too.*

Why are they doing this? Asked Tomiya.

To get his status back. If we don't return to Dextra when we said, he'll just move in and claim we lied to them and stole their people away in revenge. Then when these two saboteurs learn to control the ships, they were to bring them back for their use.

And what about us? Tomiya asked again.

They were probably ordered to get rid of us one way or another, I answered.

Yes, either make zombies out of us during our sleep or kill us some how.

How awful! And we're trying to help them!

Let's call Dalcamy, I said as I switched on the screen in control.

Dalcamy appeared. "What's up, Weather Man?"

"How have you been sleeping, Dalcamy?"

"Not too good, must be the crowdedness of the ship."

"Bad dreams?" I asked.

"Yes," he answered rather slowly starting to get suspicious of my questions now.

"I bet you can't remember what they are though, huh?"

"What is this? How do you know about my dreams?"

"Because I've been having them, too and we found out why."

He leaned forward in his Captain's chair. I had his full attention. "Why?"

"You're being interrogated while you're asleep." We told him everything.

As we spoke I could see the anger building in him. "Those little---," he wouldn't vocalize the rest of his thought.

"You have better control than I do, Dalcamy. I would have said it out loud."

"Mocki and I will find him tonight. Thanks, Weather Man."

What are we going to do with him? Asked Tomiya.

I know exactly what we can do with him, I announced. *We are going to feed him a nice big meal,* Caltomacoe began to grin before I could finish, *and an hour later we are going to put him to sleep until we get him back to Dextra.*

Tomiya's eyes got big. "That would be for two years, maybe more!"

If he's asleep he can't hurt us, I said. *He'll be all right; we'll monitor him. We'll have a meeting with all the Dextarians and tell them everything. They can watch him go to sleep. Did you get all the names, Caltomacoe?*

Yes, Dalcamy can give Dr. Bella their names when he returns to Dextra.

We took Formald to the kitchen and laid out a large meal in front of him of all his favorite foods. "I hope you're hungry Formald," I said.

"Why are you doing this? Is it poisoned?"

I laughed and took a sample of every dish, "if you don't want it, I'll eat it, it tastes pretty good."

He looked at me and then at the food. He tasted it, then started eating. We sat down and drank asil and watched him eat while we chatted as though nothing happened. He finished it all and we continued to chat.

"What are you going to do with me?" he asked again. He was trying to read us, but we wouldn't let him. Caltomacoe had joined me and was able to strengthen my block. When the hour was up we called a meeting of everyone on ship to the medical room. We prepared the sleeping chamber while they were gathering. No one but the Artarians knew what it was.

Caltomacoe started his speech directed to the Dextarians. "We have a saboteur amongst us."

The Dextarians looked at each other and then at Formald as he stood between Caltomacoe and I. Caltomacoe proceeded to tell all the details leading up to his capture and the information we got from him.

"On your planet, what would you do with someone like this?" I asked.

"He would be executed. He put all our lives in danger," answered one Dextarian.

"He would have ruined our chances of our race being saved!" another one said.

"He should die!" yelled another.

"Do all of you agree he should die?" I asked.

"Yes!" they shouted.

"We are not executioners," Caltomacoe explained. "So we decided, for our Captain's peace of mind," he looked over at me and smiled, "we are going to put him to sleep until he arrives back at Dextra. Then your people can deal with him."

"That seems more than fair," said Bruno. "I would like to see him executed, myself, but I think your decision is a better one."

"All of you have decided against me without even giving me a chance to disprove what they have been saying!" Formald shouted at them.

"I recognize that voice!" said Bruno. "You were my inquisitor! I'll never forget that voice!" Captain Bruno stared at Formald angrily. I received his thoughts of vengeance and saw Formald being strangled to death as Bruno joyfully squeezed his scrawny little neck.

Formald stood looking at Bruno, he couldn't have helped seeing the same pictures, then turned to the others. "They're telling lies about me! I found out that they really aren't going to Thrae at all. They're going to another planet to make slaves of us. Why else would they ask for just 'healthy young men'? They want to get rid of me with your help! Don't you see that?"

"That won't work, Formald," Cosca said. "We voted for them to kill you and they refused. If what you're saying is true, why would they insist on keeping you alive? No, I think you are guilty."

"Yes," said Haben, "I know for a fact that you worked very closely with Alma, and Captain Bruno recognizes you. You're lucky you're not dead now."

Formald turned to me and said, "That's why you gave me that big meal!"

"That's right, it'll help provide nourishment for you while you sleep." He shot such a force of thoughts of pain at me it made me stagger back and grab my head.

"My gift to you, Captain Packard! Something to remember me by!" Caltomacoe slapped him so hard he was lifted off his feet and thrown to the floor stunned. The pain in my head stopped immediately. "You all right, Mike?" Caltomacoe asked.

"Yes, I'm okay, let's get him to sleep before he does anymore damage."

He regained his senses as we were strapping him into the sleeping chamber and attaching the monitor sensors to his body. He looked up at me as I worked and said very calmly, "Someday I will kill you, Captain Packard."

We closed the lid and set the chamber for sleep. Only moments later he was in suspension and will remain there until we wake him.

Caltomacoe insisted on my going back to bed, my sleeping time was over and his was supposed to start. I slept very soundly and felt good when I awoke to take command.

"Weather Man," Dalcamy appeared on screen in control during my watch. "We found him. He admitted to everything you got from Formald. I didn't have to have the computer read him."

"What did you do with him?" I asked.

"Same thing you did. Have you worked on your sore spots yet?"

"No, I just woke up. Caltomacoe wouldn't let me take my regular shift. Don't worry, I'll get on it."

"I'm sure you will. Talk to you later, Weather Man." We signed off and I started my inspections and routine duties. Tensions on the ship eased a lot since we put Formald to sleep. I wondered if he was behind them all along.

"Captain, can we interest you in a game of Quise?" it was Mebnia, one of our Dextarian passengers. Quise is a lot like poker.

"I have about two hours of work yet, after that I'll be free."

"Fine, we'll wait for you in the recreation room."

I arrived two and a half hours later to a party in my honor. "Funny way to play Quise," I said laughing.

"We just want to show how much we appreciate you," Cosca said. "Most Captains all of us know, including the Boros, would have killed Formald. And would have been justified in doing it." The party was a good one and I enjoyed every moment of it.

CHAPTER 23

Caltomacoe and I started to work on my 'sore spots' as Dalcamy had called them, a very apt description. We were in my quarters, in my sitting room. I made sure Tomiya was busy with her duties. As we probed, memories started coming of discussions with Formald in my mind. *Captain Packard I'm your friend, you know that don't you? Tell me how you control your ship.*

No, who are you?

I'm your partner. Don't you remember Commodore Mackalie telling you about a partner?

I saw Commodore Mackalie talking to me. "You will have a partner, Captain Packard. He will work with you on everything. Both of you will be in constant communication."

I am your partner. How do you direct the ship?

A code.

What is the code?

Secret. The word 'secret' formed in my mind as a large picture. I had deliberately conditioned my mind to project that word whenever I thought about the code. Knowing my telepathy and defenses against intrusions were weak, I had to come up with something that would protect the operating code of the ship. I worked on it all during my preparation for

Captainship. The conditioning was so strong, it took an immense effort of concentration to get through the word and remember what the code was.

I know its secret. But you can tell me, I'm your partner.

Can't tell anyone, it's a secret.

But I have to share all your secrets for us to work together. If you don't tell me, I'll have to make you tell me.

Secret. I felt pain starting somewhere in the darkness like a small rock starting to roll. It grew larger as it rolled and the pain grew more intense. I wondered what would happen if the rock got larger than I, would it roll over me and crush me.

I don't really want to cause all this pain in you, Captain Packard,

But you give me no choice. Just tell me the code.

I felt he lied. His words didn't match the feelings I had from him, they were liken to pleasure. The pain grew as he spoke and my thoughts began to confuse. I could hear my name being called from far away. It started getting louder and louder.

You won't remember this when you wake up, will you, Captain Packard? You mustn't tell anyone about your partner, its secret, just like your code.

"Mike! Wake up!" Tomiya called.

"Enough, Mike. Rest now," Caltomacoe said. I looked at Caltomacoe, I was wet with perspiration. I went in and took a shower. "That was a good session, Mike, do you still remember it?"

"Yes."

"It may not be as bad next time."

Caltomacoe was right, it wasn't as bad the second time and the following times after was easier yet. Three days passed and the pain was gone completely. I remembered everything that happened. I felt a little pride when I found out I never did reveal the code. I called Dalcamy to report my cure. "Dalcamy, I'm sure you'll be pleased to know I got rid of my sore spots, with Caltomacoe's help."

"I figured you would. Yes, I am pleased."

"What about you? Did you have any sore spots?"

"I had a few," he looked embarrassed. I smiled and dropped the subject.

"You know, the more I get to know the other Dextarians the more I like them. I'm glad they're not all like Formald," I said.

Dalcamy agreed, "I guess all races have their problem people. Most of them seem to have many good qualities. They just need help. A little guidance and I think they're going to be fine people to know."

"I hope things work out for them on Thrae," I continued. "But if not there's always Artara."

"Artara!"

"Yes, Artarians are compatible, too. Did you forget, Dalcamy?"

"I didn't forget. I just, well, things will work out on Thrae, you'll see."

"Dalcamy! Do I sense a bit of prejudice in you?"

"Weather Man!" Dalcamy stopped and looked at me as I looked back at him starting to giggle, then we laughed.

* * * * *

Five more months went by and Thrae became a visible and large planet on our screen. It was twice the size of Earth and had two moons.

Dalcamy led the decent as Captain Corger directed him. I followed, keeping my distance. We landed on their landing pads and were met by armed personnel as we settled. Dalcamy tested the air and found enough oxygen content to sustain us, although lower than we were used to. We would have to keep our physical activities to a minimum until we adjusted. He lowered his ramp and I stayed put and monitored him. Captain Corger walked out with Dalcamy, the five Thrae soldiers followed. An official looking man walked up to them recognizing Captain Corger.

"Captain Corger! What's happened? Where's your ship?"

"First, let me introduce you to Captain Dalcamy of the planet Artara. Captain, this is General Avin Colar."

"I'm pleased to meet you, General Colar."

"How do you do, Sir. Why don't we go to my office where we can talk?"

They followed the General off the pad and into a strange looking vehicle and drove out of sight. I didn't see it very clearly. It was round and had a clear bubble over the top. That's all I could make out. I had Caltomacoe take over the monitoring.

Dalcamy and Captain Corger explained the whole story to General Colar. The General called the secretary to their king, King Melcombie, and requested an audience. It was granted immediately. However, when they went into the king's palace, we lost contact.

What do you think we should do, Mike?

I think we should wait this one out, I answered.

But what if he's in danger? Asked Tomiya.

And what if he's not? I answered. We could do more damage to our relationship with them if we show threats or distrust toward them right now. Let's give them time.

We waited, three hours went by. There was no sign of them. The sun was setting and still no sign of Dalcamy. Mocki came on screen. "Six hours, Mike. Perhaps one of us should ask about him. Make a show of concern."

"We'll give them one more hour," I answered.

Thirty minutes later a vehicle drove up to Dalcamy's ship and Dalcamy climbed out. "We're in, Mike! A request for women volunteers is going out tomorrow morning," Dalcamy announced as he came on screen.

"We were getting worried about you, Dalcamy. You were in there so long and we couldn't monitor you."

"I know, you should see that place, nothing can penetrate it. In three days the women who volunteer will be here. You, Captain Bruno and I and all the Dextarians will go to a banquet and meet them."

"You think that's such a good idea for both of us to go?" I asked.

"Mike, are you showing your suspicious nature?"

"Yes."

"It's all right, Mike. I could read the King and he was quite open with me. And I trust Corger I don't think we have anything to worry about."

"Dalcamy, remember Dextra. Those men didn't think they had anything to worry about, either."

The following morning I surveyed the area and found the soldiers gone. They had removed the guards. I lowered the ramp and walked outside. The thin air hit me and I found I was breathing too heavily for the little amount of walking I had done. I didn't want to show my distress so I walked slowly around the ship as though inspecting it. By the time I made a complete circle I felt a little better, getting used to the thin air. A vehicle drove up. It was General Colar again.

"You must be Captain Packard," he said.

"Yes."

"The King wants to meet you, why didn't you come yesterday?"

"Precautions going to a strange world, you understand."

"Yes, if our men had taken more 'precautions' they wouldn't have gotten into their dilemma on Dextra."

"It's difficult to know what to do when you're dealing with telepathic people, unless you're telepathic yourself. I wouldn't be too hard on them. The Dextarians knew just what to say to them."

"You speak as though you are telepathic."

"I am."

"So you know just what to say to us."

I laughed, "I suppose so, I just never thought about it."

"Do you know what I'm thinking now?"

"Should I? How many telepathic people have you met?"

"You're the first."

"Come on in and have a cup of asil with me. Let's get to know each other better."

The General climbed out of his vehicle and followed me in. I handed him a cup as I joined him at the table in the kitchen. Several Dextarians were eating breakfast, but left us alone.

"I sense you are uneasy, does my being telepathic make you uncomfortable?"

"Yes, I guess so. To be able to know what a person is thinking about, it's unsettling."

"Ok, I promise not to read you. How's that?" I grinned.

"You have a choice?"

"Of course! I don't have to read your mind, and I won't. All right?"

"All right!"

We talked for hours. I showed him the ship and my trophy and, of course, I had to tell him the story behind it. I introduced him to Captain Bruno and explained that he was another victim of Dextarian hospitality. "I'll be taking him home after we leave Thrae."

The day was ending with an orange sunset as General Colar exited my ship. "Thank you for a most pleasant day, Captain Packard. I'm glad we had this time together, I understand a lot more now."

I watched him drive away and wondered what he meant that he 'understood a lot more now.' I decided to go over and see Dalcamy.

"Mike, what have you been up to?"

"I just had a long visit with General Colar."

"What do you think of him?"

"I don't know, I have a funny feeling deep down in my bones."

"About what?" Dalcamy asked. "Didn't you read him?"

"No, I promised not to. Maybe I'm just making something out of nothing."

"He wouldn't have known if you read him."

"I know, but it goes against the grain to make a promise and not keep it."

"Then what's making you suspicious of him?"

"Something he said when he left. He said 'I understand a lot more now.'"

"And that's making you suspicious?" Dalcamy laughed.

I smiled, "like I said, I'm probably making a mountain out of a mole hill."

Dalcamy didn't understand my cliché and I had to explain it to him. It occurred to me that Dalcamy hadn't called me 'Weather Man' since he came back from seeing the King. "You . . ." I read him and almost jumped out of my seat when I saw what he was.

"What's wrong?" he asked when he saw my reaction.

"I guess I still have a sore spot. Did you get rid of your sore spots easily, Dalcamy?"

"Sore spots?"

"I guess they didn't amount to much with you, you've been in space so much longer than I."

"Oh! Those, yes I got rid of them quickly."

"How long did it take?" I asked.

"A couple hours," he shrugged.

"Took me three days. Dalcamy, I have to check on my sleeper, make sure he's still comfortable. But I need to ask Mocki a question first, where is he?"

"In control." We went to control together. "Mocki, do you keep your generator running when you're down?"

"No, why?"

"I find I run low on Fargon if I don't."

"Fargon!"

I need to talk to you privately without Dalcamy, I transmitted.

"Why don't we go over and take a look at it," he suggested. "You mind, Dalcamy? I'll be right back."

"No, go ahead. See you later, Mike."

He didn't hear you transmit to me! Mocki said when we were on my ship.

No, he's not Dalcamy. He's a robot replica.

A robot! Then Dalcamy is still in there some place.

Didn't you read him at all when he came back? I asked.

No. You know we always follow suit with the type of communication a person leads with, and he is the Captain. If he wants to vocalize all the time that's his choice.

That's were I have the advantage, being his equal in rank. I don't understand what's going on. Dalcamy should be able to free himself. After all, they aren't telepaths and Dalcamy is strong.

Maybe if one of us can get into the king's building, we would be able to find him and get him out.

Not just one of us. You stay with the ship. Sadek and I are going to request an audience with the King.

Mocki went back to his ship while Sadek and I started walking to the offices to find General Colar. I was breathing hard by the time we reached his building. The thin air didn't seem to affect Sadek as much as me. *Wait a minute, Sadek. I don't want to walk in there breathless.* When I was breathing easier we went in and walked into the office of General Colar's secretary and asked to see the General.

"I would like an audience with King Melcombie," I said as General Colar met us at the door of his office.

"Of course, is anything wrong?"

"You tell me, General Colar."

He knows.

"Yes, I do, and I don't like it."

"Look, Mike. . ."

"No! You look! I want to see Dalcamy, now!"

He picked up the phone and called for an audience which was granted immediately. We were driven to the palace of the King. It was impressive, a plush mansion. We were directed to a great hall where we could see the King sitting at a large desk. He looked just like any other Thraeian, dressed in an ornate uniform.

"Captain Packard, I've been wanting to meet you."

"I'm not going to read you right now, out of respect of who you are. I would rather you voluntarily explain your actions."

"I see you're angry," he said smiling, "and I appreciate your respect."

"Where's Dalcamy?" I asked.

"Right here, Weather Man," I heard behind me. I turned and saw Dalcamy standing behind me. I read him, it was Dalcamy.

"All right," I said with some relief, "now what is this all about?"

"It was a test," the King explained, "that proved very favorable. You understand we can't just send our women off with anyone that comes flying in without some investigation."

"And your mechanical duplicate of Dalcamy performed your investigation?"

"That's right. While you were busy with General Colar, our robot asked questions of the Dextarians. They were so excited about saving their race they were quite free with all their information, and the discussion with you helped, also. It showed us what kind of people you are."

"I see."

"We knew you would catch on quickly if you spent any time with Dalcamy's double. So we had to keep you away from him just long enough. Tell me, what made you suspicious of him?"

I looked at Dalcamy's smiling face. "He didn't call me Weather Man."

"Ahh, yes, I imagine that was Captain Dalcamy's insurance that this wouldn't go too far. We were able to hear and watch everything, I'll show you." He pushed a button on the console on his desk and a large curtain uncovered a monitoring complex in the wall behind.

One of the monitors was inside Dalcamy's ship, his double was in control talking with Mocki. "What was wrong with Mike's generator?"

"Just a minor adjustment. I'm surprised he didn't think of it. I guess the experience of the interrogation made him forget about it. Maybe he should go through some testing when we get home to see what else he might have forgotten."

"Yes, that's a good idea, I'll bring it up to him."

"What about you, Dalcamy? It might be wise for you to be tested, too."

"Why? I'm all right."

"You had some bad sore spots. You don't really know if you are all right until you find out you've forgotten something. Better to be sure."

"Yes, when we get home."

The king spoke into a microphone, "Come back, Dalcamy." Dalcamy turned, walked out of control and headed for the ramp. "What are sore spots?" asked the King.

Dalcamy and I explained, "- - -and they can cause some memory loss."

"So, are you going to go through some testing when you get back?"

"Probably, wouldn't hurt," said Dalcamy.

"Would if we failed," I said smiling, "then we wouldn't be Captains, anymore."

"And what is the name of your companion?" asked the King looking at Sadek.

"This is Sadek, one of my crewmen."

"You brought him in case of trouble?" asked the King.

"Nothing like having a strong telepath on your side," I answered.

Dalcamy's double walked in. "Go to the lab, Dalcamy," the King instructed. Dalcamy's double walked out.

"Interesting," I said.

"Would you like to see the lab, Weather Man?" asked Dalcamy.

"Yes."

He transmitted it to me. It was a large room set up like any scientific lab. There were large chambers much like our sleeping chambers with mechanical robots in them. They had no outside coverings and all their circuitries showed. The metal skeletons were visible as they lay in the germ-free atmosphere of the chambers. I understood that they remained this way until needed, then they were programmed and the outer skin was applied. They used Dalcamy as a model by having a computer view him as he stood in a circle that was marked on the floor. Dalcamy had agreed to only specific information to be given to the robot. The mannerisms and basic speech patterns were added so all together he had just enough to get him by.

"So that's what took so long, producing the covering," I said.

"Yes," the King answered, "this telepathy of yours is fascinating to me. You just showed him everything through your mind, didn't you, Dalcamy."

"Yes."

The King brought up the monitor in the lab and we watched as Dalcamy's double laid down in a chamber and the skin began to disintegrate and his memory was erased.

"What about the memory in the computer?" I asked.

"You're very thorough," observed the King. "Our agreement with Captain Dalcamy was that the computer would not retain any information, and it didn't. It's nearing our evening meal. Won't you stay and join us?"

"I should report to my men first, they're waiting to hear from me and Dalcamy."

"Yes, of course, I'll walk out with you."

We stood outside the mansion and I conversed with Caltomacoe and Mocki as Dalcamy joined us. Dalcamy explained everything to them and that we would return together after the evening meal.

"We can go back in now," I said to the King.

"That was fast."

"Telepathy is fast," Dalcamy said, "much faster than vocalizing."

CHAPTER 24

The king was young; I judged him to be in his early thirties. He was most handsome with black hair and eyes. He showed an awareness or experience beyond his years, still being friendly and quick with a smile.

We had a delicious meal and good conversation. King Melcombie directed the conversation around the political history of his planet. And asked many questions about our planets and Dextra.

The notice to the women had gone out as first announced to us so there would be no delay because of the "test" that was conducted.

"You don't anticipate any reluctance from the women?" I asked.

"No, some areas are so under populated the women greatly outnumber the men. Many women would accept an invitation like this just to have a husband."

"You will tell them about the insemination so their first children would all be girls," I said.

"Yes, of course. It was included in the announcement. They will know everything before they arrive."

A vehicle was waiting to take us to our ships when we were ready to leave. I took the time to look at it this time. It had four wheels, one in front and rear with one on each side in the middle. A section of the dome swung up and a door opened beside the driver. I stepped in and walked to a bench seat large enough for two. Dalcamy had to stoop down a little as he entered. The vehicle could be driven from either end, there was no need for reverse. Dalcamy and I faced each other while the driver faced the front with his back to us at my left. There was room for five passengers, comfortably. The second driver's seat in the rear swiveled around and locked, making room for a fifth passenger. Sadek sat there.

You handled that very well, Weather Man, Dalcamy transmitted as we rode.

It made me very angry, Dalcamy, I don't like games.

Well, neither do I, but he had to have his proof and it seemed the simplest way.

I guess. Anyway, there was no harm done. But he took a chance, suppose I came in blasting?

I was counting on you using discretion. I think you'll pass your testing higher now than the first time.

I'd better after this!

We were met by Mocki and Caltomacoe as we reached our ships. Both Mocki and Caltomacoe read Dalcamy to make sure.

All right, it's me, he laughed as he transmitted.

Then they read me. *I wasn't missing!*

You could be, we're just making sure. We feel better now.

* * * * *

The women arrived just as the king had predicted. We prepared for the banquet and donned our dress uniforms. I thought about taking Tomiya with me.

Would you have taken Bocha? She asked.

No, but you're my wife. It's different.

No different, I'm a crewman just like Bocha. You go ahead, Mike.

I met Dalcamy out front. *Where's Tomiya?*

She claims she's a crewman just like Bocha.

That's going too far. Wait here a minute.

Dalcamy went up my ramp and twenty minutes later returned with Tomiya dressed in a red dress to match my uniform.

"That's more like it!" I said. "You look beautiful," and kissed her.

Some Captain you are, she said smiling, *no favoritism, remember?*

Oh well, that's the advantage of being a Captain.

We climbed into their odd looking vehicle and the driver turned to us. "Are you aware that this will be an all-night affair?"

"No, we weren't aware of that," I answered.

"Perhaps you should inform your men so they wouldn't become concerned."

Dalcamy and I transmitted the message to our Second-in-Commands and waved as we drove off.

The Dextarians had gone earlier to prepare. There was a little ceremony they had to go through to meet the women. It was the custom of Thrae that each prospective groom be sponsored. The women had secretly viewed them and made their choices. Each Dextarian was given an armband that matched the color of a ribbon that the women wore in their hair. Then the sponsors will introduce the couples.

We entered the large hall and found several people standing around talking and all the women with their various hair ribbons. A doorman met us as we entered and he announced us just like the old custom of Earth.

"Captain and Mrs. Packard of the Planet Artara!" All eyes turned toward us as we walked in.

"Captain Bruno of the Planet Boro!"

"Captain Dalcamy of the Planet Artara!"

General Colar was the first to step up and welcome us. "Your wife! I had no idea you brought your wife."

"She's a crewman aboard my ship, we work together."

"That's incredible! You never cease to amaze me. Why didn't you introduce us when I was on board? She's beautiful!"

"This is General Colar, Tomiya."

"My great pleasure to meet you, Mrs. Packard."

"Thank you, I'm honored."

Music started and refreshments were passed. About an hour later the king made his entry. Tomiya was introduced to him. He was as surprised as General Colar. He gave the signal to have the Dextarian men come in and the introduction to the young women began. It was done very well and smoothly as though they did such things all the time. The Dextarians entered one at a time with their sponsors. The woman wearing the matching ribbon would step up to them and be introduced. Then the three would walk into the hall.

"Would you do me the honor of the first dance, Mrs. Packard? You see, I have to dance before anyone else can and I have no lovely wife like you to dance with."

"But I don't know your dances."

"That's all right, I promise not to step on your feet, but you can step on mine all you want."

He took her hand, led her to the center of the room and nodded to the musicians. They began to play. It was a beautiful graceful dance and Tomiya had no trouble following him. After they had danced for a while the others joined in. The King brought Tomiya back at the end and another piece started.

"That was delightful, Mrs. Packard, thank you."

"Thank you, Your Majesty."

We stood talking with the Generals and the King, enjoying cocktails and watching the dances. Dinner was announced and again the King turned to Tomiya. "Will you accompany me?" he asked as he extended his arm to her. "Please gentlemen, you will follow us?"

We followed as he led us to the banquet hall. There were large tables of food and smaller tables where the guests were to sit. The very center of the room was clear. Servants lined the walls waiting.

The King led us to the 'Kings Table' and placed Tomiya on his right and me next to her. Dalcamy sat on the King's left with Captain Bruno. Then the Generals filled the rest of the table. No one sat until the King did. As soon as everyone was seated the servants began going about their duties and music started again.

"Tell me, Mrs. Packard. Have you and your husband worked together long?"

"No, this is our first trip together."

"Wonderful! Then I trust it will be one of your greatest memories when you leave here."

"I have no doubt it will," answered Tomiya.

"Tomorrow," continued the King, "there will be a wedding ceremony for them and then preparations for the trip will be made. I assume you will be going back to Dextra?"

"Not right away. We have to make a stop on the planet Boro first. We are taking Captain Bruno and his five men home to their planet."

"That's right, I remember now, General Colar told me after meeting him the other day. They will send a Captain to fly his ship and the rest of his men home from Trok."

"Yes."

"I wonder what kind of test they will have."

After dinner we were entertained by a group of dancers, beautiful young women in frail flowing gowns. Their dance was provocative and they had eyes only for the King.

I wonder if this is the King's harem, I thought. I heard Dalcamy choke on his drink as he caught my thought.

"Your Majesty", I started, "I understood you're not married." He nodded. "I can see many young ladies that would be willing to fill that place for you," I said smiling as I nodded to the dancers.

"Yes," he laughed, "I'm sure they would."

Mike! You should be ashamed of yourself, Tomiya transmitted.

Darling, I answered, *that's the privilege of being King!* I heard Dalcamy choke again.

"Is there something wrong, Captain Dalcamy?" asked the King. "You seem to be uncomfortable with your drink." He ordered Dalcamy a fresh drink with a snap of his fingers before Dalcamy could respond.

"I'm fine, thank you. Just swallowed the wrong way." A fresh drink was placed in front of him immediately. "Thank you."

Careful, Dalcamy, he'll have enough drinks in you to share his harem with you.

"Are you married, Dalcamy?" the King asked.

Dalcamy looked up surprised after getting my thought, "No, Your Majesty, I'm not."

"Perhaps you would like a companion then?"

Told you so!

"Your Majesty, I--,"

"Fine," he said smiling, "I'll have a room prepared for you," he snapped his fingers and two servants left.

Don't offend him by turning him down, Dalcamy, I cautioned.

You think it would?

If he's anything like the Kings of Earth, I know it would. Watch his face before you speak.

"Your Majesty," Dalcamy started, "I---," the King stopped smiling as he turned to Dalcamy. "I'd like to pick the one, if I may."

"Be my guest," the King beamed with a broad gesture toward the dancers.

"The one in blue."

He picked out a beautiful redhead with emerald eyes. The King made a signal to her and she danced toward Dalcamy.

"Her name is Ludena. You have chosen well, Dalcamy."

She continued her dance with eyes only for Dalcamy. She made seductive moves and gave signals of what she had to offer him. The dance ended with her kneeling in a bow at Dalcamy's feet. She offered her hand to him as she lifted her face. Dalcamy took her hand and she rose to join him. The Generals moved to make room for her beside Dalcamy. The King was pleased and rose to go back to the Ball Room for more dancing as he offered his arm to Tomiya. I walked beside Dalcamy and his escort.

Look what you got me into, Weather Man!

Enjoy yourself, Casanova, I grinned.

I watched the King and Tomiya dance and then everyone joined in including Dalcamy and Ludena. The King returned Tomiya to me when the dance was over. Dalcamy disappeared. I didn't see him again that night.

The evening wore on and as I was dancing with Tomiya I noticed a guard walk up to Captain Bruno and talk to him. Captain Bruno looked over at the King, set his drink down and followed the guard. I turned Tomiya to see the King smiling as he watched them walk out.

It looks like Captain Bruno just received a special invitation, I transmitted to Tomiya.

Do these things always happen on other planets? She asked.

Sometimes, he's a gracious King.

We continued dancing. After the dance we were enjoying a drink and watching the others when a guard approached us.

"The King has requested you to follow me."

I guess it's our turn, I transmitted to Tomiya as I took her drink and set it down with mine. She took my arm as I smiled and nodded to the King.

The guard led us out of the Ball Room and up a magnificent staircase that turned gracefully as it rose. We walked down a hallway that was lined with pictures and tapestries. The floor was covered with a plush, thick piled, green rug.

Our guard stopped at a door and opened it for us. Four lovely ladies from the dancing group met us. Two of them took Tomiya and led her to an adjoining room.

Mike, what's happening?

It's all right Tomiya; go with them. They're going to prepare you for me.

The other two girls led me to the opposite side of the room and through a door. They had drawn a hot bath and proceeded to undress me. They bathed me with soap and water to which fragrant oils were added while giggling and humming. They had me chose the oils and scents. Then they dried me and helped me dress in silk-like garments. When I was ready one went to the door and peeked out.

"Not yet," she giggled, "a few more minutes please, Master." I waited. She checked again. "Yes, now, Master."

I was led to a large wood framed bed. There was a wooden canopy supported by four large bedposts and draped with layers of fine netting. It was truly a bed for a king. Tomiya lay half sitting supported by pillows in a lovely pale yellow negligee that spread out nearly covering the surface of the bed.

She smiled as I went to her. Three of the ladies left and the fourth brought us each a drink. "This will intensify your pleasure," she explained.

I took them and handed one to Tomiya as the netting was held back for me. I sat on the edge of the bed and looked at Tomiya as we sipped. I never heard the young lady leave as I became intoxicated with the look and scent of Tomiya.

We were awakened early the following morning with breakfast. Two ladies that had attended us the night before brought our trays and waited on us. Their timing was perfect. The four of us seemed to arrive in the foyer at the same time. Dalcamy descended the stairs with a very satisfied look on his face and his redhead on his arm. As he joined us, she smiled, kissed him on the lips and walked away.

CHAPTER 25

We were driven back to our ships. Dalcamy and I transferred my sleeper to Dalcamy's ship for transport back to Dextra. The wedding was to start at mid-day. A vehicle picked us up and took us to the palace. Ushers directed us to seats. The great hall was completely decorated with flowers. The King sat in a huge throne at the opposite end of the hall facing us.

Remarkable, I said to Tomiya. *Earth's history had many kings just like this. It's amazing how similar this world is to Earth.*

Does Earth still have kings?

Some, the people dethroned most of them; they were too cruel. There is only one powerful country now that still has royalty, England. But they don't have the same power they used to.

This king doesn't seem to be cruel, stated Tomiya.

I hope not, I've never read him to see. At least we haven't seen any physical signs of it.

Music started and the wedding couples started down the center-carpeted isle. They were spaced far enough apart that each couple had their moment of glory as they approached the king. They formed two half circles around the king one behind the other and staggered each couple so they could all see him. The King rose and addressed them.

"This is an extraordinary day for two planets, a joining of minds and bodies. The covenant you make today will be binding no matter what planet you reside on. Who speaks for these women?"

"I do, Sir," the Grand General stood at attention.

"And who sponsors these men?"

Forty-eight men rose in silent consent.

"Do you women consent to live with your chosen men for the rest of your lives and bear their children? To share their burdens and comfort them? To be subject to their commands?"

All forty-eight responded, "I do," and it echoed within the walls of the hall.

"Do you men consent to protect and love these women for the rest of your lives? To put their needs and life over yours?"

Again, the "I do" rang throughout the hall in masculine response.

"Then as the King of Amacall, Planet of Thrae, I pronounce you husbands and wives."

Trumpets sounded and billows of confetti fell from the ceiling. People stood and cheered and the chairs were taken away quickly. The lights dimmed, music started and the wedding couples began to dance a slow dance holding each other closely in their arms. The King disappeared from sight. I looked around for him, but couldn't find him. The couples continued to dance until the music ended. When the second song started everyone joined in and I danced with Tomiya.

Dalcamy came over after a couple of dances and asked permission to dance with the most beautiful woman in the room.

"Of course, Casanova, I would be honored to have you dance with my wife," I said smiling.

Dalcamy looked at me as they danced off together and I stepped out front to see what happened to the king. I found him supervising the decorating of the vehicles that were to transport the couples to the ships. I walked up to him.

He turned and looked at me, "Come with me, Captain Packard, we are preparing the ship as well."

We climbed into a vehicle and headed for the landing pad. They had moved out the largest ship I have ever seen. When I climbed out of the vehicle I stood gaping at it. I started walking around it. People were busy working, moving in and out of the ship. Vehicles packed with supplies were driven inside the lower level. It had two complete decks and viewing ports all around. Four ramps on each side touched the ground. There were massive blasters in every angle. The control area was on the very top and extended out past the decks on all sides.

"You seem impressed," the King said.

"Impressed! How about speechless! She's beautiful!"

"Our transport ship, we have four of them. They will hold approximately a thousand people."

"A thousand! There are only ninety-six passengers, why are you using such a big ship?"

"We don't have anything in between. Our war ships are too small, then there's this. There will be two war ships to escort. Would you like to see inside?"

"Absolutely."

"Where would you like to begin?" he asked as he led the way.

"Control?"

"Yes, I thought you would say that."

We entered control. It was lined with panels of flashing lights and monitors. Men sat at them flipping switches and reading digital meters and writing things down as they listened to head sets and watched the monitors. There must have been fifteen men in control and it wasn't the least bit crowded.

"Boris," the King commanded. "Activate the screen for Captain Packard."

The main screen came to life and the outside surroundings began to rotate three hundred and sixty degrees until it was back to the start. Then it began rotating at angles covering every direction possible. The screen split and showed the bottom view from the ship. Right now all it showed was the ground, but out in space it would pick up anything that would be approaching in any direction.

"The angles are being controlled manually now, but out in space the computer takes over and monitors automatically." The King explained. "We can have the screen stationary on one object while the computer continues to monitor all other directions. If it sees anything approaching, it will split the screen and give you both views. It can show up to four different views at a time with coordinates, so you know what angle and distance you're viewing."

The tour continued as he explained everything in detail. He knew the ship inside and out as though he built it with his very hands.

"You certainly know your ship. Are you just as familiar with the war ships?"

"I know them all, and I can command them all."

"She's a magnificent ship."

"I'm proud of her, she was my first creation."

"You designed her?"

"Yes. It started as a hobby when I was a child. When I became King, I made it a reality. I designed all our ships. I have another one I'm working on now, its mid-size between these two. It would have been better for this trip, but it isn't ready yet. Another year perhaps."

The infirmary was complete with their latest medical equipment. "We have some medical technologies you may be interested in seeing," I said as he explained some of their equipment. "We'll have to show them to you when we have more time."

There was a huge banquet hall with an adjoining kitchen capable of preparing food for the thousand passengers that this ship was built for.

"Have you ever used her to capacity?" I asked.

"Yes, several times. We have a neighboring planet that we are colonizing. These ships are used for transport of personnel and vacationers several times a year."

"Would you consider joining an Interplanetary Space Fleet?" I asked as we climbed back into our vehicle.

"What would be its purpose?"

"Exploration and mutual protection. Artara is thinking of forming one with the planets we have contacted. Each planet would have a fleet and would work together exploring and meeting new races gathering and sharing information."

"Where would it be based? Artara?"

"Yes, for now."

"Sounds interesting, I would like more details though. Perhaps when you work it out, you can come back and we'll discuss it."

"How did you become king?" I asked.

"I was born to it."

The dance was in full swing when we arrived. Dalcamy and Tomiya still danced.

"Looks like everyone is still having fun," the King said as we climbed out.

"Sir, shall I stop the music?" a butler asked as we entered.

"No, this is their day."

I followed him into the hall. As he entered the people stepped aside immediately opening a path for him. He started mingling with the people and talking to them like an old friend. He asked after the health of certain family members that he evidently knew. The people seemed to like him.

Two hours later the dancing ended and the wedding couples exited to the waiting vehicles amid shouts of best wishes. The King joined us and insisted we ride with him as he offered his arm to Tomiya and we followed the last of the newlyweds out.

Dalcamy was as impressed as I at the size of the transport ship. I transmitted to him all I was shown. Just before the wedding party entered the transport ship, the King told them to be happy and have lots of babies. We watched as the massive engines roared and the ship lifted to wait for us at orbiting level.

"I hope I see all of you again, Captain Dalcamy, Captain Packard, Captain Bruno, and especially, Mrs. Packard."

"I'm sure we will be back, Sir," Dalcamy answered.

Especially if Ludena stays single, I transmitted.

Mike! Will you stop it? Or we'll have to have a serious discussion.

Fine, I want to hear all about it. Your ship or mine? I asked smiling. I looked at the King and he looked as though he was about to break out laughing. *Are you sure he's not telepathic?* I asked Dalcamy.

"I hope your night with Ludena was a good one?" the King asked.

"Very good," Dalcamy answered smiling.

"You have given me much pleasure, gentlemen. I look forward to your return, and Ludena will be yours whenever you come, Dalcamy."

"But, Your Majesty!"

"Now, don't offend the King, Dalcamy," he said raising his finger and smiling.

Dalcamy looked at him and smiled, "I wouldn't dream of it."

"Have a good journey, gentlemen," he turned and walked toward his vehicle as we entered our ships.

Dalcamy came on screen as we prepared to lift. "Weather Man, what do you think about King Melcombie?"

"If I didn't know better, I'd suspect he's telepathic. His comments were too responsive to what we were transmitting."

"Well, perhaps someday we'll know for sure. What does Casanova mean?"

"Look it up!" I said grinning. "It should be in the English vocabulary," I signed off.

I lifted after Dalcamy and joined them at orbiting level. Dalcamy and I led the transport ship with the war ships one on each side of her. It was an impressive display as I viewed them on screen.

CHAPTER 26

Boro is three months away and I will be leaving our group one month out. We started learning the language of Boro as we traveled. We have been keeping the Commodore updated and he was pleased to learn that the King of Thrae was interested in hearing more about the fleet.

"We have almost completed the structure and chain of command," the Commodore explained. "In another month we will be sending representatives to each planet to invite them to join."

"Commodore, if I may suggest, when you approach Earth, go to Russia first. I have already brought up the possibility to General Buyemsky and promised he would be the first of Earth."

"Thank you, Captain Packard, I will make sure he is contacted."

"How are the Troks doing? And Lor Direna?" I asked.

"Very well, they learn quickly and are ahead of schedule. I heard a story about you and Heise having an interesting conversation," he said.

"On self-worth?" I asked.

"Yes."

"It was most enlightening for both of us," I said.

"Better be careful, Weather Man, you will be inheriting another nick name," Caltomacoe said as he joined us.

"Lor Direna has become the official representative of Trok on the council of our new fleet," Commodore Mackalie continued, "he and his wife will be staying here. He has been a tremendous help in setting this up."

"How did he like the Island?"

"I'll let you ask him when you come home," he answered with a smile.

"Did Dalcamy mention to you about he and I being tested when we get home?"

"Yes, I'll have it arranged for you. I'm also looking into some kind of protection to prevent that from happening again. We can't have our Captains being interrogated while they sleep, a sensor to be worn or something. We'll have it figured out by the time you return, I'm sure."

"I don't expect to be at Boro too long, Sir. Do you want me to mention the fleet to them?"

"If you think it's wise, use your judgment. Until next time, Captain, good journey."

"Thank you, Sir."

The time came for us to split and head for Boro. I called Dalcamy, "tell Borkalami hello for us, Dalcamy, and keep your guard up. I'll be expecting a full report when I see you again."

"Don't worry. I've heard from Borkalami, he said there was some trouble. General Alma is spreading rumors that they will not see their fifty men again. Borkalami spoke with Dr. Bella and he is waiting until we return with our sleepers before making any major moves. Are you heading home after Boro?"

"I imagine, I'll check with the Commodore and see what he says."

"Good journey, Weather Man."

"Good journey, Casanova."

I made my turn and they were soon out of sight in my viewer. Captain Bruno came in as I watched them disappear.

"You know," he said, "I think that is the hardest sight to watch, when you break apart like that."

"Yes, I think you're right," I answered.

Tomiya came in with a report, I read it and signed. Two months later we approached Boro. Captain Bruno gave us the radio frequency and I had him make contact.

"This is Captain Bruno requesting permission to land."

"Captain Bruno! Where did you get that ship?"

"It's a long story, Sir. The ship belongs to Captain Packard of the Planet Artara. He will be landing her."

"Permission granted."

Captain Bruno directed us in. A ground crew met us as we disembarked. A vehicle drove up and a General stepped out greeting us. He didn't say much as we were driven off the landing pad. We entered a building and were shown to a room that looked like a briefing room. There were several other officers waiting for us.

"Captain Packard," Bruno said, "this is General Marco, General Falk, Lieutenant Fabbro, Lieutenant Griffith and Captain Hogan."

"Welcome, Captain Packard," General Marco said as he shook my hand. "Now that the introductions are over, perhaps you'll tell us what happened, Captain Bruno."

Captain Bruno related the story to them with me filling in the missing parts. "So the rest of your men are on Trok recuperating."

"Yes, Sir."

"And your ship is still on Dextra."

"Yes, Sir."

"Interesting." The General seemed very displeased with the turn of events. "How many men do you have aboard your ship, Captain Packard?"

I looked at him surprised at his question and read him. He didn't believe Captain Bruno's story. I turned on my shield.

"Why is that important?" I asked.

He smiled at me and reached for my shoulder, "why, we have to OUCH!" he pulled his hand away abruptly. Anger flashed in his eyes and then became calm again.

I continued to read him. He thought I was controlling Captain Bruno and was holding his men prisoners. He smiled again, "as I was saying, we have to provide accommodations for you and your men."

"That won't be necessary, we are quite comfortable in our ship."

"What is this - - - energy?" he asked still shaking his hand.

"I'm sorry it distresses you," I answered. "Perhaps you shouldn't touch me." I looked around at the other men and read them. They didn't believe us either. "It seems your people don't believe us, Captain Bruno."

"Don't believe us! Why don't you believe us? There are five of my men, just outside, that will substantiate my story. Have them come in."

"They are being talked to now. If their story matches yours, then we will talk again. Meanwhile, Captain Packard will stay with us." Two soldiers walked in and stood one on each side of me.

"General! This is outrageous! The man has saved my sanity and the lives of my men!"

"I understand that is your story, Captain, but until we substantiate it, he will remain."

"I do not wish to be rude by declining your hospitality General, but I do not intend to spend time in your prison. I will return to my ship and when you decide to believe us, I will be happy to give you the shortest route to Trok." As I started to walk out the soldiers tried to grab me and felt the energy of my shield.

"Halt! Or I'll fire!" one of them shouted.

I stopped and turned to look at two blasters aimed at me. "Those won't harm me gentlemen, but they may harm you when the blast is deflected from me. It's rather close in here to have the energy from a blaster ricocheting around." I walked out the door. I walked down the hallway and could hear footsteps following me. As I stepped out of the building into the sunlight, the soldier fired his blaster. The shot hit my shield in the middle of my back. I stopped and turned to face the soldier.

"Hold your fire!" screamed General Marco as he ran out of the building toward me. He stopped and stood facing me.

"I am becoming very angry, General Marco," I said, "and that could be bad for you. You are either a very brave man or a very stupid one. Do you realize I can explode your head completely off your shoulders with a mere thought?"

Fear flashed across his face and he took one step back.

"You are a stupid man then, you don't know what you're dealing with. Very well, I'll give you some time. My people and I are telepaths. Do you know what that is?"

"No."

I stepped up to him and pushed him away with my mind about five feet, he almost fell down, but caught himself. I advanced toward him again.

"Sir!" screamed the soldier as he raised his weapon.

I turned to him and said, "Go ahead soldier! Give it your best!" He fired and hit my shield over my chest. "Do you understand now, General?" I walked up to him. "And I'm the weakest one on the ship!" I yelled.

"Captain Packard," General Falk walked up to us, "I apologize, Captain Packard." He looked at General Marco and continued. "I will take you back to your ship."

A vehicle drove up after his signal and we climbed in. The General offered his hand.

"I don't believe you'll find contact comfortable, General."

He withdrew his hand and lowered his eyes momentarily. We didn't speak until we reached my ship.

"What do you intend on doing, Captain Packard?"

"I don't know yet, I'm too angry to make that decision now." I walked into my ship and closed the ramp. I went to control and set the shields. Caltomacoe came up to me and touched my shield over my arm. He felt the energy, but didn't let go. I turned it off.

I'm all right, Caltomacoe, just tired and angry. I went to my quarters. Three hours later I went back to control refreshed from a short nap and shower. *Any activity?* I asked looking at the screen.

No. Have you made any decisions?

No, I'll just wait and see what happens.

A vehicle advanced with Generals Falk and Marco. We lowered the ramp as they climbed out. Caltomacoe and I waited at the entrance for them to come in. They slowly climbed the ramp. They spotted Caltomacoe first and surprise flashed in their eyes and then they saw me.

"Welcome," I said extending my hand. General Falk took it without hesitation. I led them into the conference room. "Have a seat, gentlemen." Sadek brought refreshments.

General Marco cleared his throat. "I want to apologize, Captain." I read him, it was very difficult for him to say that. He's a very proud man.

"Apology accepted," I answered. "How do you wish to handle getting your ship and men back?" They relaxed and we started making plans as they enjoyed the refreshments. "You will probably only need a Captain," I said. "The crewmen should be all right by the time you get there. They'll have an eighteen month recuperation period."

"The Troks will be expecting us?"

"Yes, we have one ship on Trok now. Captain Borkalami and several ships on Dextra. We are helping the Dextarians build cities. I can let Captain Borkalami know when you should be arriving so he can have your men ready for you."

"You won't be going with us, then."

"What's the point? You know how to get there." I read them again, still a little distrust. What if it's a trap and we don't even have him as insurance.

I smiled. "Why would we want to trap you? What do you have that we don't have already? I thought my planet, Earth, was a suspicious race, but you beat them."

"Captain," started General Falk.

"No, I'm not angry. I understand," I interrupted, "but you have to trust sometime and this is the time. Gentlemen, Artara is setting up an Interplanetary Space Fleet. Every planet we meet are being invited to take a look at it and join. Do you realize the potential that such a fleet has? It would mean what happened to your men would never go as long as it did ever again. You would have the help and protection of millions. You would be flying the best and fastest spaceships ever invented with protection capabilities that you haven't even dreamed of yet. Your technologies would advance ten times, information would be given to you and new teaching techniques for your children that would advance your whole world."

They looked at me astonished. "Is this for real? You're serious aren't you? That would be an incredible force of personnel."

"That's right, you wouldn't need to ever fear a new being coming in contact with you again. In fact, you would be looking for them, to make the same offer. There would be no end to the new information and technologies we would learn from other planets and new peoples. You would be involved in helping them like we're helping Dextra right now."

"When is this fleet starting?"

"Representatives have already been sent to the worlds that we have been to so far. I can have one sent here as well to explain the whole set up."

And I tried to stick him in our stinking jail, was the thought I received from General Marco.

"We need to discuss Captain Bruno," I said. "He was in trauma when I first saw him. His mind was locked up. I suspect he probably has some memory loss. You should test him. I'll be willing to help re-educate him. It will give you an idea of the technologies I've been telling you about."

"How can you re-educate him? You know nothing about us."

"You would have to give me the information, I'll show you." I led them into the library and had General Marco sit at the panel. "This is Artarian language," I explained as I loaded it in and handed him a cap to put on.

"What does this do?"

"It can record your thoughts into the computer or it can transmit information into your brain, don't worry, it can't hurt you. I learned your language in a week and a half through this. First I have to record your brain waves so it can transmit at the proper frequency." He set the cap on his head and the waves appeared on screen. "Now we're ready to transmit."

He looked up at me, "it won't record me?"

"It can't do two things at once, I have it set to teach now. But by changing this switch and pressing this button," I made the changes as I spoke, "it is now recording you."

The look on his face was indescribable as he realized he was being recorded. I waited just long enough and switched it off. Then I took the cap off his head and handed it to General Falk and reset the switches. "Now if you'd put this on, I'll record your waves and you will receive General Marco's thoughts as I recorded them."

I took the necessary steps and General Falk began to choke trying to contain his laughter when he received General Marco's thoughts. Finally he turned his back on us and his shoulders shook from laughter. The computer shut down when the recording ended. General Falk removed the cap and turned back to us. "You," still choking on laughter, "have a remarkable sense of humor, Captain Packard." He looked at General Marco and laughed again. "I'm sorry, Colis, do you want to listen to this?"

"No," he answered. "I know what it recorded." He looked up at General Falk and laughed with him.

"So, how would we get the information specifically intended for Captain Bruno in this?" asked General Falk.

"You would have to have someone recorded that knows that information, then feed it to Captain Bruno. We did it very successfully with a Trok Captain that had the same experience as Captain Bruno."

"Thank you, Captain Packard. We will find out what he's forgotten. And I believe we would be interested in hearing a representative from your fleet. Have him ask for me when he arrives." They drove away still laughing.

CHAPTER 27

The following morning several vehicles came up to our ship full of men. They jumped out and surrounded the ship. Five of them started to ascend the ramp after we lowered it.

"Welcome, gentlemen," I said as they entered.

They looked around at the ship and us. One of them came up to me, watching Caltomacoe and me. "Do you have any weapons?" he asked.

"Physical weapons?"

Why do I always get them? "Yes, physical weapons." He answered very patiently.

I smiled at him and answered, "Only the ones on the exterior of the ship, why?"

"Our Leader will be here in one hour. I want to know everything you have on board that may be a threat to him."

"There's nothing on board that would be a threat," I answered. I read him again as he complained about the Leader not meeting us on their ground. He had to come aboard the ship instead. I laughed. "Your leader sounds like some of ours. They will have their way no matter what anyone else says. You needn't worry about your Leader, we won't hurt him."

He looked at me, "you know what I'm thinking!"

"Yes, didn't they tell you?"

"No."

"Sorry, I suppose they didn't tell you a few other things, either."

"Like what?"

"Like this," I took control of him and led him into the conference room and sat him down in a chair, then released him. "You like that?" I asked.

He sat there staring at me, not knowing what to say.

"I don't like playing games, keeping secrets and playing cloak and dagger stuff. You are in no danger from us. We came to help your world, not hurt it. This leader of yours, does he control the whole planet or just a part of it?"

"The whole planet, we are all one nation."

"Good, that will make it easier."

"Make what easier?"

"Communications, I don't have to worry about going all over talking to other nations. Have some asil and relax." Caltomacoe had brought it in. I had intended to have some before we were descended upon. "Thank you, Caltomacoe, I need that. What's your Leader's name?"

"Sedillo, Lync Sedillo. We call him Mr. Sedillo."

"And what's your name?"

"Ned Patak."

"I take it you're ahead of these men that are looking my ship over."

"Yes."

"Good," I said as I finished the asil. "I'm going to my quarters to put my dress uniform on and get ready for Mr. Sedillo. Now, are you supposed to stay with me or do you want to talk with your men?"

"I'm supposed to wa..uh..stay with you."

"Fine," I said smiling, "we'll go to my quarters."

We went to my quarters and I showered and changed. "You been protecting your Leader long?"

"Seven years."

"You like him?"

"Everyone likes him. He's the best we've had." I came back into the sitting room while slipping my shirt on. "That's a nice uniform."

"Think he'll like it?"

"Yeah, he'll like it."

"Tell me about him."

"Tell you what?"

"What kind of a man is he? Is he fair in his judgments? Do people fear him? That kind of stuff."

"He's quite fair. Some people fear him, especially when they get caught trying to take advantage of him or undermine his authority."

"Do you have much of that?"

"No, like I said, most of the people like him. He cares about the people. There are always some that want his power and because he's easy to get along with they think he's soft and can be tricked, but he's not."

"How did he get into office?"

"The military put him in after the old one died. He used to be the High General like Falk is now."

"Oh, Falk is High General. He must be like Second-in-Command then."

"Yes."

"No wonder General Marco listened to him."

He sure asks a lot of questions. And why am I answering him? I'm supposed to be in control not him.

"You're answering my questions, Ned, because I'm making you answer them. You are extremely easy to control.

I felt his panic as he realized his helplessness. *Mr. Sedillo mustn't come here!*

I do not intend to control Mr. Sedillo, and I won't ask you for any secret information. I'm going to release you completely now and answer your questions."

If I didn't know he had control, how do I know he's released me?

"You won't know for sure, unless you refuse to answer when I ask you a question. However, you can choose to believe me. I have released you."

"What other things can you do besides control people? I want to know all your defenses and weapons that you have."

"Very well, follow me." I led him to control. "Caltomacoe, I would like you to show Ned everything."

"Please sit here, Ned," Caltomacoe instructed, "and put this on your head." Caltomacoe handed him a cap as they sat at the control panel and placed a cap on his own head. "We will be in mental contact, Ned, through these caps."

Caltomacoe recorded Ned's brain waves then flipped the communications switch and proceeded. I sat down in the captain's chair and waited. When they removed the caps Ned stood up and turned to me. He was shaken from what Caltomacoe showed him. "I- - -," he cleared his throat, "thank you, Captain Packard and Caltomacoe. I'll inform our Leader." *I must warn Mr. Sedillo, he must not come here!*

"I'll accompany you," I said as I rose and we walked out of control together.

"The others are different than you."

"Yes, I'm originally from Earth."

"You have the same powers as they?"

"They're much stronger than I, but yes, I can do about the same things."

"And you possess this shield, also?"

"Yes."

He walked down the ramp, climbed into a vehicle and left while the men still guarded the ship. I went to control and waited for Sedillo to come. A vehicle stopped at our ramp about an hour later and four men got out. Two of them stood outside and two started up. Caltomacoe and I met Mr. Sedillo as he entered with Ned.

"Welcome, Mr. Sedillo," I said as I shook hands with him, "I'm Captain Packard and this is my Second-in-Command, Caltomacoe."

"I'm pleased to meet you, Captain Packard and Caltomacoe." I led him and Ned to the conference room and Sadek brought refreshments.

"All the comforts of home," Lync Sedillo said smiling. "I understand you're telepathic."

"That's correct."

"Then you probably already know why I'm here."

"No, I haven't read you."

He raised an eyebrow and smiled while shifting a little in his seat. "Well, I would like you to stay a while."

"Stay? How long?" I looked at Ned and knew he was watching for any signs of control from Mr. Sedillo.

"Oh, perhaps and year or so."

"Why?"

"We are very interested in getting to know you better. I understand you're forming a fleet."

"Yes, our representative will be coming here to explain the details to you. I see no reason for us to stay here for a year. I can show you everything about us in less time than that."

"Yes, I heard about your caps, but I was thinking of a more personal level."

"You can think of a more personal level than joining minds?" I asked smiling.

"I can stay a few days, but I don't think for a year."

"Then perhaps you would consider leaving a couple of your men with us, as teachers."

"No, Sir, I don't leave my crewmen behind. If you want, I can have a technical ship come and help you."

"And what would this technical ship do?"

"Show you different technologies. It would take them about nine months to get here."

"No, I don't think that will do," he answered.

"How is Captain Bruno?" I asked.

"Captain Bruno? Oh, he's fine."

I read him. Captain Bruno was in trouble. They had him in a cell and the other five as well. "Has he been tested yet to see what memory loss he has?"

"They are about to do that," he answered.

I saw him being shot with blasters. "When is this testing to take place?"

"In the next day or so."

Caltomacoe, I transmitted, *see if you can find out where this jail is.*

"Please excuse me, Mr. Sedillo. I've just been informed of a problem I must take care of," Caltomacoe said as he rose from his chair.

"Of course. This telepathy is quite remarkable," he said to me as he watched Caltomacoe leave the room.

"Yes, it saves a lot of time. Would you like a tour of the ship?"

"Yes, I would enjoy that."

I showed him everything making sure we avoided the area where Caltomacoe was speaking with several of the Leader's men on a friendly tone and reading them for the information. By the time we reached control, Caltomacoe was running an analysis in the Computer.

"Very interesting, Captain Packard. And what is your computer doing now?"

"It's running an analysis on the quantity of energy needed for our return trip and time to produce that energy." Caltomacoe started the engines. "We need more." There was a turmoil outside as the engines started and voices came over the portable radio that Ned carried. He answered and explained. "Sorry to upset your men," I said.

"That's all right, it's good for them once in a while," he smiled. I walked down the ramp with Mr. Sedillo to his vehicle at the end of the tour. "I wish you would reconsider, Captain Packard. However, perhaps a few days will suffice." They drove off as I returned to my ship and Caltomacoe.

Did you find out? I asked.

Yes, it's in the lower level of the same building they took you when we landed.

Good, we'll get them out tonight.

Mike, you think we should interfere?

Caltomacoe, I can't let them kill him.

Sadek, Konteaky, Tomiya and I met at midnight to break Bruno and his men out of jail. I'm to cover only one man. We didn't want to risk weakening my shield too much. Tomiya will also cover one man. We left the ship and started walking the two miles. We kept our conversations to mental transmissions. As we entered the building two armed guards approached us. We smiled and acted very friendly and stood facing them.

"Why are you here?" one asked.

Sadek and I took control of them. We led them to an empty office, sat them down at a desk and put them to sleep. We took their weapons and hid them in a closet. Then continued down a stairwell. We went down two levels and Sadek picked up mental activity.

I think this is the floor, he transmitted.

We walked down a hallway and came to a heavy metal door with a small window in it. We could see two guards on the other side about thirty feet away at a desk. One was writing and the other was standing beside the desk talking to him with his back to us.

We'll have to rush them, Konteaky said.

Okay, Konteaky explode the lock, I said, *Sadek and I will take control of them.*

The door lock exploded with a sound equivalent to a .45 hand pistol and we rushed in. The guard standing spun around and raised his blaster too late; Sadek took him. I continued to run forward while the other guard stood up and reached for his blaster, but I took control before he touched it. As I turned to lead my captive, I saw a camera over the door we just came through. *Konteaky, destroy that camera.* It blew up.

We led our captives to a small room off the hall and put them to sleep.

I hope they don't decide to kill them when they find them asleep, said Tomiya.

I looked at Tomiya in surprise. I hadn't thought of that, but there wasn't anything I could do about it now. There was another heavy door and beyond that, a barred gate.

That must be the jail, I said.

Konteaky exploded the lock and we looked for a camera as we walked in. Sadek found and exploded it. We approached the gate and could see a line of cells on both sides of a passageway. Bruno and his men were sleeping. Sadek exploded the lock on the gate and everyone woke up.

"Mike! What are you doing here?" Bruno asked as I approached his cell.

"I've come to get you out," I explained as Sadek and the others proceeded to explode the locks on the other cells. "Get back Bruno." I concentrated and got a sound like a firecracker.

Sadek laughed out loud then sobered immediately not meaning to offend me. "Let me, Mike."

I stood back as he exploded the lock. "I guess I need more practice." I went in to Bruno and turned my shield off. "I'm going to cover you with my shield. You'll feel the energy, but don't lose contact with me." I took his arm and turned my shield back on.

"That's awful," he said.

"It's better than being dead," I answered.

We all started out and as we entered the hallway of the last two guards, we were met by five armed soldiers.

"Halt! Or we'll fire!"

We stopped and waited for them to approach us. Then we took control of them and put them to sleep. We continued up stairs. We could hear running footsteps as we reached the second level. We flattened against the wall.

They must have seen us on camera, I transmitted.

What now? The place is crawling with them, Tomiya said.

"Bruno," I whispered, "is there another way out?"

"Yes, we don't use it anymore."

He led us back down stairs and through an office. We came to a door that was locked and bolted; it looked like it hadn't been opened for years.

"We can't explode it," Sadek explained. "It'll make too much noise. I'll melt the lock."

Melt the lock? I could feel Bruno's wonder as he watched. We stood back from Sadek as he worked. Finally he got it opened and there was another staircase behind the door. We started up and entered an office at ground level.

"We can climb out through a window. This is the back of the building," Bruno explained.

We scrambled out a window and eased along the building. There was a vehicle parked in the shadows.

"Let's take this," I said.

We climbed in and Bruno started it up. Bruno took the long way around to our ship, but we didn't see any more soldiers. We ran into the ship and closed the ramp.

"Bruno, tell us what happened," I said as we sat in the kitchen.

"I don't really know what happened. After you left we were taken down stairs and put in jail. We've been there ever since."

"No explanation? Nothing?"

"Nothing."

The other five men agreed with what Captain Bruno said. None of them seemed upset about it. As I read them they thought it unusual but not alarming.

"You weren't worried about being locked up?" I asked them.

"No, we didn't do anything wrong."

"I just figured they wanted to talk to us more."

"I admit I thought it strange," said Captain Bruno.

"Your Leader was here today," I said. "I asked him questions about you and when he answered I read him. They were going to kill all of you. That's why we broke you out."

"Kill us! I can't believe that! Why?"

"That's what I'd like to know," I said.

"He wouldn't do that. It's just not his way. Besides, there would be questions. Too many people would be involved and want to know why. I don't believe it." The other five substantiated Captain Bruno's statements.

"Nevertheless, we saw it in his mind."

"What about the men on Trok?" Asked Konteaky.

"I'm not having them come back here to be killed," I answered.

Caltomacoe came in. "There's soldiers outside that want to come in."

"Tough. Let them stay out there," I answered. "Bruno, has anyone from your planet ever gone through anything like what you and your men faced on Dextra before?"

"No. Not that I know of." He looked at the other five as they shook their heads.

"Maybe they were afraid you were changed somehow. Turned into spies or something, alienated in some way."

"But still," said Calla, "wouldn't they have said something to us about their suspicions?"

"Maybe not," I shrugged.

We have been on ship twenty minutes when General Falk showed up. "We'll let him in, Caltomacoe."

He walked in grinning as I met him at the airlock. "Very good, Captain Packard, not one casualty."

I looked at him and closed up the ship. Captain Bruno's men came to attention as he walked in the kitchen with me. "At ease men," he said as we all sat down. "I must say, it amazed me how you pulled it off. Putting them to sleep was a nice touch. You should have seen their faces when they woke up and saw me."

"Why were you going to kill them?"

"We weren't really going to kill them, we just wanted you to think that. It was a test."

"Really?" I said. "Then you wouldn't mind going through a 'test' yourself?"

"What do you have in mind?" he asked smiling.

"Being recorded while you explain," I answered.

"Not at all. I suppose it'll record everything else as well?" he asked.

"Yes, it will." We all went to the library and I connected him to the computer to record. "All right," I said, "what was this all about?"

"About five years ago Lync's son, Gagne, was asked to join forces with a group of reptilian men to ward off an impending attack against one of their colonies. Well, to make a long story short, he and his men were beaten. Gagne was badly wounded and would have died. One of our ships happened to be in the area and picked up his distress call.

"The men that he was helping picked up their own wounded and abandoned Gagne and his men. Most of them died from lack of medical attention. Gagne has been in constant pain ever since from nerve damage."

"Have you seen these reptilians since?" asked Sadek.

"No, Gagne said they came from so far away that they had to use suspended animation to get here. They were trying to colonize a planet in a neighboring solar system of ours.

"Who were the attackers?"

"An enemy of theirs from their own solar system. They wanted to destroy the reptilian colony and their ship. They fought it out on the planet."

"So what does that have to do with us?" I asked.

"You're asking us to join your fleet. Also, you come here with six of our men and tell us we have to go nine months away to pick up the rest. How do we know you're telling the truth?"

"Your own men!" Tomiya said motioning to Bruno and the others.

"You're telepaths you could have done something to them to make them believe the story themselves."

"So what did you prove by making us believe you were going to kill them?" I asked.

"It proved you cared about them. You made the effort to save them. And you cared enough not to hurt anyone else."

"You still don't know if our story is true," said Sadek.

"No, but I believe it now."

"Now, question is;" I said, "do we believe him enough to let these six men leave with him? If he's lying, they're dead."

"It's true about Gagne," Bruno said, "and I still can't believe they would really kill us, Mike. It would be out of character for Mr. Sedillo to do that."

Caltomacoe took the cap from General Falk and listened. "He already sent the ship to pick up his men thirty minutes after you walked out of your meeting with him. He told the truth, Mike. Why don't you bring Gagne here, General Falk, we might be able to help him."

"Can you?"

"If your understanding of his condition is correct, I think so."

Dawn was breaking when General Falk left with Bruno and his men. They stood out front talking for a few minutes then Bruno and his men were driven away in an awaiting vehicle. General Falk dismissed the soldiers guarding our ship and climbed into a vehicle. Our jailbreak group and I went to bed.

Late in the afternoon of the same day Lync and his son arrived with General Falk. Gagne walked with two canes and there was no overlooking the pain that showed in his face with every step. Caltomacoe and I helped him into the opercule and started the examination.

"We can help," Caltomacoe announced afterwards. "There will be some permanent numb spots were some nerves will be destroyed completely, but their destruction won't cause any serious effects on his body. Other nerves are causing pain because they're pinched, we can free them. Also, there is a chemical imbalance that needs to be corrected. Once the nerves heal, the chemical balance will maintain itself, the pinched nerves caused it. He should stay with us for about a week."

"Only a week?" asked Gagne. "You mean the pain will be gone in a week?"

Caltomacoe smiled. "No, the pain will be gone when you wake up in about twelve hours."

They consented to the procedure and Gagne went to sleep with a smile on his face. It was a very intricate procedure and took three hours to complete. Lync stayed with us until Gagne awoke that night.

"What in the world did you do to Ned Patak?" Lync asked as we waited in control.

"I just answered all his questions."

"He insisted I was in mortal danger coming on your ship." He laughed. "Did you know he was fully armed when we came on board?"

"Yes, I knew," I said smiling. "Did you notice how watchful of you he was?"

"Yes. He thought you were going to - - - control me. That's what he called it, control."

"That's because I controlled him when he came the first time. It shook him up."

"Then you do have all the powers he told me about?"

"Yes."

"No wonder he didn't want me to come near you." He laughed again. I looked over at him smiling and he laughed harder.

"Would you like some coffee?" I asked.

"All right." He wiped the tears away that his laughter caused and followed me to the kitchen. "Mmm, kind of bitter."

"Try some sweetener in it."

"Ahh, that's better."

"You must have your hands full ruling the world."

"I have help. I have a counsel and ambassadors, readers of the law. You'd be surprised. No one man can handle a whole world alone. My Generals are a great aid to me, also. They planned our little test for you."

"I bet General Falk thought it up."

"He enjoyed it." Lync nodded.

"He took a risk, suppose we hurt someone?"

"I brought that point up to him. He said if you were as caring as Captain Bruno said, you would find a way. I don't think he expected his men being put to sleep." He laughed again and this time I joined him.

"I can imagine their reaction when they woke up."

"Pure panic. Can you imagine being awaken by the High General himself?"

"He woke them?"

"When they found the first guards asleep he issued orders not to wake them. He went and woke them all himself."

"I wish I could have seen that."

"You recorded him didn't you?"

"Yes! Come on, we'll both listen to it."

We went to control and donned the caps. Lync and I laughed several times together. When the recording went into personal memories and other information I switched it off.

"That's a remarkable machine." Lync said still smiling from the recording.

"Yes. We can . . ."

We were interrupted by the computer announcing that Gagne was awakening.

I had a numbing disk with me just in case, Caltomacoe joined us as we entered his room. Lync stood at the foot of his bed and waited. Gagne opened his eyes and looked at Lync. "It's gone! The pain's gone!"

"Move your legs," I said.

He moved them up and down. "Nothing, no pain at all."

"Sit up, then."

He sat up and still no pain. "Shall I walk?"

"No, not yet," said Caltomacoe. "You still have some healing to do, let's not push it. You're hungry; Konteaky is bringing you a meal now. Just stay in bed for another couple of days and then you can get up."

CHAPTER 28

Captain Bruno was tested for memory loss and we started gathering information to re-educate him.

Gagne learned our language in the week he lived with us while recuperating. He was also a big help in putting information into the computer. He was very knowledgeable on the structure of their spaceships. "Mike, I've been making a comparison of our engines and yours. If you add our drive system to your engines, it should boost your velocity to twice it is now."

"Let's take a look." Caltomacoe and I joined Gagne as he brought up the schematics and computer analysis on the screen in control. The computer also made the recommendation for the changes. "You're right, Gagne. That means we could get home in four and a half months instead of nine. Can your mechanics make these changes?"

"I don't see why not, you want me to start them on it?"

"I should check with our Commodore first, we're due to make a report in about three hours. Why don't you join us and we'll show it to him."

"Yes, I'd like to meet your Commodore."

General Falk came into control as Gagne and I were going over the blue prints to determine what had to be done to make the changes. "Planning on making some changes?" he asked.

"Hi, General," I said. "Gagne was showing me a possible improvement on my engines. If only your engines worked on the same power as ours, we could add some improvements to yours. Ours just won't work with your set up."

"Well, when we join your fleet, won't we be getting some of your ships as well?"

"Most likely."

"Lync is having a party in a couple of days celebrating Gagne's recovery. He sent me to invite you and your crew. You'll come won't you?"

"Sure thing, there's something else I want to talk to you about. You're going to have to pick out a representative to sit on the governing board of the Fleet. He'll have to live on Artara. Might start thinking about it now."

"Each planet has a representative there?"

"Yes, that way everyone knows what's going on and has a voice in the decisions." We discussed the changes for an hour and took a lunch break. When it was time to call the Commodore, the three of us went to control. I made the introductions when the Commodore appeared on screen. We spoke Artarian and I translated to General Falk. Commodore Mackalie explained more about the set-up of the fleet and stated that a ship had been sent and should be arriving in a little less than six months.

"Meanwhile, if you want Captain Packard to bring your representative back with him, it would save you some time. When do you think you will be starting back, Captain Packard?"

"Well, there's something Gagne discovered I think you might find interesting." I sent him the comparisons and recommendations on the engine changes.

"How long would it take to make the changes?"

"I figure about a month," Gagne said. "There are some fittings that have to be redesigned and tooled, but once we get our machinery set up it should go quickly. After it's tested, we could make the changes on the other ship when it gets here if you want."

"Have you considered structural stress on the ship?"

"Yes, the structure should be able to handle the stress. According to my calculations the structure should take ten times the pressure. I'm interested in the metal you used; it has outstanding resilience."

"I would like my mechanics to go over this first. I'll get back to you tomorrow. If my mechanics come up with the same answers, you'll have my approval on both ships."

Commodore Mackalie gave us the 'go ahead' the next day. Gagne had the work crew start immediately.

The party was very lively. Lync Sedillo made a speech about his son being healed and the new fleet being organized. The rest of the time was spent on food, drinks and dancing. Tomiya and I thoroughly enjoyed ourselves.

"I see you brought your companion in jail breaks," said Lync as we were returning to our table after a dance.

"She's my wife," I smiled. "Tomiya, this is the Leader of Boro, Lync Sedillo."

"Hello, Mr. Sedillo."

"Your wife! Well, you're a lucky man indeed to have a wife that loves adventure as much as you. Most women want to stay home safe and secure."

"Tomiya is an exceptional woman," I said proudly.

"Yes, I agree. May I be so bold as to ask for a dance of your exceptional wife?" I nodded and Tomiya took his arm.

Captain Bruno and I started a conversation and were interrupted by a loud explosion outside. Everyone ran out to see what it was as the sky was lit up with fireworks. It was better than any 4th of July celebration I've ever seen on Earth. Lync stood with Tomiya and smiled as she enjoyed the sight. People cheered and applauded the displays. When it was over they returned to the dancing.

"That was really something," I said to Lync, "I've never seen anything as spectacular."

"I'm glad you enjoyed it. General Falk told me about having a representative live on Artara. I've decided to send General Kimber Nadalin and his wife Ana."

"Good, they can come back with us." We partied until late then Tomiya and I left to have a private party of our own.

* * * * *

We had been working a week on the ship and were moving some heavy machinery with a hoist. Gagne and I were standing to one side watching when he turned toward me and belted me hard in the stomach causing me to double up and fall to the ground. He went down with me.

"What did you do that for?" I asked when I got my breath back.

"Look," he answered pointing to the wall. There was a large gear embedded to the hub in the wall, "it would have hit you." Then we heard screaming. A man was lying on the floor a few feet from us holding a bleeding stump of his right arm and writhing in pain. We ran to him and I tied a tourniquet around his arm. It was severed mid-forearm. The rest of his arm laid on the floor.

"Grab that arm and bring it to my ship!" I yelled as Gagne and I lifted the man. By the time we reached medical, the man had stopped screaming and gone into shock.

"You'll be all right," I said as we put him in the opercule with the severed arm. The opercule worked on him for three hours as he slept. Work stopped for the day and the men waited. Gagne and I stayed in medical and kept reports going out to them. The opercule finished and lifted. Posch's arm was secured to a metal plate from the fingers to just below the shoulder and was completely immovable. Instructions appeared on the screen to keep the plate on for six weeks. We took him to a room and turned on the monitor.

"His arm will be all right," I told the others as they looked at him. "He'll sleep now for at least nine more hours. You can all come back when he wakes up."

Gagne and I stayed on ship watching the monitor. "Thanks, Gagne," I said. "You saved my life."

"Sorry I had to hit you, I couldn't think of any other way to get you down fast."

"Hey, you can hit me anytime to keep me alive!"

Eight and a half hours later the monitor signaled, I grabbed a numbing disk and we went to Posch. I was numbing his arm as he woke up. "How do you feel?"

"I feel good, what about my arm?"

"It'll be fine in about six weeks and some exercises. Does it hurt anywhere?"

"No, I can't move it."

"You're not supposed to."

"But I can't feel it either."

"I just finished numbing it with this." I showed him how to use the disk.

He looked at his arm and was surprised to see it attached to him. "Was it my imagination? Or was it really cut off?"

"It was," Gagne laughed, "but its back on now."

"Feel like eating?" I asked.

"Yes, I'm hungry."

"Good, I'll be right back." As I prepared a meal for Posch, the workmen started coming in to see him. "Come on, he's awake now and hungry."

They came with me and joked with Posch as he ate. "You should have ducked, Posch."

"Just wanted time off with pay."

"You'll do anything for attention."

General Falk and Lync Sedillo entered in the midst of our laughter. "Must be good news with all this joviality," said Lync. The men came to immediate attention. "At ease men," said Lync. "Posch, I see you're in one piece again." Everyone started laughing all over again. "You're going to have to watch those gears," he continued. "They're hard on the walls."

"I think we'll leave it there as a memento," said General Falk. "We'll call it 'Posch's Gear, thought it could make him a lefty.'"

Posch remained with us to monitor the healing while work continued on the engines.

"One of the main veins is trying to heal itself closed," I said after about three days, "I'll have to put you back in the opercule to open it."

"Will it put me to sleep again?" he asked as he laid down on the table.

"No, it'll give you a local, you won't feel anything."

"That's some machine," he said as he sat up twenty minutes later.

"Yes, it has come in handy many times. Think you could use something like this?"

"Why don't you show it to our medical men?"

The next time I saw General Falk I mentioned the opercule to him. The following day General Hewes and several doctors arrived to see the opercule. They talked with Posch and examined his arm. Then they watched the recorded surgery of Posch and the opening of the vein it did two days ago. "Think you could use it?" I asked.

"Definitely! How much would it cost?"

"Nothing, we'll give you all you need."

"Give it to us?"

"We would have to install it though, our technicians can use some of your workers and show them how to maintain it."

Tomiya came into medical while I was explaining some of the controls. "Mike, can you get this out?" She showed me her hand. There was a large sliver of wood broken off deep inside.

"Tomiya! How did you do this?"

"I was moving some boards and my hand slipped."

"Next time use your telekinetics." I put a stool up to the table of the opercule, had her sit and stretch out her arm as I lowered the opercule. The sliver was out and the wound sealed in five minutes and she felt nothing.

"Thank you Mike," she said with a kiss and a smile as she left.

"She's my wife," I explained as I felt my face become extremely warm while looking at the smiling faces of the doctors.

The following weeks were busy as we worked on the ship and watched Posch's arm heal. He was up and watching the job. I went over to him one day as he was using the numbing disk. The day was a hot one and his arm was a little more swollen. "Why don't you rest for a while Posch and lift your arm. It's swelling from hanging it down too much."

"It's starting to annoy me when I want to do something and I can't."

"You only have another couple of weeks, don't push it."

"You'll be ready to go before then."

"I'm going to stay until you can use that arm."

"You'll be late getting home, why stay? We have medical men to help me with the exercises."

"You're my patient. I'm not going until I know you're all right. I'll still get home sooner than scheduled anyway with the faster engines."

The work was finished and the ship was ready to test. I had everyone leave the ship except Caltomacoe and Nakano, Boro's head mechanic. Nakano and I went to the engine room while Caltomacoe started her up. They had a different sound, a deeper hum. "They sound powerful," I said.

"Everything is reading normal," he answered. "Let's take her up."

We joined Caltomacoe in control and lifted her slowly. As we rose we tried some maneuvers. "Responds the same," Caltomacoe reported. We rose higher and picked up speed. We hit orbiting level and stabilized. The readings were still good.

"All right, let's see what she does," said Nakano.

I took control and headed out to deep space, opening her up and stabilizing at each level. "Look at those speeds! And she isn't fully opened yet."

"Hold her here, Mike," said Nakano. "I want to check the engines again." More readings were taken, still everything looked good. "Take her three-quarter now."

I made the setting and accelerated. We were pushed back into our seats as she took off. She kept accelerating. A slight tremor went through the ship and the engines quieted, but the acceleration continued.

"Mike, turn on the screen," said Nakano. The screen came alive with specks and streaks of lights flashing by. "We did it!" screamed Nakano. "We hit hyperspeed! I've been trying to figure that out for years! And we did it!" Caltomacoe and I looked at him not understanding what he was talking about. "Cut it down, Mike, slowly." I followed his instructions and the tremor came again as we slowed then stopped.

"Explain this to me," I said.

"Hyperspeed. It's much faster than the speed of light. You go so fast it's almost like jumping from one solar system to another. Mike, it takes you nine months to get home?"

"Yes."

"With hyperspeed, you can get home in nine WEEKS! You'll have to be very careful programming your computer for this; you can overshoot your target and not even know it. You did record this trip didn't you?" He stared at me with almost a trace of panic waiting for my answer.

"Yes, of course."

"Good," he sighed. "We can get back the same way we came. Let's see where we are first."

We brought the galaxy into view and estimated we had gone about a half day out in one hour and fifteen minutes. "Now just set the computer to do the exact opposite and we should be home in one hour and fifteen minutes." Again, I followed his instructions and ignited. The acceleration was the same with the tremor. When we automatically shut down we were back to orbiting Boro.

"Congratulations, Nakano!" I said as I shook his hand.

"Not me! Gagne discovered the changes, but he underestimated the potential. Maybe he didn't know about hyperspeed. Now we really have some work to do," Nakano said. "All your programming in control has to be redone. We'll start on it as soon as we get back. We better let your Commodore know right away. If someone should test without recording, they could get lost."

CHAPTER 29

I called the Commodore as soon as we landed. "Have you completed making the changes on any of the ships yet?" I asked.

"No."

"I just finished a partial test and found the changes produces 'Hyperspeed' conditions."

"What's 'Hyperspeed'?"

"Oh, nothing special. It just means I can get home in nine weeks instead of nine months." I sat back and watched him as my statement sunk in. The five-minute delay between our transmissions made it even more enjoyable.

"Nine weeks?" he said as he lifted out of his seat. "You did say nine weeks, correct?"

"I said nine weeks," I answered grinning, "and that wasn't even at three-quarter power yet. We shut down to come back and reprogram the computer to handle it."

"Nine weeks, what about stress?"

"None, less in fact, than before. Once you hit Hyperspeed the engines only have to maintain. They're not constantly pushing. Go ahead and finish the changes, but wait until you get the new programming from me before testing. A ship could get lost at these speeds. I would also like to recommend a gift to Boro of a couple of ships or so for what they've given us. They aren't able to hit these speeds with their ships."

"How many ships do they have?"

"Twenty," I relayed to the Commodore after asking Nakano.

"Fine, I'll take care of it. Nine weeks," he repeated as he disappeared from screen.

Nakano, Caltomacoe and I started work on the programming. We were able to determine from the recording of the flight the speed we were traveling at the time of the tremor. We estimated a maximum setting of ten times that and proceeded to program the computer to accept and monitor these new speeds. We named each level 'Gagne' in his honor for the suggestion of making the changes.

Besides working on the programming I started Posch on exercises and kept close monitoring in the beginning. When we removed the plate, his arm was so stiff he couldn't bend his elbow, wrist or move his fingers. "Don't use the numbing disk before exercising, Posch. The pain will stop you from pushing it too hard."

Posch showed marked improvement at the end of one week of exercises. The fingers came back much quicker than the elbow movement. We got him involved with our programming the writing helped his finger control.

"Will your sensors reach out far enough to pick up debris and meteors at these speeds to give you enough time to maneuver?" Posch asked.

I consulted the computer and found we had to boost the energy for the sensors and screen display. We devised a program that would automatically adjust the amount of energy needed for the new speed levels. Three weeks later we were ready for the big test.

Posch joined us this time in control as we strapped in for take-off. Once we were clear of orbiting level I set the computer to Gagne 1 and felt the acceleration with the tremor and then leveled out. Gagne 2 the pressure of the acceleration was much less with no tremor and Gagne 3 we felt nothing. The engines seemed to rev up each time with the acceleration and then settled down to an even purr at the top of each level. It reminded me of the sound of shifting gears in an automobile. Nakano and I were in the engine room when Gagne 4 started and we watched the readings of pressures and energy use as we peaked.

"These speeds actually conserve energy!" I was astounded. We held at Gagne 4 for twenty minutes then proceeded to Gagne 5. The engines strained a little harder this time and as they peaked they didn't have the even purr.

"They're at maximum," said Nakano, "better not go any faster than this. In fact, I wouldn't use this speed unless it was an emergency, it's putting a lot of strain on the engines."

We returned to control and cut the rest of the levels and started to slow down. Slowdown has to be done gradually as it puts more pressure on the engines. Recording this aspect is vital for programming specific destinations. We monitored all readings as the computer slowed us to a complete stop. The test lasted four hours in one direction. We took our bearing and programmed our return trip to orbiting level around Boro in two hours. The computer plotted the speeds necessary and the breaking point. I set the controls and activated.

We sat back and watched the screen as streaks of light streamed past us. We traveled at Gagne 3 for one and a half hours and started breaking. We were in orbit in exactly two hours. Caltomacoe took her down and Nakano started to leave the ship immediately. "Where are you going in such a hurry?" I asked.

"I want a work crew on those engines first thing in the morning. I want them pulled down and thoroughly inspected."

I eliminated Gagne levels 6 through 10 from the computer programming and called the Commodore giving him a full report. I transmitted the new programming and we signed off. Fifteen days later we had the engines back together and Commodore Mackalie called me. He ordered me to stay on Boro until further orders.

"What do you think that's all about, Caltomacoe?" I asked.

"I don't know. I've never known him to give an order like that without some explanation."

"I hope nothing went wrong on their end with the engine changes."

"I guess we're just going to have to wait and find out."

We sat it out for three months. We made our regular reports and still the Commodore gave no hint as to when we could start home. Then Captain Morvellance took our reports.

"Where's Commodore Mackalie?" I asked on the third report to Captain Morvellance.

"He's working on a special project. He wants me to handle all the reports for a while. He'll be back," he said smiling.

"Caltomacoe, I don't like this," I said as we signed off.

"It is unusual, but I don't know what we can do about it. He did order us to stay here."

We waited, and fifteen days later we heard a roar of engines as Caltomacoe and I sat in the kitchen having lunch. We went outside to see what was landing and I saw an Artarian Explorer Ship come down. I was about to go out to it when another one came down. Ships kept coming as I stood watching. Lync Sedillo and General Falk joined me. I didn't hear them drive up over the roar of the landing ships.

"They're all from Artara!" I said. "What's going on?"

Thirteen ships landed. Eleven Explorers, a Technical Ship and a Freighter.

Commodore Mackalie descended from the lead ship in his dress uniform and we went to meet him.

"Welcome, Commodore Mackalie," said Lync Sedillo as they shook hands.

"Thank you, Mr. Sedillo." After the formalities I asked Commodore Mackalie how long it took him to get here. "Fourteen days! We kept a steady Gagne 3 all the way. By the way, I would like to meet Gagne and thank him personally."

"He's my son," answered Lync. "He's not here now, but you'll meet him tonight. What Mike has done for him is thanks enough, Commodore. He has a normal life again." Lync explained as we walked to his vehicle.

Mr. Sedillo held a reception welcoming Commodore Mackalie and it was quite a celebration. All the Artarians were there in dress uniforms and Tomiya wore her red dress to match me. Commodore Mackalie sat with General Falk, Lync and his son Gagne. Caltomacoe, Tomiya and I were with Nakano and Posch. Speeches were made after we ate. Artara is giving Boro ten Explorer Ships and enough medical computers for all their hospitals.

"Your Commodore is very generous," said Nakano.

"Why not? You've improved our whole fleet with hyperspeed and made it possible for us to reach more planets. And you're joining our fleet."

The following morning Commodore Mackalie and I met on his ship. *Mike, you are to go to Trok and meet Dalcamy and Borkalami. I have Naygee and some of his men here to go with you. He will make the changes on their ships. Is your ship ready?*

Yes, Sir.

It'll take at least three weeks to make the changes. You should be back to Artara in time for the first meeting of the Board of Councils of the Interplanetary Fleet.

That sounds exciting. Did Russia join?

They certainly did, they said yes before we even finished explaining how it works. China joined too. America and England are sending ambassadors to look at it and then decide.

Once they see Russia in it, they'll join, I said. I feel like I've been away from home so long, how is everyone doing?

Larry Hendricks returned with his wife and we gave him a honeymoon. On the island, he added before I could ask. *Gloria is planning on taking a vacation on Artara. Her improvements on computer systems have made her rich on Earth and she's taking a year off work to come.*

Sounds like she has a soft spot for Artara.

More like a soft spot for Dakama, Mackalie smiled.

Really? What about her career?

What is a career when your heart is on another planet?

Didn't Ikomacoe take care of that?

Yes, but when it comes to love sometimes nothing can make them forget.

I thought about Tomiya, *I agree with that.* We laughed together.

The next day I left for Trok and arrived exactly fourteen days later. Borkalami and Dalcamy met me, *Weather Man!*

Hi, Casanova, Borkalami. It's good to see you guys.

Casanova? Asked Borkalami. *What's this all about?*

Nothing, Borkalami, answered Dalcamy.

Nothing! I said. *How can you say nothing?* I proceeded to tell Borkalami the story.

Borkalami laughed and looked at Dalcamy. *Casanova! That's a good name. I've also heard you made some changes on your ship.*

I'll say, how do you like fourteen days from Boro to here? Naygee came to make the changes on your ships. Borkalami and Dalcamy greeted Naygee as he joined us. *Tell me what happened on Dextra,* I said.

Let's go to the Lor's Lounge and we'll show you everything, Dalcamy said.

As we walked I noticed the Trok soldiers saluting me. *Amazing,* I thought, *they still remember me.*

I'll say they still remember you, answered Borkalami. *The first thing everyone asks is 'do you know Mike?'*

If there were a Chamber of Heroes here, you'd be in it, said Dalcamy.

Chamber of Heroes? I asked.

You know, explained Dalcamy, *like you have on Earth.*

Hall of Fame, I said laughing. *You got it mixed up with Chamber of Horrors.*

That's right, Hall of Fame.

Just for saving one Trok? I'm sure lots of Troks have saved each other's lives. And besides, I have a shield.

But you're not a Trok that makes a difference.

Suppose your shield failed? Asked Borkalami.

Or you didn't get it on quick enough? Said Dalcamy.

I didn't consider that, I said.

They do, and to be shredded by a Macao is one of the most hideous thoughts to them, said Borkalami.

We sat down at one of the tables and Borkalami started telling me about Dextra. *I just happened to be talking with Alma when the first Thrae ship landed with Dalcamy's. You should have seen the look on his face and heard his thoughts!* Borkalami started laughing. *He knew his plan failed and decided to make himself scarce, but I wouldn't let him.*

Borkalami started transmitting his memory of the event to me. "Come on Alma, let's go greet them," he said as he put his arm around his shoulders and headed out to join Dr. Bella and the others to welcome their guests. Of course Alma obliged Borkalami; he had no other choice.

"Alma," greeted Dalcamy after greeting Dr. Bella. "I'm glad you joined the welcoming party. I have two of your men sleeping comfortably inside. Perhaps you'd like to be there when they wake up."

"Two of my men? I don't know what you mean," he lied.

They went in to Dalcamy's ship and listened to the recordings.

"Do you have anything to say about this Alma?" asked Dr. Bella.

"No."

"I think it's time to wake them up," said Dr. Bella to Dalcamy.

They went into medical and began to wake up the two Dextarians. They were surprised to see Dr. Bella.

"Dr. Bella! How did you get here?" Formald asked.

"You're on Dextra, Formald," was Dr. Bella's reply.

"Oh."

Dalcamy released both of them and helped them climb out. They were a little weak and needed food. After feeding them, a group of men came and took them away.

What happened to them? I asked when Borkalami finished.

We don't know yet, they locked them up. Gathered up the other eight and had some kind of trial, answered Dalcamy. *They're supposed to let Mocki know by computer when they reach a decision. It should be sometime today.*

What about the couples?

There was a big celebration and they were treated like royalty, answered Dalcamy.

So tell us about Boro, Borkalami said.

I transmitted everything that happened.

I'll have to remember that trick when I want to get you down fast. Dalcamy said when he received the vision of the accident in the machine shop and Nakano belting me in the stomach.

Well, it worked, I answered grinning; I'm here to tell the tale.

And Posch's arm is all right? Borkalami asked.

Last time I saw him, he was back at his job.

Lor Sham walked in as we were conversing, "Mike! When did you get here?"

"A few minutes ago." I said as I stood to greet him.

"I'll have to let Kafka know. Have a drink with me?" he invited all of us.

As we were relaxing with Lor Sham, Dalcamy received word from Mocki that all eleven men are to be executed.

"Executed," said Borkalami rather sadly.

"I don't think you're going to be able to save them, Borkalami," I said.

"Why would you want to?" asked Dalcamy. "The damage they did warrants their death. You know there would be no control over them to stop them from hurting others in the future."

"Yes, you're right," answered Borkalami.

"You have a soft heart, Borkalami," said Lor Sham. "Don't let it get you in trouble."

"While we're together," I said. "There's something I want you to show me. How to mirror thoughts and change minds."

"Changing minds works a lot like your hypnosis that you used with the computer," explained Dalcamy. "Join with me and we'll do something with Borkalami," he said grinning.

Borkalami grinned back at Dalcamy. He was in the middle of the drink that Lor Sham had given him and was apparently enjoying it. I joined Dalcamy. *You don't like that drink do you, Borkalami. It tastes bitter to you.* I understood it was a type of mind control. It starts the same way in having their complete attention.

Borkalami looked at the drink after taking a sip and set it down on the table dissatisfied with it.

"What's wrong, Borkalami?" asked Dalcamy.

"It's bitter all of a sudden."

Lor Sham looked at Borkalami, "you mind if I taste it?"

"No, go ahead."

"Tastes all right to me. You did that. You changed his mind."

"All right, Mike, your turn. Make it taste good to him again," said Dalcamy.

I concentrated. *Your drink is delicious, isn't it? In fact, you want another one just like it. Go ahead and take another taste.*

Borkalami picked up his drink and tasted. He drank it down and asked for another. Lor Sham obliged him.

"That's remarkable," Lor Sham said as he came back.

"Of course, Borkalami was cooperating with us. He's strong enough to block the suggestion," Dalcamy explained. "Now, for mirroring thoughts. Join me again, Mike. Borkalami, send pain thoughts at me." Dalcamy closed his mind up and created an echo effect, which bounced Borkalami's pain thoughts right back.

"You got it, Mike?"

"I think so."

"If you don't do it right, it'll hurt. Ready?"

"Yeah." I concentrated and received a banging pain.

"You didn't do it right," Dalcamy laughed.

"Okay, try again," I said. We tried three more times and it still didn't work.

"I'll join you and have Borkalami shoot at you," Dalcamy said. I still received the banging pain and so did Dalcamy. "You're not strong enough, Mike. You're doing it right, but we're getting through your block. Your transceiver must be getting close to its recharge time isn't it?"

I figured it out on paper. "I'm about ten months past," I said.

"You'd better get it charged again when we get back, it'll help you get stronger."

"I'll have it charged," I nodded.

"This is really interesting," Lor sham said. "Can you teach this to our men?"

We told him how I became telepathic and that there was no guarantee it would work for everyone. "Would you be willing to try if we got volunteers?" he asked.

"Probably," answered Borkalami. "We would have to ask the Commodore, and your men would have to live on Artara for a year or maybe two at most. We should be able to tell after two years if it'll work or not."

"Any special age?"

"The younger the better."

"I'll have a talk with Kafka about it."

CHAPTER 30

Naygee started on Dalcamy's and Borkalami's ships the next day. Lor Sham offered some additional chikes to help, which made the work go much faster than he expected. Two weeks later the ships were back together. The day the work was finished, two ships from Boro arrived. I accompanied Lor Sham to greet them. Lor Sham had learned the language of Boro in preparation of their arrival. General Roth Voll stepped out of the lead ship and approached us.

"Welcome to our planet, General Voll," said Lor Sham, "we've been waiting for you. I presume you would like to see your men right away."

"Yes, I would."

"Please come with us then."

Lor Sham led us to a barracks where most of the Boro men were. They came to full attention as the General walked in.

"At ease men." He looked them over and said a few words of greetings and encouragement to them and came back to us. "They look like you've taken good care of them. They told me how you helped them with their injuries, thank you."

"It was our pleasure to help, General. We had the same experience on Dextra as they. I'm glad none of your men died from theirs."

"You lost some?"

"Yes, we had several suicides when we got them home. But we watched these men closer to make sure that didn't happen. Also, Borkalami was able to work with the ones that had some psychological problems."

"Who is Borkalami?"

"He's an Artarian Captain, I'll introduce you to him later," I answered.

Three more Boro soldiers came in laughing and spotted the General. "Sir!" one responded as they came to attention.

"At ease."

"Sir, may I speak?"

"Go ahead."

"How's Captain Bruno?"

"He's fine, he's at home. I've brought another Captain to fly you home."

"He's not blank anymore?" another asked.

"Blank? I don't understand." The General looked at us and I explained the condition Captain Bruno was in the last time his men saw him. "He wasn't in that condition by the time he arrived home," the General explained to them, "he was perfectly normal."

The whole barracks echoed with their cheering. The General looked at them and smiled. He turned and started out of the barracks. There were several Trok soldiers standing outside as we left. The Boro soldiers started out after us and mingled with the Trok soldiers like old friends. The General turned and watched them as they spoke to each other. There was apparent friendship and sharing of good news among them. The General smiled and continued.

"Would you like to join us in the Lor's Lounge for our evening meal, General?" asked Lor Sham.

"Yes, thank you."

We entered the Lounge and met with several other Lors and I made the introductions. I also introduced him to Dalcamy and Borkalami. "How long did it take you to get here?" asked Borkalami as we ate.

"Six months," General Voll replied.

"That's pretty good. It would have taken us nine if it wasn't for the improvements."

"What improvements?"

"Gagne suggested we add your drive system to our engines," I explained. "It gave us Hyperspeed."

"Hyperspeed! You have that?"

"You do too, now," said Dalcamy. "We gave you ten ships with it. You'll see a lot of changes when you get home."

"Why don't you let me take you to Dextra in my ship?" Borkalami suggested. "I could get you there faster and you'd be able see what hyperspeed is like."

"That sounds good, have you looked at the ship?"

"Yes, the Dextarians camouflaged it so we had to find it with metal detection. It looks like it's in good shape. We'll help you run your tests."

After dinner we talked and had a few drinks. By the time General Voll returned to his ship he knew everything that happened to the men and the condition that now exists on Dextra.

Dalcamy and I went with them in Borkalami's ship to Dextra along with a couple of mechanics from Boro. The six of us were in control with Mocki when we hit hyperspeed. Borkalami became alarmed at the tremor.

"It's all right, Borkalami," I said. "There is a tremor when you enter and leave hyperspeed."

The screen displayed the same flashing lights. We were at Gagne 1 and stayed there three hours then the ship started braking. Dextra appeared on screen when we left hyperspeed and approached orbiting level. The whole trip took four and a half hours. I felt both Dalcamy and Borkalami's amazement as we descended.

General Voll inspected his ship and started her engines. After about three hours of testing he ordered her up for a trial run to orbiting level and back. We waited on Dextra for his return.

"It's good to see you again, Mike," said Dr. Bellow as he walked up to us.

"How have you been?" I asked as I shook his hand. "Very well and very busy. I have to warn you, Mike, Formald escaped. He's determined to kill you."

"Escaped, how did that happen?"

"He overpowered a guard and made him open his cell. His mind is extremely powerful. I didn't realize how strong he was. The guard died. There was considerable tissue damage to his brain. I think Formald experimented on him." He looked down at the ground shaking his head. I saw pictures of a damaged and blood clotted brain from the autopsy he just finished. The sight made me turn away for a moment.

"Where is Formald now? Do you have any idea?" I asked looking at Borkalami's ship.

"No, we know he has some friends. Perhaps they're hiding him."

"What about the others?" Borkalami asked. "Think he'll try to get them out?"

"They were executed yesterday. You should leave, Mike. If he knew you were here he would definitely try to get to you. That's all he talked about was what he would do to you. It makes me shudder just to think about what he said. If I were you, I'd leave right now."

"Maybe I can help catch him. Let him come to me, we can set a trap."

"I don't think that's such a good idea, Mike," Dalcamy said. "He could destroy you. You have no defense against him. Better go back to Trok and let us take care of this."

"Mike, you won't be showing cowardice," Borkalami said as he picked up my thoughts. "I'm going to insist on you going back right now." He took my arm and turned toward his ship.

"Borkalami! I don't want to run away from him like this, damn it!"

"If you don't go willingly, I'm going to take control of you and make you go."

I looked at him and knew he meant it. I had no choice in the matter. I let him escort me to his ship and watched as he told Komi to take me to Trok and then return. We lifted as soon as Borkalami left the ship. Four hours later I watched Komi leave again for Dextra. I went to my ship and met Caltomacoe in control and told him what happened.

"Cheer up Mike, they're right you know."

"Yeah, I know, but I feel like such a coward doing this."

"No Mike, smart. You're out matched by Formald, he could kill you easily and he wouldn't hesitate."

"Where's the General's ship?"

"They took the Boro soldiers home. He left orders to get the soldiers home as soon as possible. And he would come in the other ship."

I decided to go to my sleeping room. I was feeling tired and thought I'd take a nap. Dalcamy called us on screen just as I was leaving control. "Did you see General Voll's ship on the way back to Trok?"

"No, why?"

"It's been four hours since he left and he hasn't returned yet."

"He was only going to orbit level. Do you think Formald might have been hiding on his ship?"

"We better make a search for him."

We notified Mocki and lifted. Borkalami joined us as we orbited over Dextra. He laid out a search pattern and we split up to begin. Five hours later we found General Voll's ship headed in the direction of Boro. We approached his ship and surrounded him. Borkalami made contact with Formald.

"Turn the ship around, Formald."

"Is Captain Packard with you?" he asked.

"Go back to Dextra, now."

"There is a planet up ahead . . . thirty minutes and we'll be there. Have Captain Packard meet me there and I won't kill General Voll."

"Captain Packard is not going to meet you."

He brought the General up in front of the screen, "fine, then watch him die!" The General screamed and grabbed his head.

"All right!" I yelled, "I'll meet you. But you have to let him go if I do."

"Agreed, Captain Packard, you come alone. No other ships or I'll kill him." The screen went blank.

Mike, Caltomacoe transmitted, *you're going to your death.*

Maybe not, I have a few tricks of my own you know.

Tomiya's eyes met mine as I rose from my chair, *I'm sorry Tomiya, but I have to go.* It was in her mind to ask to come but stopped. *I love you, and I intend to come back.*

We searched the computer for information about the planet we were headed for. It had been given a number TU4. Dextra solar system, Uninhabited, 6th orbit from the sun. The atmosphere contained just enough oxygen to sustain me. We watched the Boro ship descend and we followed, landing 40 meters away.

I'll go with you, Mike.

No, Caltomacoe, he'll kill the General if you do. I walked out of my ship and started toward the Boro ship and up the ramp. Formald opened the airlock. "Let the General out Formald."

"After you come in." I entered.

One of the mechanics laid on the floor and the General was standing on the other side of him. I went to General Voll.

"Are you all right?" I asked.

"Yes."

I bent over the mechanic and turned him over, he was dead.

"He killed him. He just looked at him and killed him. How is that possible?"

"Go to my ship, General, and wait for me," I said as I led him to the airlock.

"He's not leaving, Captain Packard."

"That was the agreement."

Formald stood laughing. "Agreement? What makes you think I'm going to keep any 'agreement'? He stays! He's going to take me to Boro. After I deal with you." He took control of me as I looked at him.

Mind control, I was surprised he knew it.

I know many new things since the last time we met, Captain. I had lots of practice on my guard. I learned how I could cause extreme pain without killing right away. I can prolong it almost endlessly. To demonstrate. My left arm felt like it was being ripped from my body. I wanted to scream and couldn't. *Interesting isn't it, Captain? You can't scream, you can't move. You can't do anything, but feel.* I started to black out. *Oh no, Captain,* the pain eased, *you're not getting out of it that easily. Are you ready to tell me the code for your ship now, Captain?* He laughed. *You fought so hard to keep it a 'SECRET', remember? I didn't know this trick then.*

Yes, I remember, Formald.

You can still think! Good, I wonder if your wife would still be able to think with this much pain.

My anger filled me as he mentioned my wife and I began to push the pain away.

Good, Captain, you're becoming a challenge. Anger will give you strength to endure more pain. Yes, I'll get your wife over here when I tire of you.

My other arm began to hurt. I concentrated harder. My anger built and I stared at Formald.

"What are you doing?" He vocalized his question.

I could see fear in his eyes and my pain eased. I concentrated harder.

"No! That's not possible!"

The pain increased and started to confuse my thoughts. *I'm going to kill you Formald! You're dead meat!* His head exploded. I collapsed to the floor. I picked myself up and staggered over to the screen. "Caltomacoe!" I sat hard on the floor.

Caltomacoe picked me up and set me in a chair. "Mike, look at me."

I looked at Caltomacoe. *I won, Caltomacoe. I killed him.* My face felt wet and I wiped my upper lip with the back of my hand thinking it was sweat, my hand came down bloody. *Must have a bloody nose,* I thought. *I don't remember getting hit in the nose.* I looked at the General. He stood staring at Formald with a shocked expression on his face. "General."

He looked at me and backed away. "You blew up his head! Just by looking at him! His head!"

"I had no choice General, it was either him or me."

Borkalami and Dalcamy came running in and slowed a little as they saw Formald's body. "Come on Mike," said Dalcamy. He practically carried me out. They took me to medical on my ship and laid me down on the table. I caught a glimpse of Tomiya, but they moved too quickly for me to talk to her.

"What are you doing? I'm okay."

"Just relax, Mike." I felt a tube enter my arm and went to sleep.

CHAPTER 31

I woke up and Tomiya was lying beside me. I turned to hold her and my arms hurt so much I moaned. She immediately placed a numbing disk on my neck and the pain eased.

"What's going on?" I asked.

"You were hurt, Mike, he hurt you badly. He made you hemorrhage, you have to be very quiet for a while. Go back to sleep, I'll be here with you."

They made me stay in bed for a week. We were back on Trok. Dalcamy and Borkalami came daily to see me.

What about General Voll? Is he all right? I asked.

He was in shock for a couple days. He wants to come see you, but he's afraid of you. He's afraid of all of us now.

Because he saw what I did.

I've tried talking to him about it, but whenever I mention it he makes an excuse and leaves, Dalcamy said. *I guess he just needs more time.*

When is he leaving?

I talked him into staying for another week that I wanted to make sure he was all right. Actually, I was hoping you two could get together before he leaves.

Yes, well if you would let me out of bed!

All right, they laughed, *you can get out of bed. But no work, take it easy.*

I threw the covers back and started to get up and felt the pain in my arms again.

See! Borkalami said, *move slow and easy.*

I can't believe he did that much damage.

Mike, your eyes and nose were bleeding when we got to you.

My eyes?

Yes, several blood vessels were ruptured; you would have died.

Okay, I promise to move slow and watch everything I do. Did you examine General Voll for any sore spots? I asked as I dressed.

He's been so frightened of us I doubt he would allow it. I didn't want to force him, Borkalami explained.

Did Caltomacoe show you his technique that he learned from the computer?

No.

It's very thorough. Have him show you before we leave.

We walked very slowly toward the Lor's Lounge, a soldier drove up. "May I have the honor of giving you a ride, Mike?"

"I'm only going to the Lounge."

He jumped out and opened the door for me. The three of us climbed in. "Thank you very much," I said as he opened the door again. He saluted and drove away.

"Mike!" Lor Sham came over. "How are you feeling?"

"Pretty good."

"I tried to come visit you, but your Doctors told me you needed quietness and rest."

"I guess they were right. I didn't realize how weak I was till I started walking over here. Have you seen General Voll?"

"He usually comes in about this time," he said as he looked around. "There he is now, I'll get him." Lor Sham left as I sat down in an easy chair and relaxed. A few minutes later he returned with General Voll.

"Hi General," I said. "How have you been?"

"I'm fine. I . . . Well, thanks for saving me from Formald."

"Have a drink with me?" I asked.

"Yes, what would you like?"

"Lor Sham knows the drink, I can't remember the name of it."

"I'll get it, Mike," said Sham.

I could feel General Voll's nervousness although he tried to conceal it. He sat in the chair across from me.

"General," I said after Sham brought the drinks, "I'm sorry you had to see that. He wasn't going to let you go."

He immediately rose from his chair to leave. "I'm glad you're all right, Mike, but I have to---,"

"I'm going to be rude and ask you to stay, General. We need to talk about this."

And if I don't will he force me like, him?

"I won't force you, General."

"You won't have to," interrupted Lor Sham, "I will. This has gone far enough, General, the man saved your life."

"You didn't see what he did. What they are capable of doing with a mere thought."

"General, does it make us any different?" I asked. "We are the same people that met you when you landed. You just didn't know our power then. You do now, but we haven't changed toward you. And besides," I continued in a lower tone, "it takes more than just a mere thought."

The General looked at me for a long time thinking and remembering. "I'm sorry, Mike, I'm being a fool. You aren't different. It's just that I didn't know such power existed. And to see a man's head explode like that, it was gruesome."

"It was the first time I ever did it, General, and I hope the last."

"None of us have ever done it," Borkalami said, "but Mike had no choice. If he hadn't, he would be dead now and you on your way to Boro with a man that would rule your world with horror and cruelty."

"You think he would have killed Mr. Sedillo and taken his place?"

"It was in his mind to do just that," I said. "He had it all planned."

"And he had the strength to do it," added Dalcamy. "He could have done it easily."

"A good example of why a fleet like ours is needed," I continued. "If I wasn't able to stop him, they would have. Did he do anything to you, General?"

"What do you mean?"

"Control you in anyway, talk to you in your mind?"

"He did something, I didn't understand what was happening."

"I would like you to let Borkalami examine you, General. Mentally, just to make sure he didn't hurt you."

"Wouldn't I know if he hurt me?"

"Not necessarily, but this examination would make it show up."

"What will happen?"

"You'll daydream," I said smiling. "I found it rather pleasant."

He looked at Borkalami, "and if he finds something wrong? Then what?"

"Then we help you make it right again," Borkalami answered.

"What do I have to do?"

"Nothing, just sit back and relax." Borkalami examined General Voll completely and found no sore spots. "You're all right, General. Let's have another round of drinks to celebrate." He left with Lor Sham to get them.

A week later General Voll left for home and so did we. Caltomacoe still wouldn't let me do anything strenuous. He continued to scan me every eight hours. *You're healing too slowly, Mike, maybe by the time we get home there will be some signs of healing. Do you remember everything that happened?*

Yes, I remember, and no, it doesn't hurt to remember, I added laughing.

Well, at least he didn't succeed in amputating your sense of humor.

We arrived at Artara in seven days. Caltomacoe kept us at Gagne 4. The Commodore met us and personally escorted me to Medical. *I'm all right, Commodore.*

Sure you are, you always walked this slowly.

They put me in the opercule and examined me. When they finished, they put me to sleep. I woke up confused, someone came over and looked at me. *Don't move around too much, Mike, go back to sleep.*

"Where am I?"

Medical.

I don't know what that is, I thought. *I guess it doesn't matter. I am sleepy.* I woke up again and saw Tomiya sitting in a chair at the foot of my bed. A nurse walked up to me. *How are you feeling?* The nurse asked smiling.

Fine. I sat up with her help.

Feel hungry?

Yes.

Good, I'll be right back.

I reached for Tomiya and we held each other. I could feel her concern, fear of losing me. *Hey, what's this all about? I'm okay, see? Stop worrying.*

She drew back and looked at me, still holding on to me. *Yes, you're all right . . . now.* We hugged again.

The nurse returned with a tray of food and I ate every last morsel. I felt like I hadn't eaten for a week. Tomiya and I visited as I ate. *That was good,* I said as the nurse took the empty tray.

Do you know where you are?

Medical. She sat down on the edge of my bed and looked at me. I knew she was reading me. *Sorry, I'm already spoken for.*

She smiled and asked, *do you remember what happened to you?*

Yes. I remembered Formald's head exploding. I tried to stop the thought so she wouldn't see it, but I couldn't. I started remembering the whole ugly incident. Then I realized she was making me remember it. *No! It's too ugly for you to see!*

Don't worry about it, I'm prepared. We continued and I relived the whole experience. *Do you remember coming here to Medical?*

Yes. I started to remember the landing and walking with Commodore Mackalie. I remembered waking up and being confused and then there were other memories that I didn't know about. Snatches of pain and people around me. Times of darkness and bright lights that hurt my eyes, she stopped. *What was all that?*

Do you have any idea how long you've been here?

Didn't I just get here yesterday?

No, you've been here two weeks. Most of the time you've been asleep. What you just remembered were the times you woke up. You will remember more as you heal. It's a good sign that you remember as much as you do.

I looked at Tomiya as I realized what she must have been through. *What's wrong with me?*

We had to replace some of the main blood vessels in your brain. They were too badly damaged and weren't healing. Borkalami kept you from having any brain damage by sealing the exterior of the vessels so you had good circulation, but they just weren't healing.

So now I have plastic blood vessels?

No, she laughed, *we took them from your legs.*

Commodore Mackalie walked in as my first visitor. *It's about time you woke up. Your wife took up residence here while you slept,* he said smiling.

I looked over at Tomiya with so much love my chest felt it might burst. I *guess I missed the meeting, huh?* I said.

Afraid so, Mike. It was a good one and you were missed by everyone. We added a new office and rank, Commander General. He's second to me and will take my place when the time comes.

Who is it?

Borkalami.

That's great! You made a good choice. Did he know before the meeting or did you surprise him?

It was a surprise to him. We had a little celebration after the meeting. Two fold, Borkalami's promotion and the start of a new fleet.

How many representatives were there?

Eight. One from Trok, Thrae and Boro. Five from Earth; America, Russia, England, China and Australia. Dextra will join eventually, but they have enough to do right now just getting their world established again. Their titles are 'Korbid'. The Artarian word for Councilman.

How long do they serve?

That depends on their planets, we haven't set a term. That way their governments can make changes if they become dissatisfied.

You're Chairman?

Yes, Artara will always retain control.

It should, that's safer. How are the Trok students coming along?

Very well, they only have another year to go and they will be returning. I have enjoyed their company many times. I expect you will be having many visitors from them, they think very highly of you.

They are outstanding people. When I think about the first time I saw one of them. Well, I'm glad it turned out the way it did. What did you think of Thrae?

I suspect the King is telepathic, judging from your reports.

You do. I had that thought too, but he doesn't admit to it. My wife and I had a very good time there, I said smiling at Tomiya. *Didn't we honey?* She nodded and smiled back.

I *understand Dalcamy did, too,* he transmitted laughing.

I'll never forget the look on his face when the King offered him a 'companion', I laughed. *The timing couldn't have been better.*

We may be able to establish coexistence there.

Good, they are compatible, too.

Yes, but I'm finding out that some of our people want us to remain pure. Hope there won't be trouble in the future.

Give them time, they'll adjust. But it would be a shame to see the pure Artarian disappear. There's a sense of pride in being pure.

I don't think that will happen. We're too heritage minded to allow it. You should get into our history sometime.

That would be a good study while I'm recuperating.

I don't think they'll let you do that, they want you quiet. You'll just have to wait. You have another visitor outside. I'm going to leave so he can come in, I'll see you tomorrow.

My visitor was Lor Direna and his wife. We had a good visit and he told me how surprised Borkalami was about his promotion. Everyone agreed it was a good choice. Direna told me about the good time he and his wife had on the island, "I never dreamed such a place existed."

We visited for about an hour and the nurse came in and chased them out. She said I had enough visiting for a while. I was tired and fell asleep shortly after they left.

I woke up and found the nurse had pulled the curtains making the room semi dark. I happened to glance over at the chair in my room and could see someone sitting there.

Someone there? I transmitted. There was no answer. "Is someone there?" I vocalized.

"Yes, I didn't want to wake you."

That voice, I know that voice. I commanded the lights on. "General Buyemsky!"

"Not General anymore, Korbid Buyemsky"

"That's great! How did you swing it?"

"It was the Premier's idea. Since I was the first to tell him about the fleet he figured I should be the one to come. I'm glad he picked me."

"I am too, it's good to see you again."

"It's good to see you, also, but I didn't expect to have to see you in Medical. I was shocked when I heard what happened to you. I came several times when you were sleeping, but they would only let me see you through the monitors. You know you almost died, Mike, it was that close."

"No, I didn't know. I had no idea I was hurt that badly. You know everything that happened?"

"Yes, I pushed Borkalami into showing me. You did the right thing, Mike. Only you should have done it before he hurt you so badly."

"Well, it's over now and I'm going to be fine. Let's talk about you. I'm curious to know what happened when the American Representative found out you were here."

Buyemsky started laughing. "You should have seen his face, Mike.

"Let me read you. I'll be able to see everything you remember about it."

"All right. What do I do, just think about it?"

"Yeah."

We all gathered in a reception room before going in for the meeting. Everyone had on their dress uniforms. There were no mistaking the countries represented. We mingled and introduced ourselves. When the Trok came, everyone from Earth just stood and stared. I walked up to him and offered my hand.

"You must be from Earth," he said.

"Yes, that's right. Russia." I couldn't tell if he was pleased to meet me or not. How can you tell with an expressionless face? He reminded me of an insect. I was glad he wasn't telepathic like the Artarians.

I broke Buyemsky's thoughts with my laughter. "I'm sorry, I couldn't help it. I thought the same thing when I saw the first Trok. Being telepathic helps to understand their feelings easier. He probably was pleased by you. Especially if everyone else just stared at him. Go ahead, show me more. I'll try not to interrupt you."

It took him a little bit to start again. He backed up to the handshake.

"My name is General Buyemsky"

"I am Lor Direna, from Trok."

"I'm glad to meet you, Lor Direna. Come meet the others." I introduced him and stood smiling as he shook hands with each person.

The Englishman was hesitant to touch him. I wondered what his thoughts were.

The American was the last to arrive. A diplomat dressed in a business suite. I walked up to him and shook his hand while saying, "I'm glad you made it. I was beginning to think America wasn't coming, and it would be a shame to lose out." He had no idea that Russia was a member. Surprise showed clearly on his face. The raised eyebrows and the slight opening of his mouth. He inhaled quickly and silently. However, he had the presence of mind to respond quickly.

"I wouldn't dream of missing such an auspicious meeting, General."

"I don't think anyone knew who was coming except the Commodore," I said laughing.

"It was good to surprise him, the Premier got a good laugh out of it, too."

"I'll bet America is a member now."

"Absolutely."

As I healed more visitors were allowed in and after a month I was allowed to go home. They re-energized my transceiver just before I left Medical. The Commodore insisted I stay home for at least two months before even thinking of reporting in. I started exercising again with Tomiya, in every way possible. It was good to be home.

I reported in for testing after the two months home and passed with a much higher score as Dalcamy predicted. We have three hundred ships now. Korbid Buyemsky met me at my ship and I showed him the new drive system and my trophy.

"Vyacheslav has been ordered back to Russia, Mike."

"He has?"

"He doesn't seem to want to go, I don't think he will."

"Are you going to do anything about it?"

"No, I think it should be his choice. He has built a life here. A medical technician, I hear he's very good at it. Strange, I would not have thought it of him."

"That doesn't sound like the Buyemsky I first met in Russia," I said.

"This isn't the same Buyemsky. I told you there were a lot of changes in Russia. Did you know we tore down the Iron Curtain?"

"What?"

"That had nothing to do with the Artarians. Our new Prime Minister has been working on it for some time. We are now a socialist government with elections."

"Elections. The same Prime Minister I met?"

"No. He is no longer called Prime Minister. He is called President."

"How did the people react to all this?"

"Many left Russia. Later, there has been trouble between people from different providences. The old prejudices are free and surfacing again."

"The Russian people are strong, I'm sure they will overcome these problems."

"I agree. There are a lot of changes all over Earth because of the Artarians. I can see a time coming when all the nations of Earth will truly be united, but I may not live that long."

"Artara has changed, too," I said. "I brought up the status of Artara and they are out of danger of stagnation now. The future looks good for everyone."

"We should celebrate, Mike. Why don't you get your wife and the four of us go to a Recreation Center tonight?"

That sounds good, I've never met your wife."

"Yes you have, remember Tonya?"

"How could I forget Tonya? She's your wife?" I asked surprised.

He nodded smiling. "She wasn't then, that was the first time I used her and she was crushed by your rejection. She didn't want to work for me anymore, so I married her instead."

"That's a good way to keep your agents." We laughed together as we walked off the landing pad.

THE END